D0974951

The Woman Who Would Be Pharaoh

A Novel of Ancient Egypt

William Klein

CLEARWATER | FL | USA

For information, contact Kunati Inc., Book Publishers in Canada.
USA: 13575 58th Street North, Suite 200, Clearwater, FL 33760-3721 USA
Canada: 75 First Street, Suite 128, Orangeville, ON L9W 5B6 CANADA.
E-mail: info@kunati.com.

FIRST EDITION

Designed by Kam Wai Yu
Persona Corp. | www.personaco.com

ISBN 978-1-60164-189-2 EAN 9781601641892
Fiction

Published by Kunati Inc. (USA) and Kunati Inc. (Canada).
Provocative. Bold. Controversial.™

http://www.kunati.com

Library of Congress Cataloging-in-Publication Data

Klein, William (William Richard)
The woman who would be pharaoh : a novel of ancient Egypt / William Klein.
-- 1st ed.
p. cm.
Summary: "Based on historical events at the time of Pharaoh Tutankhamun, this meticulously researched novel brings to life the ancient glory of Egypt and the ruthless men and women who schemed and murdered to rule her"--Provided by publisher.
ISBN 978-1-60164-189-2
1. Ankhesenamen, Queen of Egypt--Fiction. 2. Queens--Egypt--Fiction. 3. Tutankhamen, King of Egypt--Fiction. 4. Regicides--Egypt--Fiction. 5. Egypt--History--Eighteenth dynasty, ca. 1570-1320 B.C.--Fiction. I. Title.
PS3611.L452W66 2009
813'.6--dc22

2009003819

To Sheryn

With love, respect, and gratitude

May you spend millions of years
You lover of Thebes, sitting with
Your face to the north wind, your
Eyes beholding felicity

Inscription on wishing cup
Tomb of Tutankhamun

BOOK 1

1342-1339 BC

Prologue

1342 B.C.
Amarna, Egypt

The platform stood on the gravelly flatland between the police barracks and the great temple of the Aten. The audience, mostly clergy from the temples of Egypt, had been waiting two hours beneath the full glare of a pitiless sun. Whispered complaints broke the stillness of the hot air, tempers flared; and Simut, the second high prophet of Amun, bored and angry, counted the puffs of dust that billowed up where each sun-struck victim fell.

The delay in the ceremony did not surprise Simut. Pharaoh Akhenaten was famous for keeping people waiting outdoors in the sun. Pharaoh never apologized. What better way to show one's love for the disc of the sun than to bathe in its splendid rays? Simut shook his head in disgust. Was it for this that he had left the comfort of his Theban home, and sailed downriver to the new capital city?

A trumpet blared, and Simut looked back over his shoulder. Pharaoh Akhenaten and Queen Nefertiti were borne across the field in a golden palanquin. A second palanquin followed, bearing Princess Ankhesenpaaten, one of Akhenaten's four surviving daughters. Akhenaten's mother, Queen Tiye, the widow of the third Amunhotep, Mighty Bull, sat across from the princess. The bearers lowered the palanquins near the platform steps. The royal couple, their daughter and the queen mother mounted the platform.

Akhenaten turned to his guests with a rapturous smile. He wore a heavy pleated robe the color of gold, and the blue battle crown, the Khepresh. The audience clapped politely.

Simut stared at Akhenaten. He had learned to hate the elongated, smiling face, the excessively full sneering lips and cold black eyes. It was the face of the heretic Pharaoh, the ruler who repudiated all the gods of Egypt and squandered the wealth of Amun-Ra's temple to finance the building of his new city of the sun-god. What new damning decree would the heretic announce?

Simut waited. He counted two more puffs of dust. Akhenaten, joyous at the applause, allowed things to quiet down. At last the waiting was over.

Pharaoh raised his arms and began in a voice that seemed distant and hollow. "I've called you here because the Aten, creator of all things and sole god of the universe, grieves. He grieves because there are many among you who have not abandoned the false gods of Egypt. This being so, I've devised a loyalty test that all must take to prove their loyalty to the Aten."

Akhenaten glanced at his queen and daughter, standing to one side near the edge of the platform. Nefertiti stared away, a blank look on her face. Akhenaten smiled at his thirteen-year-old daughter, Princess Ankhesenpaaten. She smiled back.

Akhenaten continued in a cold, distant monotone. "I've sent my soldiers up and down the Nile gathering bricks and stone upon which are chiseled cartouches inscribed with the name of Amun-Ra. Most were taken from temples dedicated to that false god."

Pharaoh pointed to a cloth-covered mound on the platform. A pedestal stood next to the mound. He motioned to his high priest of the Aten, Meryra. The high priest stepped forward and stripped off the cloth, revealing a pile of rubble—broken bricks and tiles of various shapes and sizes. The guests looked at the rubble and then stared at one another, and Simut wondered if everyone shared his thoughts, that Pharaoh had descended to a new level of madness.

Akhenaten continued with a smile that looked strangely prankish. "As your names are read out, you will ascend the platform, receive a mallet and chisel and then each one of you will obliterate the name of Amun-Ra from its cartouche."

A long low moan swept through the audience. Simut could not have imagined this request in his wildest dreams. Pharaoh was asking the most important priests of the temples to repudiate a god worshiped by their families since the beginning of time. His mouth went dry, and his heart pulsed against his throat.

Two foreign dignitaries standing next to Simut, wary of the ceremony, stared at one another, eyes wide with wonder, all the while shaking their heads. Simut watched them. One was the foreign minister from Naharin, and next to him, the chief of Wawat, dressed in leopard skins, a felt hanging down his copper-colored back. Simut could understand their astonishment. They would not understand that for an Egyptian, the obliteration of a person's written name was a literal death for the person or god who bore it, a stripping away of identity, and, in this case, the stripping away of all past memories and spiritual knowledge of the god.

Simut's hatred for Akhenaten and his family boiled over as he considered the blasphemous request. Did Pharaoh intend for him, the second high prophet of Amun, to step forward and take up the chisel and mallet and repudiate his beloved Amun-Ra? Never!

Akhenaten, seated on the platform, nodded to Meryra. In a surprise move, the high priest handed off the mallet and chisel to Nefertiti. She accepted the proffered tools, looking tired and indifferent, as though all resistance had been beaten out of her. The look on her face would only feed the rumor of a rift in the royal household. A guard held a tile in place on the pedestal. It bore Amun-Ra's name. Simut thought he could see tears gathering in Queen Nefertiti's eyes. Three quick strokes and the tile was defaced.

The chisel and mallet were handed off to Princess Ankhesenpaaten. The young princess grasped the tools without hesitation. A determined look in her eyes, she struck hard at the tile. It snapped with the first stroke. She turned to her father with a proud smile.

The bitch! Simut thought. Pharaoh's bitch daughter! He silently thanked the gods that Akhenaten had not sired a son. Everyone knew that young Tutankhamun, Mighty Bull's only surviving son, would wear the crowns of Egypt. But there was concern back in Thebes that the new pharaoh's wife would be found among the daughters of Akhenaten.

Toward the end of the strange ceremony, Akhenaten stunned the reluctant audience when he called out his mother's name. This was the great lady, the proud widowed queen of Mighty Bull. Only last year she had been forced to leave Thebes and live with her son in Amarna.

Queen Tiye looked at her son in disbelief. Meryra took her arm and escorted her forward. A sandstone block containing the cartouche of Amun-Ra was brought before her and placed on the pedestal. The queen mother drew back in a state of fright. Amun-Ra had been the state god for generations, and her husband had become one with the god, and was anointed in his name as the third Amunhotep.

Queen Tiye began to shake. She looked over at her son, eyes pleading for mercy. Simut had never seen the proud great lady in such a state. Helpless, his hands instinctively formed a fist. Akhenaten ignored his mother's plea. The widowed queen reluctantly accepted the chisel and mallet, but at the same time, all of the strength seemed to drain from her frail body, and the tools sagged in her hands. She sobbed.

Akhenaten motioned to Meryra. The high priest held the queen's hands and guided the chisel toward the cartouche. The queen's cry mellowed into a low moan as she fell like a dead weight to the platform floor. A murmur spread across the audience. Several priests cried openly.

Slowly, painfully, the queen, with help from Meryra, rose to her feet. Again she looked at her son. "Akhenaten," she cried out, gesturing with a hand raised to the sky. "He ... he was your father!"

Except for Queen Tiye's gown fluttering in the hot breeze, there was an awkward stillness, a pause in time.

Resigned to a fate worse than death, the queen mother turned slowly toward the pedestal, the mallet cocked in her hand. She brought it down on the head of the chisel held by Meryra. A piece of sandstone splintered out of the cartouche. She dropped the mallet with a shriek. Looking more like a helpless commoner than a queen, she fell to her knees.

The cries of despair from the audience were muted when a young man appeared from out of nowhere and raced up the platform steps. Simut recognized him. It was the queen's young steward, Huya.

Legs spread apart, hands on hips, Huya stared hard at Akhenaten, then he raised his fist and cried out: "Woe to you, Pharaoh! You've assailed our lady and our good god, Amun-Ra. You and your sun-god shall be cast out! Thebes endures, and so shall Amun-Ra."

Tears of anguish rolled from Huya's eyes as he bent down and slowly raised Queen Tiye to her feet. He put his arm around her waist and helped the old lady down the platform steps. No one attempted to stop them.

Simut smiled. Pharaoh had suffered a public rebuke from a servant. He watched as Akhenaten pursed his lips, dumbfounded by the unexpected turn of events. He sensed a feeling of restlessness and fear spread across the audience. Quietly, with no outward display of hostility, Pharaoh turned to his captain of guards and nodded.

Simut shook his head. Huya was as good as dead.

The guards waited until the queen mother was seated in the palanquin, then they seized Huya, bound his hands behind his back and led him away. Simut watched in dismay.

❧

At the hour of noon on the following day, the queen mother's faithful steward, Huya, was taken into the Eastern Desert to meet his fate. There had been no trial, no announcement of an execution.

Medjay guards staked Huya spread-eagle on the pebble-strewn burning sand. In no time at all the midday sun began to broil his olive skin a deep maroon. For a few blissful minutes he fell into a delirious sleep, but the tugging grip of a will stronger than his own dredged his reluctant spirit back to a place of blinding light and unbearable pain.

His eyes fluttered open to the hell he had momentarily left behind. His vision cleared. The dazzling sun was blocked from view by a Medjay guard towering above him, the guard's indifferent beefy face and tawny bare chest etched against a hazy yellow sky. The red-glazed amphora cradled in the guard's arms tipped downward. A long glutinous tongue of honey oozed menacingly over the lip, hung motionless in the still air and then rapidly descended.

Huya's screams for mercy were silenced by the amber wave of honey crashing like a hot fist against his face, laving his seared body in a heavy sticky-sweet warmth.

Huya was the first to hear the flies.

They came slowly at first, one or two at a time, and then in swarms. They hovered over him like a translucent shroud. The glaring sun flickered and grew dim. Huya felt the feather-soft beat of busy wings across his cheeks. The flies carpeted his eyes in thick animated black swatches, swarmed over his lips, scurried into his ears and drilled against his brain with a frantic high-pitched whine.

Huya's suffering intensified with an awful pricking at his flesh. Mercifully, he could not see the two scorpions sharing a meal in the tenderness of his crotch, or the copper-colored ribbon of ants spreading out across his thigh.

He wailed a curse to Pharaoh Akhenaten. His high-pitched wolfish howl rolled eerily across the parade grounds and out onto the endless barren desert. Battle-hardened guards gazing down at the writhing young man faltered in their stern watch and feared for their souls.

That same afternoon, unaware of Huya's execution, Simut decided to return at once to Thebes. He sat amidships of his state vessel, wondering why Akhenaten had not called his name out at the ceremony. Perhaps the misshapen monster knew he would be reaching too far, and that the second high prophet of Amun would never come forward to renounce Amun-Ra. What happened was undoubtedly meant as a warning. The coward did not want to create an incident. But there was an incident, thanks to an obscure steward in the service of Queen Tiye. The ceremony was botched, and Simut was glad.

Free of the harbor, he stared back at Amarna, basking beneath a dull lemon sky. Then, silently, he cursed Pharaoh, and swore in the name of Amun-Ra that the heretic would be brought down, and that none of his line would wear the crowns of the Two Lands.

1340 BC
Thebes, Egypt
Two years later

1

On a warm summer day the royal scribe Menkhara sat at a cedar workbench in the scriptorium of Karnak's House of Life. Head resting on two clenched fists, he gazed down at a dull yellow papyrus sheet he had been writing on in neat hieroglyphic script. The papyrus was flanked by two piles of small pillow-shaped limestone tablets. The tablets were heavily marked with an obscure form of Babylonian cuneiform. His eyes shifted from the papyrus to the tablets and back again.

This was the second year that Menkhara, the nineteen-year-old son of a commoner, had worked for the temple. It was his first assignment since his elevation to royal scribe, an exalted office for one so low-born, and he never ended a day without first thanking his favorite god, Thoth, the scribe of the gods, for his good fortune. He was especially grateful to Simut, a priest from Karnak's House of Life, who took time from his priestly duties to teach at the Kap. Simut had taken the scholar under his wing, befriended him, and even invited him to his villa. When Simut inherited his father's office and became the second high prophet of Amun, he used his influence to obtain Menkhara's appointment as a royal scribe.

Menkhara's brow furrowed as he pondered the tablet he had been translating. A quick mind and a mastery of Akkadian and Babylonian cuneiform had already marked him as one of the brightest young scholars at Karnak. But on this assignment the going was slow and yielded no information of value. Pharaoh Akhenaten had over the years ignored the pleas and complaints of Egypt's vassal states, and when he died, Egypt's foreign affairs were left in an unsolvable mess. Nothing could be done to repair foreign relations unless the unanswered limestone dispatches recovered from a pit behind Akhenaten's House of Correspondence in Amarna were found, translated, and the thoughts of chieftains and vassal kings made known.

The study door opened. Menkhara looked up. A young woman stood in the doorway. She held a basket of cake-bread and a clay vessel brimming with sweet beer. Menkhara lowered his reed brush and smiled at her fondly. He knew the hour of the day by Mayet's appearance, and was always grateful for the food she brought. It was better than what he would have gotten for himself with the few deben of copper he made in wages.

Mayet, age fifteen, was not beautiful, but she had a pleasant open face and lustrous hair, cut to shoulder length. She had bright shining eyes, a pert mouth and an innocent smile that set his heart racing from the day he first set eyes upon her. She wore a single garment of homespun cotton that reached to her ankles. Her bare breasts were moderately large, with nipples as pink as lotus buds.

Their marriage terms and dowry were arranged long before Menkhara thought of her as a lover. For years, she was nothing more than the deputy foreman's brat child. But the time came when Menkhara began to look at her differently. To their parents' surprise, they fell in love.

Mayet set the food basket down on a small table and poured beer into a stone jar. Menkhara left his workbench and slapped at his kilt, causing plumes of limestone powder from the shards and tablets to hang in the still air. He sat down across from Mayet and reached gratefully for a jar brimming with cool sweet beer. He broke off a piece of cake-bread and ate hungrily.

Menkhara did not speak until he had finished his beer and a

loaf of cake-bread. "I know that we've been invited to a party with our friends at the Lion's Tooth Inn tomorrow night," he said hesitatingly, "but I've been invited to dine with the second high prophet, Simut. He wants to confer with me about a new project. I will have to go to Amarna for a while. I won't be gone long."

The smile on Mayet's face faded. "You expect me to go alone to the Lion's Tooth?" she said, staring pensively at Menkhara.

Menkhara thought about that, and then he smiled. "Well, I hope I'll be gone no more than three weeks. We'll go to the Lion's Tooth Inn on my first night back, and every night thereafter, if you wish?"

Mayet's face relaxed. "It's not drinking beer at the Lion's Tooth that excites me, Menkhara. I want to be with you."

Menkhara reached over and took her hand. "And you shall be, every day of our lives."

There was a silence, and then Mayet said, "What will you be doing in Amarna?"

Menkhara shrugged. Mayet was not really interested in his work. Perhaps she saw that he was expanding his circle of friends and was fearful of losing him. Her thoughts were on marriage. She looked too sweet staring at him from across the table, and he wanted to gather her in his arms and tell her not to worry. Instead, he explained his assignment as simply as he could.

"I'll be poking around the town's House of Correspondence, trying to find discarded incoming correspondence. Our late Pharaoh Akhenaten cared nothing for foreign affairs, and his indifference to our allies may have cost Egypt an empire. No one is able to assess the damage without knowing what was said of us by governors and kings of our vassal states."

"Tutankhamun's betrothed, Princess Ankhesenpaaten, lives in Amarna. I hear she is very beautiful."

Menkhara looked at her with a touch of amusement. He

brushed crumbs from his chest. "I would imagine so."

"She has a reputation. If she lays eyes on you, she'll want to sink her teeth into you."

Menkhara laughed. "She's a solar princess. What would she have to do with a commoner? You are being silly."

"I don't feel good about this."

Menkhara sat next to Mayet and put his arm around her. Don't you bother your head with ridiculous rumors. I love you."

Mayet smiled. "You must think me an awful goose."

Menkhara returned her smile, his large brown eyes twinkling. "I think you're the loveliest girl in the world." He kissed her gently on the lips.

Mayet left, and Menkhara went back to work, but he had lost his ability to concentrate. His mind drifted.

What he had told Mayet was true. Well, almost. He never once doubted his affection for her, but he had mixed feelings about the effect their marriage would have upon his future. It was its inevitability that bothered him. The marriage would bind him forever to the hot tawny hills around Deir el-Medina, and a society of tomb builders, no matter how well he succeeded at court.

He wanted more for himself, something he could not find among the rough villagers who labored for Pharaoh. He longed for the company of important Theban priests and the high-born class of people who lived in their fine homes at Malkata and the District of Karnak. Simut had opened doors for him, made possible his advancement to the status of a royal scribe, and introduced him to a few important people, like the treasurer, Maya, and the vizier of Upper Egypt, Ay, who now served as regent. Working for the temple of Karnak and the Theban clergy offered the promise of a better life. Also, it had gotten him out of the workers' village, and away from Father and the neighbors, who always smelled of burnt gypsum and sweat.

Menkhara loved the idea of waking every morning in the splendid glitter of Thebes. He dreamed of possibilities unthinkable in the village of workers. But the only reality was marriage to Mayet. Could he be sure that with the daughter of a deputy foreman of workers as his wife, men of influence and power would deign to welcome him to their homes? It was only in her absence, away from that alluring sweet smile, that he dared to dream of a life well beyond the reach of his birth.

2

Wearing a new white pleated skirt and new sandals, Menkhara hurried toward Simut's villa. He was fresh-bathed and his body glistened with oil of lily. A cool evening breeze felt good against his skin.

Simut's villa was not far from the east wall of the temple of Amun-Ra. Menkhara was no stranger to the place, yet each time a servant led him behind its courtyard doors and down the walkways, he always paused to admire the lush beauty of the garden and the pond and the lilies floating on water as bright and clean as the Green Sea.

Menkhara and Simut dined at a low ebony table set in a candle-filled room. The food was as good as he expected, and there were the usual ewers of fine wine and flasks of honeyed beer. But where were the musicians? Simut always insisted on music when he dined. And the cheery conversation that always accompanied their meals was absent, giving a kind of texture to the silence. Menkhara sensed that something wasn't quite right. Later, they had honey cakes, grapes and sweet wine beneath an arbor in the garden. Simut began to open up.

"I went to see Ay the other day," he began softly. "The vizier received me in the audience hall in the palace at Malkata."

Simut shook his head. “My uncle treated me as though I were a suppliant, a visitor. He sat on Pharaoh’s throne the whole time. Can you imagine that?”

Menkhara looked into his friend’s fixed dark eyes, and then he laughed. “I wouldn’t read too much into it.”

“With his granddaughter as queen, he’s one step closer to the Horus crown. I had hoped that he summoned me to say that he had put an end to Tutankhamun’s betrothal to Ankhesenpaaten, but the subject never came up.”

“Perhaps the regent simply wanted good company?”

Simut smiled cynically. “It was hardly a family visit. He wants a progress report on our translation of Akhenaten’s foreign correspondence received by Pharaoh during his reign.”

“Much of it is missing,” Menkhara said. “The letters I’ve translated are mundane.”

“He won’t brook excuses, Menkhara. I told him you were working on the few tablets we have, and that I planned on sending you to dig near the House of Correspondence in Amarna.”

Menkhara watched Simut sip his wine. The goblet looked miniature in his large beefy hands. Everything about Simut was large, except his height. He had a fleshy face with small black eyes. He was born with a clubbed leg shorter than the other, causing him to walk with a noticeable limp, dragging his lame leg as though it were a dead weight. There was much about Simut that Menkhara did not like, thoughts that he did not like to dwell on. His sense of humor, for example. Simut had none. He was dour. And his table manners were awful for one so high born. He belched at will and picked his teeth.

Menkhara said, “I don’t understand why you’re so obsessed with Princess Ankhesenpaaten. Even the high priest Inmutef has accepted her marriage to the prince.”

Simut thrust his jaw forward in a showy, combative way. “My

father, Anen, whose priestly rank I inherited upon his death, was murdered in Karnak's temple, his crushed body found in the offering room of the god, and in this very temple. I'm convinced he was murdered by agents of Akhenaten. Simut's eyes narrowed. "I've sworn an oath that no descendant of that swine will ever sit upon the thrones of Egypt."

Menkhara began to realize that Simut had some terrible plan up his sleeve and wanted his help. He reached over and clasped Simut's arm. "No good can come of it."

Simut's hard stare phased to a warm smile. "I've helped you in your career, my friend. I've never asked a favor in return. I've treated you as an equal, and asked you to treat me as you would a brother, with no special deference because of my station in life."

Menkhara smiled and loosened his grip on Simut's arm. "Well, go ahead and ask."

"You'll be in Amarna to search for foreign correspondence during the reign of Akhenaten. You'll have a royal warrant signed by Ay. The warrant will gain you access to every building, place and home in Amarna. Nothing will be denied you."

"Provided my demands have something to do with foreign correspondence."

"Don't be stupid, Menkhara," Simut said scornfully. "What I'm going to ask of you is for the sake of our beloved temple at Karnak, and the god Amun-Ra that we both love and admire. There is still time to prevent the prince's marriage to the daughter of Akhenaten. Their betrothal will be aborted if it is learned that Ankhesenpaaten, a solar princess, is less than pure and therefore unworthy of marriage to the future Horus god."

"Less than pure? What's that supposed to mean?"

"That the future wife of Pharaoh has behaved like a woman of pleasure."

"How do you know this?"

Simut gave Menkhara a crafty smile. "It's common talk at court. It's just that nobody is brave enough to come forward."

"And that's what you want me to do, gather proof that the princess is a whore?"

"Yes."

Menkhara shook his head. "You've had too much to drink."

"You will go to Amarna with the best credentials, a royal warrant signed by the regent. It will admit you anywhere. You are good looking and will meet young people your age in the local inns.

"No!" Menkhara shot back.

"If we're lucky, you might even be introduced to Princess Ankhesenpaaten.

"No! Damn it, Simut. I won't do it."

Unfazed, Simut continued: "She frequents the local taverns often enough. You will have access to Kings House where she resides. You could easily develop some evidence of behavior unbecoming a solar queen."

Menkhara breathed a long sigh, all the while shaking his head in disbelief. "You want me to spy on the future queen of Egypt?"

Simut thrust his thick lower lip out and stared hard at Menkhara, then shook his head.

"Do I have to beg the son of a worker, the young man admitted to the society of the Kap through my influence; the same young man who made my friends his friends and now moves easily in their company? Must I get down on hands and knees and beg my dearest friend whom I love as I would a young brother, the same brother who owes his royal scribal rank and social connections to my love and loyalty?"

"Your kindness and your friendship come with a price."

"My father will be avenged, Menkhara. You can't show your gratitude over a plate of fine food. Show me something in return for my friendship."

Menkhara said under his breath, "Damn you for this."

Simut's face broke into a broad smile. He took Menkhara by the hand. "I knew I could depend on my dearest friend."

"I'll look around. I can't promise anything."

Simut gave Menkhara his hand. It was pudgy and felt warm and soft, the feel of a small freshly killed animal.

Menkhara drew back, heart thundering in his chest. "When do I leave for Amarna?"

"At once. I'll join you within a week of your arrival in Amarna."

"You will be recognized. Is that wise?"

"I'll be disguised."

"Why do you want to go anyway?"

Simut laughed. "Well, if for no other reason than to give you moral support."

Menkhara stood up, repressing his anger as best he could. He had always treated Simut as his superior, if for no other reason than to acknowledge the doors the second high prophet had opened for him. But suddenly he felt threatened and confused.

"I'll take my leave now," Menkhara said, staring gloomily at his friend. "Thank you for dinner."

Menkhara walked down the narrow garden path toward the forecourt, and then turned and looked back. Simut stood by the gate, as fat and as round as ever. He waved.

Menkhara gave Simut an icy stare. "Second high prophet," he called out crisply. "You've asked me to do a terrible thing. This pays back the debt. We're even." Without waiting for a reply he turned and disappeared from sight.

3

In the royal palace at Amarna, fifteen-year-old Princess Ankhesenpaaten was bored, and when she was that way, she liked to drink. She sat in the silence of her bedchamber sipping pomegranate wine from a goblet. Her handmaidens, Leta and Auti, sat across from her on large crimson pillows. The golden ewer of wine sat on a low ebony table between them.

Ankhesenpaaten wore a loose-cut transparent narrow dress that left the right shoulder exposed. Unlike most at court, she wore little makeup, largely because nature had endowed her with all the beauty any young woman could hope for. Her eyes were large, black and bright, her lips full and sensuous. As a teenager she had not learned to use her beauty and her position at court to best advantage. For older men it was precisely this mix of beauty and childlike immaturity that was so appealing.

"We're only weeks away from moving to Thebes," she said with a sigh.

Leta said: "And then our Tutare will become Pharaoh." The handmaiden was not out of place in calling Prince Tutankhamun by his family nickname, Tutare. The royal couple played with the handmaidens and other servants, and within the confines of the palace no distinction was made between young royals and their personal servants.

"You would have to remind me about the coronation," Ankhesenpaaten said. "On that same day I must wed him."

"But you love Tutare, Princess," Auti chimed in.

"Of course I love him," Ankhesenpaaten shot back with an angry glare. "I love him as a brother. How am I to love a nine-year-old as my husband?"

Leta, more bold than Auti, asked: "What is it you want, Princess?"

Ankhesenpaaten gazed upward. “I want a real lover! I want a man of the world. And I want him to make love to me. I want to make love on a bright pillow, on divans covered in fine linen. I want him in the sunlight and by the moonlight. I want him at my side morning, noon and night. I want a man!”

Leta arched her eyebrows and smiled. “And that is all?”

“No. All that, and the crowns of Egypt too!”

“You can’t have both. Tutare comes with the crown.”

“If I were a man, nothing would stop me.”

There was a long silence. Auti reached over and filled their goblets. Ankhesenpaaten smiled sadly. “How shall I kiss him the night we are wed?”

“Your make-believe lover?” said Auti.

“No, you stupid girl! Tutare. He’ll be more like a brother to me than a bridegroom.”

“The prince will not always be nine,” Leta consoled.

“Easy for you to say,” Ankhesenpaaten said bitterly. “You can marry your heart’s desire. You at least have that choice.”

Leta nodded in agreement and a slow thoughtful smile filled her face. “When I was quite young, a dear friend had a brother not more than the age of the prince, nine, I think. Once, I caught him pleasuring himself. It was so large for his age, I could scarcely take my eyes from it. But sparing him the embarrassment, I drew back before he caught sight of me.”

Ankhesenpaaten’s face wrinkled with disbelief. “You’re telling a story!”

“I swear, mistress. It’s true!”

The three girls drew into a triangle, their heads together, giggling.

Then Ankhesenpaaten drew back. “Oh, but not the prince. Tutare is such a runt.”

Leta gave Ankhesenpaaten and Auti a mischievous smile. “The

proof of the pudding is in the eating."

"Let's have some fun with dear Tutare," Ankhesenpaaten said.

Leta and Auti burst out laughing. Ankhesenpaaten's smile concealed the anger that lay behind the plan. It ached away at her heart. Tutare was nearing his coronation, and her marriage to him the only way to the crowns of Egypt. Tutare was to be her husband. It was a dilemma she could not think through; and in the turbulence of her adolescent heart quite drunk with wine, she was beginning to find relief in the silliness of her lingering childhood. She would humiliate Tutare, and find pleasure in it. That was as good a way as any to end her day.

⁂

Down the palace hall from where Ankhesenpaaten entertained her handmaidens, Tutare lay in his massive new bed, listening to the hum of the cool night wind caught in the roof vent above his head. The bed had belonged to his father, Pharaoh Amunhotep. It had been well-worn by Father's weight, and the linen covered reed mattress sagged and swayed uncomfortably under his back.

Restless, Tutare stared up to the ceiling and at the painting he had begun to hate. How many times had he counted the forty-three ripples on the shimmering water, the twelve startled wild ducks soaring in the cloudless sky? He even had names for the ducks, the names of people he hated most. The largest and fattest he called Kheri Heb, Karnak's master of rituals who had come up from Thebes to teach him the mysteries of kingship. His only pleasure came from the ever-changing crimson glow of wall sconces that seemed to set the ducks in motion, causing their wings to flap.

As the move to Thebes and his coronation approached, his thoughts turned more and more to Father's death. That was during the time of the co-regency, and the same day his uncle Petara, who called himself Akhenaten, had become the sole ruler. He was visiting in Thebes at the time, and he remembered how the whole court at Amarna had come to Thebes to pay homage to Father.

Tutare felt a pang of sadness, recalling how Simut, second high prophet of Amun, had led him through the adjoining robing room to Father's bedchamber to watch the last breath pass from Pharaoh's mouth, and the beginning of his voyage of eternity. The place had stunk of boiled leeks, the only food Father could take hold of. He had never seen Father that way, and the sight of his empty open eyes staring away at nothing, his slack open mouth and black rotted teeth, was too much to bear.

They had placed him in a bedside chair, where they expected him to grieve at the slow passing of Father. He sat feeling swallowed up in the vast chair, awkward and out of place, his chin buried in his chest, too afraid to look up. He made himself think of the friend he had hoped to play with that day, and the punt he paddled along the banks of Lake Tiye. If only he could concentrate on the lake, and how the water slapped against the sides of the punt; then he would not have to worry about Father's labored breathing or the thought of losing him.

But Father had raised himself up and begun to howl in pain. Tutare was terrified. He cried out, and slapped his hands over his eyes. His heart beat in his throat. The howling slowed to a long low moan, and Father's sweaty head fell back upon the headrest. A servant wiped the sweat away with a damp cloth. Then Father became silent, like a statue, and the only sound was the drone of a fly. The air was stifling, and he became more conscious than ever of the stink of boiled leeks. He felt sick and feared he would vomit. He remembered squirming in his chair. Finally, he felt Simut's comforting hand upon his shoulder, signaling the end of the long vigil. He'd never felt so grateful.

But since then, counting five years with his fingers, two more Pharaohs had died: his uncle Petara whom the world knew as Akhenaten, and his older brother, Smenkhara. And that was when the Kheri Heb had told him he was Pharaoh's only surviving male heir.

When Father's bed arrived, the priests took away Tutare's bed with the painting on the foot panel. The painting was of a lion chasing an oryx across the Eastern Desert. He remembered the green lion highlighted with gold leaf, and the blue oryx, always within one swipe of the lion's sharp claws, its large black eyes glistening in terror. Every night before going to sleep, he would stare hard at the painting and whisper in a taunting voice: "Lion, you will never catch my friend the oryx." But once in a nightmare, the two beasts tumbled in a spray of sand, the lion's mouth had clamped down upon the oryx's neck, and he'd screamed.

His mother, Sitamun, raced into his room, her face caught in the light of the earthenware lamp held in her outstretched hand. He felt so relieved. Mother had comforted him with a whispered song, his head pillowed upon her soft breasts until he had fallen into a peaceful sleep.

Tutare got out of the big sagging bed he detested, sat by the window and gazed down at the palace city of Amarna, with its endless villas, gardens, sandstone buildings and courtyards. Everything looked bright in the moonlight. At the town's edge he could see the high-notched wall of the granary mill, and beyond that, the palace walls, the Nile curling around the edge of the plain, and bone-white sails going upriver on a brisk wind.

He was hungry. The Kheri Heb had ordered him to bed early and without dinner. He knew it had something to do with his forthcoming coronation. Everything had changed as the great event approached.

When Father died, and he was ordered to live permanently in Amarna, he could no longer attend the palace school of the Kap with his friends, and was forced to receive private tutoring instead. Important court officials came to his chamber to bore him with lectures. The Director of Horned, Hoofed and Feathered Beasts spoke to him about Pharaoh's lands. The palace steward came to drone on about court etiquette. The Kheri Heb answered his complaints with long lectures on sacrifice and then read to him from an ancient papyrus on kingship. Who cared about sacrifices! He didn't like the Kheri Heb. He was ugly, with bug eyes, fat wet lips and a breath foul from beer and leeks. When the Kheri Heb left, Mother tried to explain the duties of kingship in a way that he, a nine-year-old, was supposed to understand. But what was the use? Nothing made sense. The only thing that mattered was his gurgling and aching stomach. "I won't make it to coronation, Mother!" he'd cried out. "I'll be dead from starvation first."

He wondered if his betrothed, Ankhesenpaaten, would keep her promise and sneak him something good to eat. It was getting late, and he was beginning to think she had forgotten him. He hoped things would get better after their betrothal.

The chamber door creaked on its hinges. He turned and straddled the window-bench, his legs dangling above the floor. Someone had come into his chamber, a human form glowing in the flickering light cast from the hall sconces.

Ankhesenpaaten stood in the doorway. Tutare's eyes grew wide. Where was the fifteen-year-old cousin he knew so well? She looked so grown up. She stood motionless, holding a bronze platter piled high with food. He seldom saw her dressed up like that, in such a fine linen gown. She looked so much like her mother, Nefertiti. Her eyes were so big and dark that when she stared at him he hardly knew what to say. When she laughed and gave him an approving smile, he thought his heart would burst, but when she was angry or scowled at him, he wanted to die. He didn't know what to think. Her hair was neatly in place and hung dark and glossy over her shoulders. How much time must her handmaidens have spent brushing it. She wore a colored glass diadem that sparkled in the firelight

The food, the way she looked—could this be another trick?

Ankhesenpaaten smiled warmly, and her large eyes shone merrily in the candlelight. She set the tray down on a small table and sat next to Tutare on the window bench. "I thought you would like something to eat," she said.

Tutare looked down at the tray. Set in a bed of lotus flowers were cakes, pomegranates, grapes and figs. "Thank you," he said, staring up anxiously into Ankhesenpaaten's eyes.

She looked down at him, smiling with her bright, thickly painted red lips. He at once forgot the mean tricks she had played on him before. How could he hold a grudge? They had played together like brother and sister. And she was very beautiful.

"Soon you shall be crowned ruler of the Two Lands," Ankhesenpaaten said.

Tutare crushed a grape in his mouth. "Yes, and you'll be my queen."

Ankhesenpaaten put a finger to her chin, and a strange smile came to her face. Tutare grew nervous.

"What sort of husband am I to expect from one so young?"

The question made no sense to Tutare, but still he tried for an answer. "Well, we shall play games to our hearts' delight, and not be told what to eat or when to go to bed."

Ankhesenpaaten, still smiling, said, "but what kind of lover will you be?"

Tutare began to form a vague notion of what she was getting at; it had to do with physical love, and having babies, and the sorts of things that grown-ups do. After a long silence he said:

"Well, one day, when I am older, yes, that too."

Ankhesenpaaten laughed loudly, and she said in an unbecoming, deep voice. "Can you get it up?"

"What?"

"That little dingy of yours."

Tutare flushed. His cheeks felt like hot coals. He felt foolish and stupid and wanted to cry.

He was distracted by a noise at the far end of the chamber. It was Auti and Leta. He looked back at Ankhesenpaaten. She responded with that mean laugh of hers. Why had she brought Leta and Auti with her? His heart beat hard against his chest. This was going to be one of those really bad times.

Ankhesenpaaten reached for the hem of his white linen night cloak. He rolled away from her and stood up. Before he realized what was happening, Leta and Auti had him by his arms and dragged him toward his bed.

It was no contest. Slightly built for a nine-year-old, he offered no resistance and they pinned him down on his bed. Ankhesenpaaten offered him the opportunity to remove his night cloak. He shook his head adamantly. "No!"

The handmaidens stared down at him with cruel smiles, giggling. Ankhesenpaaten reached over, grabbed Tutare's thin gauzy linen cloak by the neck and pulled down. Auti and Leta rolled him on his side, and in an instant the shredded cloak was ripped from his body.

Tutare covered himself with his hands and cried in earnest.

Ankhesenpaaten pulled his covering hands apart, pointed to his little peeper and filled the room with her laughter. "It looks like a toad! A dead toad!"

"When do you suppose he'll be old enough to lie with?" Leta giggled.

"Never, I think," said Ankhesenpaaten, catching her breath.

She leaned over and pressed her face so close to him, all he could see were her large dark eyes. Then she said with a satisfied smile: "I think I'll call you little peep."

Tutare twisted and squirmed but could not break free of Leta and Auti. "Don't!" he cried out.

Ankhesenpaaten took hold of his peeper. She held it between her thumb and forefinger as though it were something fished from the Nile. She gave it several quick jerks. "Little toady goes Peep! Peep! Peep!"

Tutare screamed. With a surge of anger, he found a hidden reservoir of strength, burst free, leapt from the bed and ran to a dark corner of the chamber. Tears flowed from his large dark eyes. "When I am Pharaoh I … I'll have your heads c–cut off," he stammered.

There was a standoff. The girls laughed hysterically, and Tutare stared at them in silence. A figure appeared in the doorway. Mother!

The young ladies doubled over, laughing helplessly. They did not see Sitamun. She stared past her son, her eyes fixed on the three girls, her face an angry frown. Finally one of the girls spotted her. Her laughter was abruptly stilled with a gasp. Ankhesenpaaten and the other handmaiden looked up. The handmaidens eased away from their mistress and shrank back against the far wall.

Mother stared hard at Ankhesenpaaten, her face flushed and angry. Ankhesenpaaten stared back defiantly. There was going to be a fight. He had seen them go at it before, and he would come out on the losing end when it was over. Both would be angry with him. Mother would lecture him about Ankhesenpaaten, and would swear that if she had anything to do with it, the bitch would never be queen. Ankhesenpaaten would ignore him for days, and when she finally spoke, he would be the object of her scorn.

"What are you doing in my son's chamber?" Sitamun demanded.

Ankhesenpaaten's bright red lips curled into a hostile smile. "We came looking for him, to play Senet. Then we heard a commotion outside."

"Liar! You've stripped him naked." Sitamun walked to the bed, stooped and picked up Tutare's night cloak. "For shame, Ankhesenpaaten! I would have thought you might have outgrown your stupid pranks. How dare you humiliate my son."

Tutare remained standing by the bed. He had ripped the linen cover from his bed and draped it over his body. He cringed as he watched Ankhesenpaaten take a stand and refuse to apologize. That's the way it was between the two of them, ever since the regent ordered the court back to Thebes. Mother had done everything within her power to prevent his betrothal to Ankhesenpaaten, though he was not sure why.

Mother put a comforting hand across his head, without taking her eyes off Ankhesenpaaten: "You are unworthy of his friendship."

"Friendship, Queen Mother?" Ankhesenpaaten finally said with a defiant smile. "I shall be his wife."

Mother turned pale. "Whatever the future may hold, he is a child! You've no business in his chambers."

Ankhesenpaaten gave Sitamun a look of feigned surprise. "Well, I am not here to bed down with him."

Mother's face drained white. "You and your friends have abused the prince, made a fool of him." She pointed an accusing finger at Leta and Auti quaking against the wall, and then turned back to Ankhesenpaaten. "You are loathsome and crazy, like your late heretic sun-worshipping father. I'll make you pay for this, daughter of Akhenaten!" She wheeled and pointed an extended finger at the doorway. "Now leave at once, the three of you!"

Mother crossed the room and sat at the window. Tutare waited until the scraping sound of sandals faded then he went to Mother's side. She stared out of the window, her hands clasped together so tightly in her lap that they were red at the fingertips.

Mother slowly lowered her head. "Oh, dear God," she sighed.

Tutare thought his heart would break. He did not like to see her in such a state. Momma, Momma, Momma, he said over and over again to himself. He felt guilty that he had caused her pain. He rested the palm of his hand on her shoulder and said softly: "I'm sorry, Momma."

After a long silence, Mother said, "It is a pity my dear Smenkhara is not alive today. Your brother made such a fine Pharaoh. I remember him at his coronation, dressed in his robes of state, the crown of the Two Lands upon his head. He looked so proud and powerful, so god-like! He would not let that bitch walk all over him." She gave Tutare an embittered smile and then added: "Oh no, my darling Smenkhara would never let that happen."

Tutare winced and looked away. He had only the barest memories of his older brother, and much of that memory was built upon the way Mother described him. He imagined that Smenkhara was handsome and strong, and even as a child, could talk back to his elders and fill their hearts with fear. But he could not do that. Mother would slap him hard across the face for the slightest discourtesy. Sometimes she had slapped him so hard he was sure his head would come off. But he loved her no less for it. Even when his ears were ringing and his cheeks stinging from a slap, he had cried out in tears: "Oh, Mother! Don't be mad at me. Tell me what I should do. I love you. Please tell me what I should do, Mother."

It always ended the same way. Mother would take him in her arms, kiss his brow, stroke his hair and whisper gently in his ear: "You must be strong for both of us, my little Tutare, my prince.

You must be Pharaoh!"

"Yes, Momma. Yes! Yes! Yes!"

4

The whitewashed mud-brick House of Correspondence in Amarna's central district had become Menkhara's place of work. It was a busy, small city, no more than one hour of march* in length, with a beautiful temple complex and a magnificent palace with balustrade ramps and majestic central halls.

The town was built around a broad processional roadway that formed an arc to the Nile and ran from the northern palace to the official royal palace. It had the look of a city built in a hurry. There were irregular roads and muddled housing arrangements, with estates of rich men built against rows of housing for the poor. Even the king's residential home lay near grubby government buildings and within sight of long rows of warehouses.

Menkhara managed a team of ten cuneiform scribes. He depended on his second in command, the Greek, Critias, especially when it came to handling the young volunteer scribes, who preferred horseplay to working. A senior scribe of the foreign office, Critias had spent most of his adult life in Egypt, though he could speak and read in many dialects of Greek, Cretan, Hittite and the language of the Canaanites up and down the Phoenician coast. Add to this a robust smile, a cunning mind and resourcefulness, and Menkhara could not help being grateful for his companionship.

For ten days, hired workers from Amarna dug a pit outside the House of Correspondence. Menkhara was told that it had been used by Akhenaten's minister of foreign affairs, Tutu, to dispose of foreign dispatches. As the workers dug the pit chanting ancient hymns, the scribes sifted through yellow sand and grayish gravel in

*An ancient Egyptian unit of measure equal to approximately six miles or eleven kilometers.

search of discarded limestone tablets scattered about in shards.

Slowly, a common theme began to come through from the meager Babylonian cuneiform material they had worked so hard to unearth. The vast domain of vassal states and friendly kingdoms that for generations looked to Egypt for leadership, were ignored during Akhenaten's reign, their communications and complaints unanswered. Akhenaten, the Lord of Love, indifferent to the world beyond the borders of Egypt, had all but given away an empire.

Menkhara and Critias were anxious to complete their work, but first they would have to authenticate their findings. They tried to interview former scribes in the mansion of the Aten and the god's House of Life, but all to no avail. The next best thing was to find Egyptian papyrus, which acknowledged letters from foreign leaders, and this meant searching out state documents.

What better place to look than at Kings House, a short distance from the House of Correspondence. The royal prince, Tutankhamun and Princess Ankhesenpaaten lived there. Their privacy was inviolate, and yet Menkhara had a mandate, a warrant to go anywhere. He resolved to exercise that right.

Menkhara and Critias set out for the royal residence at sunset in the evening of their tenth day at Amarna. Kings House, built of mud brick and painted a brilliant white, was not much to look at. It flanked the east wall of the palace and was joined to that building by a bridge.

When the young men arrived at Kings House, a nervous chamberlain examined their royal warrant, hesitated, then finally swung the door open. Critias decided to explore the state records room on the first floor. Menkhara followed a servant up to the second floor. The ramp was bordered on each side by carved stone balustrades of black and red granite, with carved scenes showing Akhenaten and his family worshipping the Aten.

Menkhara was shown into the late Pharaoh's study. He dismissed the servant and almost at once was drawn to Akhenaten's desk. The surface was covered with piles of documents, and Menkhara guessed that they had not been read. He began sifting through them.

From behind him, a firm demanding voice. "When you have finished, please leave my lord's things as you found them."

Menkhara slowly turned.

The young woman was immobile as a statue, her bright red lips bowed up to a smile that was at once critical and fetching. Her eyes glowed darkly, and there was about her an aura of royalty despite her obvious youth.

Menkhara guessed that the young woman was the princess Ankhesenpaaten. She looked Mayet's age, but possessed a confidence his betrothed did not have. Her gown, thin to the point of transparency, glimmered in the light of the sun, which appeared from the window as a great orange ball melting into the rim of the horizon. Her left breast was exposed, and it glistened white from fine droplets of sweat.

Had Menkhara not been taken by surprise, he would have instinctively risen to honor her with a low bow of respect. But her words were flung at him as though she were addressing an incompetent servant. Menkhara did not respond immediately, using the silence to assert his claim of independence. And then, with affected deliberation, he rose slowly from his seat.

He bowed politely. "I am Menkhara, lady, a royal scribe to the court at Thebes and the temple of the true god, Amun-Ra. I have a commission from the vizier and regent to conduct this search."

"From Thebes, sir? Then indeed you are a thief." She smiled, and Menkhara detected contempt in her manner, though it was overlaid with an air of courtesy.

"No thief, lady. Only a humble servant of the temple of Karnak."

Ankhesenpaaten smiled critically. "Tell me at once; when you're not pilfering through my father's private possessions, do your spies report to my Theban grandfather, Ay, on my behavior."

"If I offended you, lady, I am—"

"Oh, I didn't expect a straight answer." She turned away and left the room, her words trailing behind her: "Do what you have to do."

Menkhara followed her every move, his eyes fixed on the stubborn lift of her head and the way she squared her shoulders. The feeling she left behind made him more uncomfortable than the sting of her words. Then he settled back into Pharaoh's study chair, and forced his mind back to the clutter of papyrus on the desk.

❧

At day's end, Menkhara and Critias returned to their quarters in the southern suburbs of the city. It was an abandoned villa now used to house civil servants up from Thebes. It was late when they got to the villa, and the two men decided to review their findings in the morning.

Critias suggested a place he had heard about, an inn not far from the House of Correspondence. It was famous for its Syrian whores and fine wine and beer. Critias laughed. "Only the best sort of people patronize the place. It's called the Inn of the Two Brothers."

Menkhara smiled. "Why not?"

Menkhara and Critias bathed in the cool waters of the Nile, occupying their time with horseplay and water fights. Then they toweled off, returned to the villa, changed kilts, oiled their limbs and set off for the Inn of the Two Brothers.

5

Two sentries were posted at the front gate of Kings House when three teenaged girls came out of the shadows of the lawn sycamores and silently descended the short flight of steps to the forecourt.

Halfway across the forecourt, Princess Ankhesenpaaten motioned her two handmaidens to halt. "Yes," she whispered, pointing to the sentries. "They are the same two, Sahte and Khons. Must I repeat your instructions?"

"No," Auti and Leta answered softly in unison.

"No? You're too sure of yourselves, the both of you. I suppose that's because I let you get away with so much mischief, and you never take my threats seriously."

Leta and Auti accepted their mistress's criticism in silence, lowering their eyes in unison to the ground in a gesture of obedience. Ankhesenpaaten smiled. She had grown up with her handmaidens in Amarna, and was of the same age. Class lines were sometimes blurred by their affection for one another. Ankhesenpaaten preferred their company over the children of noblemen. She would confide in no one else, and she never doubted their loyalty. Sneaking out of the royal residence in defiance of Grandfather Ay's orders issued from Thebes made their loyalty and friendship more important than ever.

Left alone after her father and mother's death, she learned about young men and lovemaking, and she also developed a love for good wine and honeyed beer. Grandfather Ay wanted her in Thebes within days of Pharaoh Akhenaten's death, but she refused to go. Grandfather wrote back and said that she was as stubborn as her father. She took it as a compliment. But she had the temerity to write back and tell him that she didn't need Grandfather's agents watching after her every move. The old soldier was a stick-in-the-mud, and would never approve of anything she did. So why go to Thebes when she could lead her own unsupervised life in Amarna, in the shadows of her father's temple of the Aten?

Princess Ankhesenpaaten clasped Auti's hand and encircled Leta's waist with her free arm, drawing them close to her.

"Now listen carefully," she said, her voice lowering to a whisper. "I want the guards to quit their posts long enough for me to slip through the gates. My grandfather Ay resides in Thebes, but he has spies everywhere. If he finds that I've left Kings House against his orders, your punishment will be worse than mine. Grandfather will blame you, and have you both put out of this life in the most horrible way."

Leta and Auti nodded, and Ankhesenpaaten knew from experience that she had their attention.

Ankhesenpaaten continued: "Get them to walk you into the stand of palms, and behave as though pleasure awaits them in the shadow of the trees."

Leta said, "I recognize them. We made sport of these same two sentries two nights ago, Princess. They'll be on to us."

Ankhesenpaaten smiled. "Well then, this time give them what they want."

"My lady!" Auti said, her cry muffled behind a hand at her lips. "I would rather kiss a monkey's ass."

Ankhesenpaaten laughed. "Well, give them almost what they want. There's no end to the abuse a man will take so long as the hope of sex is fixed in his mind. Besides, they're stupid soldiers, and you're my clever friends, eager to please the future queen of Egypt. Is this not so?"

Leta and Auti nodded.

Ankhesenpaaten spoke to Leta and Auti rapidly, authority in her voice. "When I have slipped through the gates, tell the guards you are off to see a relative in Thebes. I'm going with my friends to The Inn of the Two Brothers, and will return home at the usual time. As before, you will wait for me outside the inn. There will be guards posted there by the patrons to watch their horses and chariots. You will be safe."

Ankhesenpaaten positioned herself behind an obelisk of the Aten rising out of the stone floor of the courtyard. She watched her two handmaidens walk slowly toward the tall bronze gate. Leta called out a greeting. As the sentries turned, she flattened her body against the obelisk. The deep voices of the sentries sounded surprised at the unexpected company. She knew Leta and Auti well enough to imagine the seductively giddy motion of their bodies bathed in moonlight, and how their eager smiles and large black eyes could gleam with interest. She could guess how the sentries would respond. Their behavior is predictable, Ankhesenpaaten thought with an inner smile. Young men seek the pleasures of lovemaking with the same constancy as grazing cattle search out green pasturelands. It was a lesson her father, Pharaoh Akhenaten, had drummed into her head.

Ankhesenpaaten waited. The sound of the couples talking at the gate was a steady murmuring hum punctuated with an occasional shriek of laughter. She grew impatient. *Silly girls. Get on with it*! The voices trailed off. She cocked her ear then ventured a peek. The foursome walked away, parallel to the gate. A little farther and hopefully they would dart into the line of palms.

One of the sentries stopped and looked around. Ankhesenpaaten drew back behind the obelisk and waited, her heart thumping in her breast. More chatter. She peered slowly around the obelisk. The sentries had their arms around the girls' waists, allowing their javelins to trail behind in their free hands.

With a sigh of relief Ankhesenpaaten watched them dart down a path and disappear in the shadow of the trees. Taking a deep breath, she left the obelisk and jogged toward the garden and the safety of the date palms.

A hundred meters or so inside the neat rows of palms, she waited, panting for breath. Her friends were always eager to escort her to the Inn of the Two Brothers, and sometimes they even vied for the honor. Who would it be this time?

From the long rows of date palms she could hear the muted voices of her maids and the sentries. She heard laughter and breathed a sigh of relief. The guards were distracted. She would make good her escape. She leaned against the smooth bark of a palm trunk and waited.

"Princess?" came the soft reedy voice of a young man.

A face speckled in moonlight appeared before her. It was Seba, the son of the overseer of the herds of the Aten. He flashed her a brave smile, as though to solicit her thanks for allowing him the honor of escorting her to the inn.

She had no romantic interest in Seba, but he was a friend, and a reminder of the many young people outside Kings House all too eager to help her enjoy what was left of the good life in Amarna.

Seba leaned near to her. She turned to him and, without hesitation, kissed him on the cheek. Seba flushed. She knew he considered himself in the running as one of her favorites. She liked him to think so, and had no reason to convey any other impression.

Seba said, "A chariot waits beyond the trees."

They walked quickly, hand in hand through the dense stand of palms. Then the trees began to thin, and there were scattered spots of dancing moonlight. Very soon they were out of the trees and on a gravelly road. A brace of horses and a chariot, bathed in moonlight, were secured to a nearby palm tree. The horses, nervous beneath the swishing palm fronds, bobbed their heads and whinnied.

The chariot rumbled down the road. The air was clean and cool, and Ankhesenpaaten breathed out a sigh of relief, her eyes fixed on the flickering lights of the southern suburbs.

Outside the Inn of the Two Brothers a party of friends waited for the princess. The inn was a gathering place for prominent citizens of Amarna, and a favorite of the privileged young. It was sometimes patronized by priests of the Aten as well as merchants and seamen from the Phoenician coast. All of this added just a sufficient amount of danger to excite the interests of young people with money to spend.

Smiling friends encircled the chariot after it stopped at the inn's door. Seba proudly helped Ankhesenpaaten from the chariot.

Outside a nearby barn, an Assyrian trader sat in a lowered sedan chair. He watched the young people and the princess. Ankhesenpaaten was vaguely aware of being watched. The Assyrian wore a broad purple-sleeved tunic. Ankhesenpaaten tried for a better look, but the Assyrian had gotten out of the Sedan chair presenting his back on her. She turned back to her friends with a contented smile, and disappeared through the inn's open doors.

6

Menkhara and Critias arrived at the Inn of the Two Brothers. They stood for a moment outside the open front door listening to the laughter of patrons mixing with the music of reed pipes and the sharp ringing of a sistrum.

They entered through a curtain made of strings of turquoise stones. In the center of the crowded room was a low ebony serving table loaded with pitchers of wine, beer and bowls of figs and cake-breads. Most of the patrons sat on brightly colored cushions, talking or shouting at the young serving girls for attention.

Menkhara and Critias found a small cedarwood table and ordered honeyed beer. It was not long before the two good-looking Theban men attracted the attention of the inn's whores. The whores knew that Thebans, up from the south, had money, and were away from their homes and their loved ones. Critias, with his roving eye and love of female companionship, fell at once under the spell of a seductive smile belonging to a whore from Sidon. He allowed himself to be led away, managing only a quick smile for Menkhara as he disappeared down a darkened hall.

Menkhara sat alone nursing his beer. A pack of noisy young people passed his table, headed for a chamber partitioned off from the main room by a heavy beaded curtain.

A pretty face flashed by. Menkhara watched, incredulous. Princess Ankhesenpaaten! The dour look she had given him at Kings House was gone. She was animated with laughter and conversation. Was he mistaken? Royal princesses did not appear in public inns. It was unthinkable! But there she was, her pretty bobbing head commanding attention as she passed in front of him.

The partygoers disappeared behind the beaded curtain, their laughter punctuated by occasional shrieks of delight. He felt much older than he was; older than he wanted to be, a fuddy-duddy who had never experienced the joys of youth. He ordered a second beer.

The inn entertained with music. Soon the simple tunes on the double flutes gave way to the strumming of a harp. From out of nowhere, dancing girls, slim and young, snaked their way across the room. They mounted a platform and faced the patrons, their thin oiled bodies naked except for the strings of blue beads around their waists. Wreaths of lotus blossoms crowned their long, glossy black hair.

The beaded curtain parted. The young partygoers came out to

watch the dancing and stood near the platform, full of animated discussion.

Wide-eyed, Menkhara watched Ankhesenpaaten pushed gently up the steps by her friends. They shouted encouragement, and at the same time dared her to perform. She teetered slightly, and Menkhara guessed that she was drunk.

Ankhesenpaaten mounted the platform and turned to face the applauding patrons and friends. A broad smile broke across her face as her eyes swept the audience. Shocked, Menkhara watched the future queen of Egypt stoop and pick up a pair of clappers someone had thrown onto the stage. Putting them on, she joined the girls as they formed a vigorous chorus line, their tawny, eel-like arms weaving above their heads. Two sistrums and a lute began to play.

Menkhara was struck by Ankhesenpaaten's vivaciousness. She was dressed in a simple translucent narrow dress covering her left shoulder, leaving the right shoulder bare. The wide-open cloak of linen fastened in front was so sheer that no feature of her body was left to wonder about. It was the latest fashion, and very appropriate for a woman of rank and position.

At first the princess seemed to be simply one link in a chain, but as the tempo picked up, she began a wildly ecstatic rocking of her hips and belly that fell out of sync with the smooth, coiled motions of the other dancers and the beat of the clappers. Rapacious eyes fixed on her as her movements progressed toward a bucking that left little to the imagination. There could not have been a man in the audience who did not burn with desire for the fifteen-year-old.

When the music fell silent, Ankhesenpaaten descended the platform steps, oblivious of her friends who were waiting for her to join them. She turned and walked directly toward Menkhara's table.

Surely she would not want to talk to him in a public place, he thought. But now she stood at his table, breathing hard, her gown clinging to the sweaty high points of her body, the cant of her belly and the rosebud nipples of her breasts.

"Again we meet, Menkhara. I must learn to read my signs more carefully." She smiled and added: "Will you not offer me a seat?"

Menkhara, maintaining his composure with ex-treme difficulty, stood up in an instant. He pulled out the seat across from him and waited until the princess arranged herself in it.

Meanwhile, Menkhara ordered a second pitcher of honeyed beer. Ankhesenpaaten's friends had gathered at the base of the platform, waiting for her to join them. The young men, suddenly deprived of Ankhesenpaten, stared across the room at their princess, seated across from some unknown rival, then slowly disappeared behind the beaded curtain.

"You're an accomplished dancer," Menkhara said.

"Is that why you're here, Menkhara? I would assume that you've come here to spy on me."

"Not so, lady," Menkhara insisted.

"What will you tell my grandfather; that his granddaughter, the future queen of Egypt, behaved like an ordinary woman of the street?"

Menkhara collected his thoughts. He was so taken aback by the presence of a solar princess, it was as though he had walked into a dream. This was undoubtedly the kind of thing Simut might have hoped for. But he was not thinking of Simut, his mission in Amarna, or anything else. "You mistake me," he finally said. "I have no such thoughts."

They sat quietly, drinking their beer. The princess kept her eyes on Menkhara.

"You know," she finally said, assessing him with a smile, "you really are too good-looking for your own good. I bet you've broken many hearts."

"I wouldn't want to think so."

"Do you have a lady you are bound to?"

"I am betrothed," he answered.

"To whom?"

"Your highness would hardly know her."

"Your future sovereign has asked you a question, Menkhara. To whom?"

"Her name is Mayet. She is the daughter of the deputy foreman in the village of workers at Deir el-Medina, across the Nile from Thebes."

Ankhesenpaaten pursed her lips thoughtfully. "How is it a royal scribe charged with your responsibilities is betrothed to the daughter of a worker?"

Menkhara smiled. "Because I am the son of a worker. My father is the chief foreman at Deir el-Medina."

Ankhesenpaaten laughed lightly and shook her head. "You're full of surprises. Is your Mayet pretty, Menkhara?"

"Yes, tolerably so."

"Tolerably?" Ankhesenpaaten laughed again, then sipped her beer. She put down her glass and lifted her large dark eyes slowly. "Prettier than me?"

"That's unfair, lady." He hesitated, and then added, "There's none so fair as you."

"Would you be so kind as to accompany me home?"

Menkhara did not answer immediately. Her request suggested possibilities that would have delighted Simut. But from the very beginning he had had no stomach for gathering evidence against Ankhesenpaaten, and regretted letting Simut talk him into it. For now, he was content to feed into her eyes, her youth. She was beautiful.

"I came on foot," he finally said.

"Then we'll leave on foot."

Menkhara tried to calm himself. If nothing else, he would not come off looking a fool. He breathed in and smiled. "If that's your wish, lady."

7

Disguised in the purple-sleeved tunic of an Assyrian trader, Simut sat in his sedan chair outside the Inn of the Two Brothers. His two Syrian carriers, Baladan and Lokrava, sat motionless beneath a tree, staring silently into the night. The men were from Tyre, and Simut kept them as sedan carriers and household guards. They were as dumb as oxen, but he could count on their loyalty.

Simut snoozed lightly but was always conscious enough to open his eyes when someone entered or staggered out of the inn.

Two hours passed, and Simut, at the edge of sleep, was finally roused by the rippling sound of a woman's laugh.

Princess Ankhesenpaaten was leaving the inn. A man accompanied her, walking close by her side. He was on her right, his face hidden from view. This was more than Simut had hoped for. The princess was walking into the night with a man. But who? Some disgusting, filthy merchant, no doubt! He snapped his fingers, and in an instant the carriers were on their feet. Simut pointed into the dark toward a stand of date fig trees. "Follow them," he hissed.

They followed the couple through the trees and out onto a flat gravelly field. At the far end of the field stood Akhenaten's great temple of the Aten, its roofed portico and six colonnaded courts bathed in moonlight. The princess and her escort were headed toward the temple's front gate. Simut guessed they were probably drunk and looking for a private chapel where they could be alone, unseen.

Exercising the caution of a hunter nearing his kill, Simut ordered the sedan chair lowered near the entrance to an adjacent warehouse. Pondering his options, he watched the man and Ankhesenpaaten nearing the temple gate. The man turned and gazed across the flat, pebble-strewn land, moonlight illuminating his face.

Menkhara!

Simut watched, gloating over the sudden turn of events. A plan of action quickly formed in his mind. Menkhara would be alone with her in the temple. He had doubts about sending Menkhara to spy on the princess, but now things were working out better than he could have imagined. There would be no need for spying, no need to accuse the princess in the court of the vizier; no need for long-winded testimony on the princess's character.

He would kill her either in the temple or somewhere along the road back to Amarna.

He could not have planned things better. He had made sure to tell no one he had come to Amarna. The local authorities were incompetent. They would not find her assailant. Baladan and Lokrava, his loyal stupid servants, without thinking twice on it, could rip Ankhesenpaaten's heart out. And if Menkhara got in his way, or didn't go along with it, one nod of his head and his men would put a quick end to him.

Simut embellished his plan. He could make the princess's death seem like rape—after all, she was out at night with a commoner. He would have Baladan and Lokrava have their way with her body. There would be clear signs of sexual assault. Simut could not remember when he felt so good. With the hated princess dead, Amun-Ra would be satisfied, and better still, his father's death would be avenged.

He ordered Baladan and Lokrava to lower the sedan chair, then settled back on his seat, his eyes fixed on the young couple standing bathed in moonlight outside the deserted Temple of the Aten. It was no place to attempt an ambush—too much open space and moonlight. If they ventured inside the the temple, he would send in Baladan and Lokrava to take the princess by surprise. They would make quick work of her. Now all he had to do was wait.

8

Menkhara and Ankhesepaaten stood in the moonlight outside the temple of the Aten.

"My father's temple, Menkhara. It is truly beautiful. I would take you inside, but even in the moonlight, there is much that you would miss. In the light of day it is glorious to behold. You can see from here that it has an open roof so that the Aten can send his golden rays down upon the sanctuaries within."

Menkhara smiled. "It must be lovely."

"What do you know of the Aten?" Ankhesenpaaten continued.

"I know that the priests of the Aten believe in one God, and that he is the source of all life. Your father believed himself to be the son of the Aten, but could not win the hearts of the Theban people. I suppose that's why he left Thebes and founded Amarna."

Ankhesenpaaten reached for Menkhara's hand and took it in hers. It seemed like a natural, spontaneous gesture, something waiting to happen. "All of that is true," she said in a noticeably softer voice. "My father was the son of the Aten as well as his chief prophet. He was, in the words of his priests, 'the good ruler who loved mankind.' There is not a day goes by where I don't feel in the heat of the sun his holy presence all about me."

In the shared silence they turned away from the temple and

started down the path back to Kings House. Menkhara was beginning to like her. She had changed from the moment they paused outside the temple. There was another side to her. She became serious when she talked about her god and Akhenaten. It was as though her father and the god were one. It was something she wanted to share with him, teach him, and he respected her for it.

Within sight of the royal residence they came to a stand of sycamore trees.

"Let's rest here in the shadows," said Ankhesenpaaten.

The princess sat with her back against a fat tree trunk and stretched her legs to their full length with a sigh of relief. Menkhara sat beside her and watched her peer upward through the leafy branches. She looked very young—younger than Mayet, who was her age. Flecks of moonlight danced in her black glossy hair and against the soft curve of her shoulders and arms. Her full sensuous lips, done in deep red ochre and set in a wise smile, reminded him of a bust he had seen of her mother, Nefertiti. Her small hand lodged in his.

Ankhesenpaaten said, "We haven't known each other very long."

Menkhara smiled. "I suppose not."

"If I told you that I have good feelings about you, what would you think?"

Menkhara smiled. "I wouldn't know what to think."

They stared at one another in silence then Ankhesenpaaten leaned over and kissed him on the mouth. Menkhara drew back instinctively, not out of shyness but surprise. She was a solar princess, betrothed to the future Pharaoh. If they were seen, he would be as good as dead.

Menkhara swallowed hard. "You shouldn't have done that, lady," he said sternly.

Ankhesenpaaten laughed. "If it does not matter to me, why should it matter to you?"

"Because I value my life, as you should value your position."

"If a kiss puts you in a fright," Ankhesenpaaten teased, "I suppose you would faint straight away if I offered you my love."

"I would not faint, Princess," said Menkhara. She was as saucy as she was beautiful. He regretted escorting her home. He sensed that the princess usually got what she wanted. Akhenaten must have spoiled her terribly. She could cause trouble. He pondered all that she had done, beginning with going to the Inn of the Two Brothers. She drank too much and danced for the benefit of merchants and traders. She allowed herself to be conducted home by a commoner, kissed him, and he guessed that she was prepared to offer much more. He guessed she was capable of anything, this young woman who was about to become the god's wife. He would have to reason with her as best he could.

"You are a solar princess," Menkhara began. "You're the future queen of Egypt."

"I'm a young woman."

"Nevertheless, a solar princess, uncorrupted and betrothed."

She gave him a hard smile. "You wouldn't be the first. I was both daughter and king's wife to our late Pharaoh Akhenaten."

Before Menkhara could reply, she snuggled close to him, the scent of oil of lily on her skin. Desire gripped his loins as he gazed into her eyes, shining in the moonlight. She was beautiful. Without realizing what he was doing, he caressed her silky black hair and brought soft strands to his mouth and nose. He held her tight.

A twig snapped, and Menkhara froze. Gazing up, he thought he saw a shadow flit through an opening in the stand of trees.

He stood up, pulling Ankhesenpaaten to her feet.

"What is it?" she cried in a panicky voice.

Menkhara stepped forward, peering through the trees.

Across the field, outside the protection of the sycamores, three figures hurried toward them across the moonlit field. The lead man was stout, and in the garb of an Assyrian merchant, a foreigner, his broad sleeves billowing in the wind. His face was wrapped in a cloth, and tied in the back. Running ahead of the fat foreigner came two men bare to the waist and dressed in simple kilts. A chill ran through his body.

Menkhara whispered under his breath. "Assassins, Princess. They are coming for us."

He clasped Ankhesenpaaten's hand, pausing only momentarily to consider his options. The only thing that mattered was the princess's safety. The stand of sycamores was not dense enough to hide them. He would have to get her unharmed back to Kings House. Once they left the protection of the trees, they would be spotted in the open field, and he could not count on the princess moving quickly enough to make it to the royal road.

Menkhara pulled Ankhesenpaaten close to him. "Head for the royal road, lady. There are guardhouses along the way. They'll have to break off the pursuit. I'll distract them, and then catch up with you."

Ankhesenpaaten opened her mouth to protest.

"Go!" Menkhara commanded.

The color drained from Ankhesenpaaten's face. She turned and jogged a few paces, then slowed to a quick walk. She looked back at Menkhara and then broke into a run.

Menkhara waited behind the trunk of a thick sycamore. Ankhesenpaaten broke into the open field and headed for the Royal Road. One of the pursuers pointed then raced toward the princess. Menkhara started after them, hoping to cut them off before they reached the open field.

He was close enough to see sweat glistening on the assassins' chests as they ran. The third assassin, the fat one dressed in

Assyrian robes, trudged along far behind, hindered by what appeared to be a limp.

Menkhara moved swiftly through the trees at an angle to the route taken by the men. He reached a point they would have to pass, close to the trees, and there waited and listened to the lead man panting as he approached. He let him pass. Moments later, the second man came trudging along, gasping for breath.

Menkhara sprang at him. He girdled the assassin's waist from behind and spun him around, crashing his face into a tree. The dazed assassin yelped. Menkhara seized hold of his hair, pulled back, then thrust his head into the tree again. The assassin fell silent, his body limp. Menkhara let go, and was in hot pursuit of the lead man before his victim hit the ground.

The swiftest of the assassins rapidly gained on the princess. Menkhara dashed across the open field. Ankhesenpaaten's lead had dwindled.

Menkhara closed the gap between himself and the assassin. Moonlight glittered on a polished bronze blade. The man was armed with a knife.

He reached the assassin, who at the last second turned toward him. Both men lost their balance and fell in a tangle of arms and legs. The gravel bit into Menkhara's skin as he tumbled across the ground.

The two men sprang to their feet. The assassin was no longer in possession of a knife, but he had another weapon—his fists, and he used them to good advantage, pummeling Menkhara. Stunned, Menkhara staggered backward. The assassin came for him, breathing hard and grunting like a pig. Two more body blows and Menkhara was on the ground, face up.

Dazed, Menkhara lay still, too dizzy and weak to move. Sweat burned in his eyes as he looked up at the assassin straddling him, a cold flat smile on the man's face.

Menkhara twisted to the left, reaching for the assassin's leg. The assassin grunted an obscenity in a foreign accent. Menkhara's eyes fell upon the bronze knife less than a meter away. He lunged for it and took hold of it by the haft, just as the assassin dropped to his knees and clasped his large hands around Menkhara's throat and squeezed.

Menkhara, unable to breathe, smashed his fist into the man's chest with enough force to break his grip. The assassin rocked backward, recovered and looked down at his squirming victim with a brutal smile. He doubled his large hands into fists.

Menkhara thrust the knife upward.

The blade pierced the assassin's throat. Warm blood gushed across Menkhara's chest. The assassin fell back with a gurgling sound. Menkhara waited, supported on his elbows. Small bubbles of blood formed on the assassin's lips. The dying man breathed heavily, one hand pressed against his neck. Menkhara staggered to his feet and stared down as the man's open vacant eyes turned skyward.

Nauseous from the heat, his chest covered in blood, Menkhara stared across the field. The fat Assyrian had passed him during the struggle, but Ankhesenpaaten outran him. He breathed a sigh of relief. A moment later she tripped and fell in a faint cloud of dust. The Assyrian was immediately upon her. He fell to his knees and lay across her body. Ankhesenpaaten screamed. Menkhara raced toward her.

Ankhesenpaaten twisted away from the Assyrian's grasp and struggled to her feet. The Assyrian would not be thwarted. He threw himself at her. Breath expelled from her lungs, the princess stumbled back, striking her head against the trunk of a sycamore as she collapsed to the ground and lay still.

Menkhara, enraged at the sight of Ankhesenpaaten sprawled unconscious at the base of the tree, leapt at the Assyrian, reached down and grabbed a thick strand of his hair. A wig came off in his hand, exposing the perfectly round bald head of a priest! The Assyrian turned to face him, his eyes staring from behind the cotton mask.

Menkhara sent his fist crashing into the man's face. He groaned, rolled away and tried to get up. Menkhara struck him twice more, then, breathing hard, ripped off the cloth mask.

"Simut!"

Blood flowed from his broken nose, and one eye was nearly closed.

Menkhara stared down at his life-long friend in horror, his thoughts muddled.

"For the sake of Amun, Menkhara," Simut wheezed. "What are you doing?"

Menkhara pulled Simut's face up to his and whispered harshly in his ear. "What am I doing? Damn you! If she sees your face you'll be prosecuted and broiled in the sun. Out of respect for our friendship, Simut, I'll say nothing; but get out of here!"

"I thought we were the best of friends," Simut whispered hoarsely. "Look what you've done."

Menkhara pointed to the princess's coiled, trembling body. "Look what you've done," he shouted, scooping up the wig and throwing it at Simut. "Cover your face and leave at once."

"In the name of all the gods, Menkhara," Simut pleaded.

"Go! Go! Go!"

Simut wrapped the cloth around his face, all the while threatening in a choking voice: "You will answer for this, commoner." He turned and loped away.

Menkhara imagined the grimace of hatred on Simut's face. If he knew the man, he was already planning his revenge. Menkhara stared after him, his eyes on the Assyrian gown fluttering in the moonlight. His friendship with Simut was now a thing of the past, and he knew in his heart that his life would never be the same again.

Menkhara kneeled down beside Ankhesenpaaten and cradled her head in his arms. She moaned and opened her eyes.

"They want to kill me," she said softly.

"They?"

"Everyone who hates the memory of my father and his god, the Aten. The priesthood of Amun-Ra called Akhenaten the great heretic in his lifetime, and believe that as the future queen of Egypt, I would extend the heresy and deny the Theban priesthood title to their lands and treasures."

"Not everyone hates you, Princess."

"For now, my betrothal to Tutare works to Grandfather Ay's advantage. So long as someone of his line is Pharaoh's queen, his influence at court will not wane."

Menkhara smiled at her. He had a sudden urge to kiss her. "When the Thebans see how radiant and beautiful and kind you are, Princess, you'll win their hearts."

"I don't want to win hearts. And I've no desire to be wife to a nine-year-old boy." Tears filled her eyes. "Oh, Menkhara, I'd rather be married to a ditcher in the fields who works among the cattle and the pigs and comes home at night with his stinking shabby kilt stiff with mud."

Menkhara caressed her hair. "You'll feel better in the safety of Kings House, after a bath and a good night's sleep."

"I can't go back now. The guards will see me. I always wait until dawn and the changing of the guards. I can come and go anytime I please during the day."

"We can't stay here in the open like this," Menkhara insisted.

After a silence, Ankhesenpaaten said, "We'll go back to the temple lake. It is better there by the reeds, and the water is cool. I like the night, especially when I'm close to my father's temple of the Aten."

Menkhara nodded. "If that is your wish."

The next moment she sat up and whispered in Menkhara's ear.

"Will you swim with me in the lake?"

Her breath was warm on his neck, and he delighted in the sensuous softness in her voice and the way she smiled at him. He did not answer, but stood up and offered her his hand. She came to her feet, and slowly they walked back to the temple.

The pewter-colored lake shimmered in moonlight. They stood beneath the protective drooping limbs of a weeping willow at the water's edge and watched the soft rippling water. Ankhesenpaaten rested her head against him. Menkhara put his arm around her shoulders. She looked up at him, a small smile on her lips. He kissed her on the cheek. She put her hand to his chin, coaxing him to greater intimacy. He kissed her on the lips. Ankhesenpaaten untied the sash of her gown and fiddled with a shoulder strap. The gown fell. Then with a giggle, and without looking back, she waded into the water. Menkhara stripped off his kilt and followed. When the water reached Ankhesenpaaten's waist, she plunged forward with a gentle splash and disappeared.

Menkhara dived beneath the surface. By the time he reached her, she was near the middle of the lake, treading water.

"You're a good swimmer," Menkhara said, bobbing up beside her.

"My father insisted that all his daughters swim, though he couldn't do so himself. Women are not taught to swim, especially in temple lakes since they are meant for priests to wash off impurities before entering their temples. But this is Amarna." She laughed.

The young pair swam to the far side of the lake, momentarily disturbing a duck and her ducklings paddling quickly out of harm's way. They rested near the bank, waist deep. The princess floated in circles, splashing with her feet. Then she came to Menkhara's side, and they stood together, staring up at the bright full moon.

Her breasts, wet and shining, gleamed in the moonlight. Her long black hair hung straight down her back. Whatever experience she had with men, there was a trusting side to her nature that radiated innocence.

They began to slowly swim back. A gray heron skimmed across the water, so low they could hear the flapping of its wings before it spiraled up to the sky and disappeared.

Drawing close to the shoreline, their bodies came together as though on cue. Menkhara circled her waist and drew her close. She raised her arms and clasped her hands around his neck. Their bodies pressed, the softness of her breasts against his chest. She wiggled her body, broke free and swam without stopping until she reached the shore.

Menkhara waited momentarily and then followed. He reached her, standing at the water's edge in the reeds. He waded up to her and took her outstretched hand. They returned to where their clothes lay beneath the protective branches of the weeping willow. She lay on the soft warm ground and coaxed Menkhara to a place beside her. And this time there was no coyness, no hesitation and no playfulness in her intent.

Menkhara kissed her wet breasts, all the while exploring her body with his one free hand. The princess responded in kind, her hand silking down to his loins.

They made love, and when it was over, Ankhesenpaaten lay in his arms and fell asleep. Menkhara remained awake, staring up at the sky, listening to Ankhesenpaaten breathing gently at his side. Was he crazy to love her? Her face was soft and glowed with the innocence of a child, and he thought of the great divide that separated them.

At the edge of his mind was Simut, who was undoubtedly

spending a sleepless night under the same night sky, nursing his obsessions, planning his revenge. Menkhara closed his eyes.

When he wakened, the princess stood over him, tying the sash of her gown and stepping into her sandals. It was dawn. Kingfishers and swallows sang in the willow, and ducks quacked among the reeds. The sky on the eastern horizon was a hazy pink. He quickly stood up and put on his kilt.

Ankhesenpaaten put her arms around Menkhara's waist. She looked up at him. "Thank you," she said.

They held hands and walked out to the clearing, cut across a field and turned onto a road leading to the government buildings. A few hundred meters from the gates of Kings House, the princess stopped.

"Now we must say goodbye, Menkhara," she said. "I suppose you'll be returning to Thebes."

"The day after tomorrow, lady."

"You'll see me at Malkata when the court moves upriver?"

"If it's your pleasure."

"Oh, Menkhara, I must go," she said, trying to smile. Tears came to her eyes and she put her arms around his waist, pressed her head into his chest and kissed him. She pulled herself away and walked down the road that would take her past a row of low government buildings and onto the grounds of Kings House. Menkhara watched her go until she disappeared down a narrow alley.

9

It was the noon hour, and Princess Mutnedjmet sat in naked silence on a carpet in the center of her bathing room, attended by three servants. One was busy laying out a fresh gown and powdered sandals, while the two others gently poured cool water over her head and across her torso. Her favorite servant, the mistress of her toilet box, gently rubbed her arms with open hands dipped in rose-scented water. It was Mutnedjmet's second bath of the day, and if she followed her usual routine, two more would follow before she sat down to her evening meal.

Mutnedjmet eyed the dress her servant had brought into the bathing room. It was a linen garment that by the standards of the youth of her day was a bit on the conservative side. It would cover her completely. An exposed breast, as was the custom among the younger set, would not do for a forty-year-old woman; and though her breasts had barely begun to sag, they were still a far cry from the high and full bosom of her youth. Besides, she did not want to be compared to anyone else.

Mutnedjmet hated competition of any kind, even when she was in the company of women half her age. Growing old was a dirty trick of the gods that she would elude as long as possible, except to cover up and deny in her mind's eye that she would not be forever young in body and soul.

If anyone contributed to Mutnedjmet's obsession with youth and beauty, it was her older sister, Nefertiti. How could it be otherwise? From early in life, Nefertiti was considered to be a young lady of astonishing beauty, whereas Mutnedjmet, when her face was not twisted with scowls of jealously, was merely pretty. But now that Queen Nefertiti was dead, and Mutnedjmet was her father's only living child, it was her time to shine. And how hard she tried. Sadly, not even her servants' considerable skill at toilet could roll back the years. The application of cosmetics—the bright red ochre and bands of black kohl—did little to hide the crows' feet around her eyes and the thin maze of hairline wrinkles slowly gathering at the corners of her mouth.

There were two men in Mutnedjmet's life, one all-powerful and the other a weak scoundrel.

Her father Ay, vizier of the Upper Kingdom and regent to

Prince Tutankhamun, was the most famous man in the kingdom, and held many titles granted him by the third Amunhotep, the old king who was known affectionately as Mighty Bull.

The other man in Mutnedjmet's life was her husband, Tanehes, a former Lieutenant of Infantry, relieved of his command for cowardice, and whose only occupation at court was drinking and whoring in the less reputable taverns and beerhouses of Thebes. A partygoer with no ambition, Tanehes was Mutnedjmet's husband in name only, and the reason why she sought the companionship of many men, a pastime that was the subject of whispered gossip in the forecourts of the palace at Malkata.

Washed and dried, Mutnedjmet climbed onto an alabaster bathing slab. She lay on her back, eyes closed, while two servants applied a deliciously scented oil of lily to her body.

A young nervous servant girl entered the bathing room, looked around and then trotted over to the bathing slab. "Excuse, lady, but the second high prophet of Amun has arrived for his audience, and awaits in the receiving chamber."

Eyes closed, Mutnedjmet's slack mouth suggested boredom. "Simut?" she said. "Well, keep him waiting, you silly goose."

The servant girl nodded, bowed abruptly, and backed out of the bathing room.

Simut? Mutnedjmet thought. Why would I—? Then she remembered the invitation. Simut had something to tell her about a matter of great interest. She was willing to listen to the chubby crippled priest, if only in the hope that he found some way of keeping the young princess off the throne of the Two Lands. Simut, she thought, imagining the fat priest fidgeting in his chair, waiting for her to appear. A smile broke across her face. She remembered the last time she granted an audience to Simut. She liked to keep the pompous pig waiting; anything to take him down a notch or two. He was pompous to be sure, and so dull, but he had something to offer: an implacable, obsessive hatred of Ankhesenpaaten. Mutnedjmet smiled. *The enemy of my enemy must be my friend, I suppose.*

Her reason for hating Ankhesenpaaten was a lot less complex. The young princess was an obnoxious bitch who never treated her Auntie Mutnedjmet with proper respect when she was down for a visit; and if Ankhesenpaaten married the sickly Tutankhamun, and he died, she would try to rule in her own right. The very thought of Ankhesenpaaten lording over her was simply too disgusting to think about.

Normally the long wait would have put Simut in a foul mood. He did not like to be kept waiting, especially by a woman. But Mutnedjmet was his last best hope after the mess he made of things in Amarna. The princess, thank all the gods, hated Ankhesenpaaten as much as he.

Mutnedjmet entered the room. Simut shot to his feet and bowed. She looked as elegant as ever, though less reserved than at their last meeting. This time she actually came around the desk and offered him her hand. It was cool to the touch, and Simut could smell the glistening oil of lily on her skin. She looked at him with a cool interest that left him utterly confused as to what she might be thinking.

She smiled and sat down next to him. As was her custom, she wore a sheath dress, both breasts covered, but low enough to show a magnificent bright golden collar strung with beads of gold, carnelian and feldspar. She smiled at him, a smile meant to tease and hide, only slightly, her superiority.

"Dear cousin," she said, showing more curiosity than concern, "whatever happened to your face? It's all black and blue, and your eye is swollen."

"I was attacked by thieves in a dark alley in Amarna. I managed to fight them off, but as you see, they got in some good blows."

"Poor man," Mutnedjmet said. "But what were you doing in that hateful town?"

"Your father wanted answers regarding foreign correspondence exchanged between our late Pharaoh and our allies in Syria and elsewhere. I sent some of our best royal scribes to find out what they could, but in the end knew that I would have to get personally involved."

Mutnedjmet looked obliquely at Simut, giving him the impression that she had advance information about why he sought an audience. "Is that what we are going to talk about, cousin?"

"No, lady. I'm privy to information I inadvertently obtained in Amarna—information we both must value."

Mutnedjmet edged closer to Simut. The smell of oil of lily was as strong as ever. Simut associated the scent with the first time he had sex with a woman. But Mutnedjmet was much prettier than the fat wife of the deputy treasurer he had lain with in the storeroom of the House of Life's scriptorium.

Simut described how he had seen Menkhara and Ankhesenpaaten leave the Inn of the Two Brothers, holding hands. Inspired by the shocked look on Mutnedjmet's face, his voice rose in volume, dramatizing every detail with his hands. He decided to embellish the story.

"They entered a stand of sycamore trees. I ordered my carriers to follow. I got out of my sedan chair and followed sounds of laughter and giggling. And then I saw them, as plain as ever in the moonlight, lying on the ground, bodies entwined. Their moans filled the night. Horrified at the sight of our compromised divine princess, I fled."

Mutnedjmet listened intently to Simut, signaling to him with nods of her head and sighs of understanding that she believed every word of it.

"Poor dear man," she said in a low voice. "How terrible for you to bear witness to such a thing." She reached over and took Simut's stubby hand in hers and kissed him on his fat cheek.

Simut's heart skipped a beat.

"What do you propose to do about it?" Mutnedjmet said, breaking a long silence.

Simut thought for a while. "It would be the Princess Ankhesenpaaten's word against mine. Your father would never let the matter go to court. And it is not likely the high priest would have the courage to take up the matter."

"You are right, of course. Father will not have his granddaughter cast out as impure. He wants Ankhesenpaaten as Tutankhamun's queen, if for no other reason than to preserve his influence at court long after Pharaoh is mature enough to reign in his own right."

"But he doesn't know his own granddaughter! She is willful, cunning, yes, and even cruel. She—"

"Enough!" said Mutnedjmet, cutting in with a dismissive wave of her hand. "We need not preach to each other on the subject, cousin. Neither of us wants her on the throne, and we need only work together to prevent it from happening." A crafty smile played across her face. "When Princess Ankhesenpaaten arrives in Thebes, it will be difficult for her to arrange a rendezvous with this Menkhara of hers without help. Remember, cousin, this is Thebes, and with the coronation and marriage weeks away, her every move will be watched. She cannot act alone. Father will see to that."

"Then what is the point?"

"The point, cousin, is that we will accommodate the young lady's unbridled passion. We will arrange for the lovers to meet."

A surge of excitement coursed through Simut. He fidgeted in his chair, hardly able to contain himself. He wanted to cry and laugh at the same time, throw himself at Mutnedjmet's feet and thank her a thousand times over.

"Father plans to take over a palace apartment at Malkata," she continued. "I will continue to reside here at the family villa. When the princess settles into Malkata, I'll give a party and present her to the flower of Theban society. Menkhara will, of course, be invited. We will arrange for them to be alone. And then, at the right moment, with proper witnesses ..." Mutnedjmet paused and gave Simut a broad smile.

Simut leaned closer. "Yes, lady, and then?"

Mutnedjmet smiled. "And then? Oh, Simut, you have the imagination of a toad. Do I have to spell it out for you?"

Simut flushed. Mutnedjmet had a way of putting him down just when he thought he had gained her respect. But it hardly mattered. He had gained a powerful ally, and she could pee all over him for all he cared. Ankhesenpaaten would be seen for the whoring bitch she really was. She would be cast out from court, forgotten! Praise the Lord of Thrones, Amun-Ra! Praise the gods for Mutnedjmet!

10

On his return to Thebes, Menkhara was one among many summoned to appear before the regent Ay and his council to better understand the disastrous loss of Egypt's eastern empire during the reign of the heretic Pharaoh.

Menkhara arrived early at the palace at Malkata and joined other officials milling around the forecourt waiting their turn to be called before the regent. The main palace building at Malkata was centered on a huge pillared court, including an audience hall.

After an hour of broiling in the hot sun, Menkhara was finally called up to the audience hall. He sat facing a scribe who questioned him about the House of Correspondence in Amarna. Ay was seated on the scribe's right hand. Maya, the treasurer, was seated next to Ay, and next to him sat the regent's aging cousin, Minnakht, general of the armies of Egypt.

Menkhara read his translations out loud. The scribe interrupted him from time to time to confer with Ay. When Menkhara finished, Ay smiled and thanked him, and the scribe motioned the next official forward even before Menkhara bowed low and withdrew.

Menkhara started down the long flight of steps that lead to the forecourt below. The audience was so brief that he somehow felt cheated. The regent had not asked him one question.

A servant, breathless from running, caught up with Menkhara. "My mistress, Princess Mutnedjmet, desires to see you in her apartment."

Menkhara was unsettled, confused. The regent's daughter had asked for him? "When?" he asked.

"Now, sir. I am to escort you to her villa."

Mutnedjmet waited for Menkhara in Father's bedchamber, one of several rooms in the palace complex at Malkata. She reclined on Father Ay's bed, propped up with cushions, staring on occasion into a polished bronze mirror, wondering if her new wig was right for her triangular face.

Mutnedjmet was in a good mood, confident that things would fall into place. The plan to clip Ankhesenpaaten's wings would succeed because it was too simple to fail. The princess and Menkhara were young and in love, and like most people their age, stripped of discretion and common sense. Their young hearts would send them pell-mell into trouble, and with only a nudge from wiser heads.

Her only immediate concern was Simut. He was a fool, much too obsessed and anxious. If it were not for his inheritance of his father's high office, he would not be fit to clean the temple lake. She would have to keep Simut tethered. Moments later, Menkhara stood in the open doorway.

"Menkhara," Mutnedjmet said with a smile. "Come here and sit beside me," she said, motioning to a chair facing the bed.

Menkhara bowed and stepped into the room. Mutnedjmet was surprised. The young scribe was astonishingly handsome and quite tall. His limbs and muscular chest were more suited to a worker than a scribe, and he carried himself with a confidence that did not match his youth. She studied his face, the large, dark, wide-set eyes and the black mane of hair that fell over his tawny broad shoulders. His appearance confirmed in her mind's eye that Simut had not exaggerated Ankhesenpaaten's attraction to him. Of course she fell in love with Menkhara. What woman would not fall in love with the young scribe, given any kind of encouragement?

Mutnedjmet sat up and smiled. "Do you know me, Menkhara?"

"I've not set eyes upon you until now, lady."

"Undoubtedly not. I don't participate in any of the festivals, and I stay out of the sun as much as possible. Do you know why I've summoned you?"

"No, lady."

"I'm disposed to do a favor for my dear young friend, Princess Ankhesenpaaten, and by that motive help you as well."

Menkhara's brow furrowed. "I don't understand."

Mutnedjmet gave him a broad smile. "The princess has told me everything."

Menkhara's lips parted slightly. He unconsciously ran the palm of his hand down his thigh and over his kneecap. Mutnedjmet could see that the young man had lost his composure. It was a good sign. He had something to hide.

"It's all right, Menkhara," Mutnedjmet continued, showing bright white teeth. "Ankhesenpaaten is my dearest friend. We know each other's secrets. I am her aunt, you know. She's sent me a letter and told me all about you. She described you as handsome. She did not exaggerate. You've broken many hearts, I'll wager"

"No, lady."

"Well, to the point, then, young Menkhara. Tutare and the princess will arrive here in Thebes in seven days and will establish residence here at Malkata. She wants to see her lover, and I'm certain you desire to see her. This is not Amarna. She will be watched and protected, especially in light of Tutare's coronation and her marriage to our new king on that same day. But Auntie Mutnedjmet to the rescue." She paused long enough to pour wine into a goblet and hand it to Menkhara.

"I'm going to give a party for her shortly after she arrives. She will spend a night at my villa. My father is now living here at Malkata to best serve the new Pharaoh, and I've the family home to myself. I'll invite you to the party. I'll arrange for you to spend the night together if that is your wish. You live within the precinct of Karnak?"

Menkhara hesitated and then said quickly: "With my parents at Deir el-Medina."

"Oh, your family are working people?"

"Yes, lady."

Mutnedjmet lowered her eyelashes, a lifelong habit that signified her disdain. She gave him a brittle smile. "And now you are a royal scribe and work at the scriptorium in the House of Life.

I'm sure your parents must be very proud."

When Menkhara left, and the servant waiting outside in the hall closed the door, Mutnedjmet let out a long sigh and scowled. "Bring me a goblet—no, bring me a ewer of pomegranate wine. The gods only know, I deserve it!"

11

Princess Ankhesenpaaten sat in silence across from Grandfather Ay, in the study of his Theban home. She waited respectfully as he wrote, hunched over a papyrus, unmindful of her presence.

He had summoned her to his study undoubtedly to upbraid her for some obscure breach of good manners. In the back of her mind she had considered that it might be something more ominous, something that had to do with her sneaking off to the Lion's Tooth Inn the night before. Had Grandfather found out?

She would not soon forget the day of her arrival at Thebes. The royal golden falcon ship, Userhat, had come assertively around a bend in the river. A huge crowd of Thebans waited for them on the quay. And when she had seen stern old Grandfather Ay heading up the welcoming party, she knew her life had changed forever.

Beginning on the day of her arrival, she was told that she could not leave the palace on her own, and if she went to the wharves to shop she would have to be in the company of a chaperon. Thinking only of Menkhara, desperate to see him again, she had slipped out of the palace and visited the Lion's Tooth, hoping to learn something of his whereabouts. Someone had undoubtedly spotted her there and told Grandfather.

Feeling lost and uncomfortable in the huge chair, she continued to watch Grandfather Ay scratch out notes on a strip of papyrus. She lifted her eyes and stared passively across the room to the alabaster oblation table.

Grandfather Ay finally set down his reed brush. He rolled up the papyrus, tied it with a linen cloth and shoved it into an oxhide tube. He clasped his hands on the table and stared at her, his dark eyes fixed and intimidating. She stared back, uncompromising, a slight smile on her face which could have been mistaken for insolence.

"You've any idea why I summoned you, child?" he asked.

"No, Grandfather."

"You've been here in Thebes less than two weeks and are already the talk of the court."

Ankhesenpaaten gave him a flat smile. "Small wonder, given my betrothal to Tutare."

"What's that supposed to mean?"

"I'm fifteen, and I am going to be married to a nine-year-old child. How do you expect me to feel? Is it unnatural to enjoy the company of young men my age?"

Grandfather Ay jerked himself upright. "I don't mind telling you that the late Pharaoh, your father, was not loved in these parts. I stayed in Thebes when the court moved to Amarna, and over the years, especially since your father's death, I did what I could to smooth over old wounds."

Grandfather Ay shook his head ominously and continued in a voice filled with frank contempt. "You've earned yourself the reputation of a frivolous coquette, willing to abandon yourself to every sort of pleasure. You were seen at the Lion's Tooth in the company of commoners, ordinary workers. For shame, child! A solar princess conversing with a commoner!"

"It was small talk. Nothing happened!"

"You were in a public tavern, a solar princess. Everyone can draw his or her own conclusions. For shame, Ankhesenpaaten. From this time on, your social outings shall be confined to the homes of the members of court. You will never again patronize the public taverns of Thebes, much less the Lion's Tooth."

Ankhesenpaaten could feel the heat of anger spread across her cheeks. "I am the daughter of a Pharaoh!" she began furiously. "I am no slave and will not be treated like one."

Grandfather Ay's face softened. He had raised two willful daughters of his own. "Of course you're no slave." He picked up his reed pen and reached for a fresh papyrus. Except for the scratching of the pen, there was a silence. Then, under his breath he said softly. "You may go, child."

Stunned, Ankhesenpaaten remained rooted to her chair. For the first time, she could not find words. She hesitated, then slid from her chair and left the study, her heart beating with rage. What could she do to get this old man out of her life?

I hate you Grandfather! Oh, how I hate you!

Mutnedjmet had heard about Ankhesenpaaten's adventure outside the walls of the palace. It was the talk of Malkata. Perhaps Father was beginning to think twice about marrying the daughter of Akhenaten off to young Tutare. What better way to find out than to wander into his study before returning to the family villa? Father trusted her, and even relied on her opinions. Well, some of them.

"Wine?" Ay asked. Mutnedjmet sat across from her father's table desk in the same seat occupied by Ankhesenpaaten moments before. He didn't wait for his daughter's response. She never refused wine. He filled her goblet to the brim.

"Well, I suppose you've heard about Ankhesenpaaten being seen at the Lion's Tooth," Ay said, setting down the ewer of wine.

Mutnedjmet could not resist a smile. "Who hasn't?"

"Well, in fairness, the child has had no real parental guidance in Amarna."

"By the eye of Horus, Father!" she said angrily. "In a few short weeks she'll be queen of Egypt. She's a solar princess, and should behave like one. Besides, from what I can tell, she is not at all pleased about marrying Tutare. Why not oblige her and find someone else?"

"I'll never understand your opposition to the marriage."

"And I shall never understand your approval."

"Why are your feelings so violent, daughter?"

"She is the daughter of Akhenaten. The Theban clergy do not want his issue on the throne."

Ay's brow furrowed. "Since when have you cared about politics?" He grunted. "I suspect that you've reasons of your own. I'll hear no more on the matter. She's my granddaughter, your sister Nefertiti's daughter. As regent and Vizier of the Upper Kingdom, I must see to it that the laws of succession are followed."

"Respectfully, Father, I think you are making a mistake."

Ay smiled. "I'm not sure that you're the one who should be telling me that. Look at that mistake you married."

"That's not fair. I was a child."

Ay set down his goblet and learned forward. "And so is Ankhesenpaaten. She will mature."

In the long silence, Mutnedjmet turned away and then stared back at Ay. "Father, you're not a young man," she finally said. "Should you pass on, your steady hand will be gone. Ankhesenpaaten is willful, proud and headstrong. She will bend young Tutare to her will. And what happens to me when you're gone? The daughter of the vizier and regent will have no place in Ankhesenpaaten's court. She will see to that. I've heard that she rejects the state god, Amun-Ra, and offers oblations to the Aten every night, and is just as fanatical as her father. She'll make life miserable for everyone."

Ay took a swallow of wine. "You put too much on young Princess Ankhesenpaaten. Do you think this old soldier should fear a slip of a girl? No, of course not. And neither should you. Now it's getting late and I'm hungry."

The conversation wasn't going anywhere. It never did, and Mutnedjmet was not surprised. She took a deep drink of wine, and felt a warm glow in her belly. She smiled at Father. Everything was going to be all right because she had a plan that could not fail, and in the end Father would be forced to find a new queen for the prince. She thought to herself: I know what is best for Father. I know what is best for me.

12

Ankhesenpaaten was playing Hounds and Jackals with Tutare when Mutnedjmet was admitted into the princess's chamber. The betrothed couple sat at a table, their eyes fixed on the game board, when Mutnedjmet paid the couple her unexpected visit. She entered the room unannounced and watched them awhile, then said, in a cool voice, "Is this how your Aunt Mutnedjmet is to be greeted?"

The prince looked up. "Auntie!" he cried out, standing up and rushing to her side. Mutnedjmet put her arm around her frail nephew and kissed him on the cheek.

Ankhesenpaaten, an annoyed look on her face, looked around, and then, recognizing Mutnedjmet, gave her an unreadable smile. "How glad to see you, Auntie. She motioned to a seat. "Wine?"

Mutnedjmet declined. "I thought we could have a chat. Alone."

"Tutare, be a dear and leave us." Ankhesenpaaten's tone of voice struck Mutnedjmet as maternal.

"Must I?" said Tutare.

"We will continue with our game later."

"Promise?"

"I promise."

Mutnedjmet watched Tutare slowly walk toward the doorway. When he was gone, she turned to Ankhesenpaaten. "I heard about your run-in with your grandfather," she began.

"It's not fair," Ankhesenpaaten pouted.

"Perhaps. But, dear child, your grandfather is the vizier and regent. He is responsible for your safety. What if something happened to you?"

"I know how to take care of myself."

Mutnedjmet smiled. "I'm sure you do. And I can well imagine that you want to meet young people your own age."

"You're right about that. Very shortly I will marry a nine-year-old." There was a look of restless anger in Ankhesenpaaten's eyes. "It will be like marrying my own baby brother."

Mutnedjmet rose from her chair and sat beside Ankhesenpaaten on her bed. She took her hand. "Dear child, it need not be such a terrible thing."

"How so?"

Mutnedjmet smiled. "There is no reason why you cannot take a lover. Despite all that is written, there is an unwritten code, and it can be very accommodating." Ankhesenpaaten cocked her head, and Mutnedjmet detected a shadow of distrust in her niece's face. "I was young once, you know." She winked.

"I don't wish to take a lover," Ankhesenpaaten insisted with tones of suspicion.

Mutnedjmet laughed. "Of course not. You already have one."

Ankhesenpaaten feigned a shy smile. She opened her mouth to speak. Mutnedjmet raised a finger to her lips.

"What do you mean, Auntie?"

"Darling girl, you have, despite your tender age, the look of a woman in love." Mutnedjmet smiled sweetly and with understanding. What can I do to help you?"

Ankhesenpaaten's jaw dropped. She looked pale. "How is that … how could you …?"

"You must not be so suspicious, otherwise you will go through life trusting no one. Why should your Auntie Mutnedjmet want to hurt you?"

"But why would you want to help?"

Mutnedjmet smiled. "You will soon sit at Pharaoh's side, filled with the divine afflatus. I know this, and so perhaps my motives are not so pure, perhaps even selfish. There will be a time when I might ask a favor of you."

Ankhesenpaaten bit her lip nervously and Mutnedjmet's heartbeat quickened. Her niece was undoubtedly pining for her Menkhara. *Simut was at least right about that.*

"There is someone, Auntie," Ankhesenpaaten said nervously. She hesitated and then burst out: "Oh, Auntie, do you really mean to help me?"

Mutnedjmet put her arm around the princess's shoulder, staring into her pensive, puzzled face. "Yes, my dear. I will help you."

Ankhesenpaaten began to cry. "He is a royal scribe, and his name is Menkhara. Auntie Mutnedjmet, I love him so. I have scarcely been able to sleep. And I am watched, so there is no hope of seeing him." She turned and buried her head in Mutnedjmet's shoulder.

Mutnedjmet could feel her niece's warm tears flow across her bosom. She stroked Ankhesenpaaten's hair. Then she sat up, forcing Ankhesenpaaten to an upright position.

"All kinds of events are planned for you and Tutare," Mutnedjmet began. "You and the prince will be introduced to the high and mighty of Thebes as well as their children. I'll plan a party in your honor. I will invite your lover. No one will dare to check my guest list. And when the evening draws to an end you will be together. I'll see to that."

Ankhesenpaaten was delirious with excitement. She looked at her aunt searchingly. "What if we are found out?"

Mutnedjmet laughed, dismissing her fear with a wave of her forefinger. "Trust me, child. Trust me." She handed Ankhesenpaaten a linen handkerchief. "Now tell Auntie all about your young man."

"The bitch is clever beyond her years," said Simut. "What makes you think she trusts you?"

"For the same reason you trust me, cousin," Mutnedjmet answered with a smile. "You need me. Ankhesenpaaten needs me; both of you need me for entirely different reasons."

They sat across from one another on cushions in a small room down the hall from Simut's study. He was grateful that Mutnedjmet had come to his villa. There was still a large blue mark below his eye where Menkhara had punched him, and he did not want to be seen in public since returning to Thebes.

"They'll have to be caught in the act," Simut insisted. "We will need more than circumstantial evidence to break the betrothal."

Mutnedjmet stretched her body to full length, her head propped against the wall. Simut observed that part of her gown had ridden halfway up her thigh, showing the smoothness of her tawny skin.

"Dear cousin," she said, "you know so little of women, especially teenage girls. They are full of passion, more than their elders would admit to. She wants her Menkhara, even to the point of not using the intelligence she was born with. Had you more women in your life, you would understand these things."

Simut flushed. It was true, of course. His infirmities had made him shy, and he feared rejection. For a time he had forced some of his female servants into bed with him. He would not have to fear rejection from servants who wished to keep their jobs. But they were not reliable, and more than one had proved unfaithful. It was easier not to get involved.

Simut continued to look for things to go wrong with the plan. "We will need good witnesses. No servants. They cannot testify against a solar princess. We will need guests. Your father will be suspicious. He will suspect a setup."

Mutnedjmet waved her hand at Simut, as though she were shooing away a pesky fly. "It doesn't matter what Father thinks. He'll have to act. And besides, he is the vizier. It will be especially hard on him to try his own granddaughter in the house of Maat. He may have to recuse himself and send the matter over to Karnak to be tried before the Kheri Heb, since the case involves a solar princess."

Simut shook his head with resignation. "You've thought it all out; and to my everlasting shame, I have offered nothing."

"To the contrary," Mutnedjmet smiled. "There is much I'm going to ask of you before this is over." Her smile grew faint, and her eyes narrowed seductively on him. She patted the pillow next to her. "Come here, Simut, and lie with me."

Simut, heart pounding in his chest, sat up and awkwardly lay next to Mutnedjmet, stretching his body to full length. In one motion she untied the sash at her waist and lifted her gown. Simut tried not to show his excitement. He was, after all, younger than she, and for all his shortcomings, he thought himself a man of the world. But when her hand reached under his gown and silked up his thigh to his groin, he shuddered. He wanted to shout with joy. Then he felt the warmth of her lips on his as she lay over his body, her weight pressing his shoulders deep into the pillows beneath him.

13

It was the evening of Mutnedjmet's party honoring Prince Tutankhamun and his betrothed, Ankhesenpaaten.

Menkhara entered Mutnedjmet's villa through the front gate and walked across the courtyard. No questions were asked by the several guards patrolling the courtyard. Inside was a large entrance hall surmounted by a loggia. Smiling servants pointed him in the direction of a large square room both sumptuous and inviting. Supporting papyrus columns were painted with plants and animals, and the ceiling was constellated with stars set to twinkling from the light of wall sconces. Low couches and brightly dyed linen pillows were scattered throughout the room. Servants bearing golden ewers of wine and baskets of food wormed their way through the noisy crowd of merrymakers.

Menkhara felt nervous. This was not just another welcoming tavern, but the beautiful private home of a princess. He was a commoner in a place where he didn't belong. He had doubts about Mutnedjmet. The invitation was too easily given.

He found Mutnedjmet surrounded by a cluster of her noisy guests. Someone whispered in her ear. Her lips, painted in red ochre, bowed to a smile, a delicate pleasant sign of recognition that flew at him with all the danger of an arrow true to its mark. She passed through her ring of friends as though they were wisps of clouds, arms outstretched in greeting.

"I'm so glad you are here, Menkhara," she said, her head tilted up to him.

Menkhara studied her face. She seemed much older than when he had seen her last. The cosmetics on her face had the unintended effect of aging her, especially around the face and mouth.

"Did you just arrive?" she asked.

"Yes."

"Then you have not seen the princess?"

"No."

"I would oblige you, but she and young Tutare are being shown around my gardens. You must not seem too anxious."

Mutnedjmet led Menkhara over to the far wall where they lowered themselves onto the soft bright luxury of duck feather pillows. Guests who seemed closest to Mutnedjmet joined them, forming a noisy semicircle. Mutnedjmet introduced Menkhara as a rising star in the Theban court.

Menkhara's goblet was filled a second time with a robust Fayyum wine. He was beginning to feel confident. A low table was set before them, and servants covered the surface with large wicker baskets draped with floral caps, mounds of cakes, pomegranates, grapes and figs. Then, from another place in the shadows of the room, the plangent sound of an Egyptian great harp mixed with the haunting call of a reed pipe.

Mutnedjmet had turned from him, stood up, and made her way to the center of the room, greeting guests as she went. She motioned to a musician sitting behind a kettledrum. He beat the drum, and the room fell silent.

"I invite you to the entrance hall for the entertainment you have all been waiting for," she said.

A tittering passed among the guests, and Menkhara understood why. Mutnedjmet's infamous dwarf servants, Renehen and Pera, were about to perform. Everyone in Thebes knew about the stunted couple. They were the centerpiece of her parties, famous for the art form they made of copulation. No one admitted to taking them seriously, but they understood the long moments of intense silent tension when private passions stirred beneath robes and gowns. Mutnedjmet took Menkhara's hand, and together they led the rowdy guests into the entrance hall.

Moments after the guests assembled, the young people clapped hands and called for the dwarfs in unison. "Pera! Renehen! Pera! Renehen! Pera! Renehen!"

A figure moved through the shadows cast by the columns.

The male dwarf Pera tumbled out of the darkness with all the dexterity of a trained acrobat. He stood in the center of the room, an alien so removed from humankind in appearance Menkhara thought it some exotic animal from the fabled land of Punt.

Pera smiled. Uneven carious teeth stretched across his mocking smile. His eyes, like those of a dead fish, shined watery and cold from an excessively large pocked face. The creature, no larger in stature than a six-year-old child, stood on bowed legs, belly extended. His fingernails were allowed to grow long and curved, so that his hands resembled the claws of a bird of prey. His cock hung between his legs like a large dark desiccated gourd. The miserable little thing circled the room on his toes, bowing to his audience with a fanciful conceit.

Pera's entry was followed almost immediately by the sudden appearance of the she-dwarf, Renehen.

She bolted into the room with a somersault, landing next to Pera. Renehen's age was lost in her ugliness. Her breasts were shriveled, down-covered sacks tipped with raisin-like nipples. Her small, gnomish body, having survived smallpox in youth, was cratered from head to foot. Sympathy was not something readily given the creature, and no amount of it could survive the leering smile or the wicked tongue darting snake-like out of the ruptured face.

From another room came the shimmering sound of

tambourines. The dwarfs faced each other and gyrated slowly. The tempo increased, their bodies lodged in each other's arms. They separated, and this brought a round of applause from the audience. The object of interest was the dangling gourd between Pera's legs. It had sprouted into a red-capped trunk, a full one quarter the size of the dwarf's body.

Menkhara stared at Pera's extraordinary organ with amazement. Mutnedjmet looked at him with an open smile and squeezed his hand. "I dare say it does something to the pride of every man here," she laughed.

Once again the shattering sound of tambourines. Renehen somersaulted around the room, pausing long enough in front of each couple to display her cavernous and not so private parts.

The room shook with roars of approval as Renehen amused the guests with one of her favorite tricks called the Kingfisher. It consisted of a running leap onto Pera's huge scimitar cock, a performance that if improperly executed, could maim one or both of the participants.

Menkhara found himself enjoying the choreographed erotica, embarrassed at his own lusts. The ugliness of the dwarfs and their screams of pleasure excited him. It was as though he was learning to breathe in a sea of revulsion and drawing satisfaction from the experience.

Princess Mutnedjmet's pet dwarfs finished their act and left the room. The guests returned to the party room. Servants trotted in with ewers of wine, and it was as though the party had begun all over again.

❦

Mutnedjmet held Menkhara's hand, insisting they wait in the audience hall until the guests had all returned to the party room.

When they were alone, she said, “And now the moment you have been waiting for, Menkhara. Ankhesenpaaten waits for you in my private sunshade in the garden. It is secure. No one may enter, and I have posted guards.”

Menkhara and Mutnedjmet entered the villa’s lush garden. It was a perfect night, with enough of a waning moon to cover the fronds of date palm trees and the fish ponds with darting flecks of gold. Along the walkway luxuriant vines with large purple grapes hung from a trelliswork built up with stone. The air was heavy with the sweet smell of flowers and the fragrance of incense trees.

They came to a pretty arbor at the head of a pond. On the other side of the arbor was something that looked like a covered shrine.

Mutnedjmet pointed to it. “Inside you will find your beloved, waiting for you.”

“What is it?” Menkhara whispered.

“A Shuyet-Re, or if you wish, a sunshade temple. My father had it built for Nefertiti and me when we were children. The screen walls allow the cool winds to enter, so that it is tolerable within, even on the hottest days.”

“I have not seen such a thing.”

Mutnedjmet smiled. “Most commoners haven’t, but having one is an honor reserved for a fortunate few. Now get on with you.”

Menkhara disappeared inside the sunshade.

A moment later, the dwarfs, Pera and Renehen scampered down the path toward her chattering like children at play. She regretted having her two precious pets tagging along. She should have ordered them locked in their chamber.

The dwarfs came to her side and placed their arms gently around her legs at the thighs. She put a finger to her lips. “Shhh, both of you! Another sound and I will have you beaten.”

Where were the witnesses? she thought, nervously squinting down the dark garden path. Everything depended on them!

Two familiar figures came out of the darkness, their white gowns plainly visible in the moonlight. One man was tall and obese, and she recognized him at once as the court treasurer, Maya. He was highly regarded by Father, and would make a good witness. The other man, a foot shorter, but no less obese, limped along beside Maya. It was Simut.

Mutnedjmet breathed a sigh of relief. The trap was about to be sprung.

Menkhara had hesitated in front of the sunshade. It was covered in a translucent linen screen, and he could see the dull shivering light of oil lamps within. He opened the linen flap and stepped inside.

Ankhesenpaaten stood near the opposite wall. An oil lamp flickering on a small table gave off an amber glow on the linen screen. The princess was dressed in a simple see-through dress, covering her left shoulder and leaving her right shoulder and breast bare. She wore a wide cloak of linen fastened in front, but thrown back over her shoulders. The smile on her face deepened.

"I thank my God that you've come, dearest Menkhara." She fell into his arms, burying her face in his chest.

Menkhara kissed the crown of her head and pressed his arms around her back.

She looked up at him. "Do you love me?" she said, a pleading look on her face as she waited for an answer.

"With all my heart and soul," Menkhara answered, wondering at the smallness of her waist, and the way sweat on her breast beaded up and glistened in the lamplight.

A light kiss, and then she slipped out of his arms, took his hand and guided him to a chair next to the table. She prompted him to sit. She sat in his lap, and he marveled at how light she was. She brought her arm around his neck and drew close. Her freshly washed hair smelled of spices, her skin of costly unguents. She seemed so like a child in his arms. Their lips met again, but this time with hunger.

Menkhara explored her body, running his hand across her exposed damp breast, and down the cant of her belly, over the small thatch of hair and then down her thighs. He leaned forward and kissed her breast.

A floor mat lay in the center of the sunshade. Menkhara guessed that his wise and thoughtful hostess had placed it there for one purpose. He circled Ankhesenpaaten's waist and legs and lifted her as he rose out of the chair. He lowered her gently to the mat.

With a loud snap the linen screen was torn back. A burst of light and a flurry of objects.

A villa guard poked his head and arm through the screen. A flickering bright light from the guard's torch filled the sunshade.

Ankhesenpaaten stiffened in Menkhara's arms as he helped her to her feet.

A sharp command ordered Menkhara outside, but not before the mischievous male dwarf Pera slipped past the guard's arm and tumbled into the sunshade with an insane screeching laugh. The dwarf, for no apparent reason, wrapped his arms around Ankhesenpaaten's leg and simulated copulation.

The princess screamed.

Menkhara clasped the dwarf's throat and chin. Pera leered at him unafraid. Enraged, Menkhara lifted the dwarf and twisted his head with a loud snapping sound. Pera went limp. Menkhara dropped the dwarf's lifeless body to the ground.

Ankhesenpaaten, stunned into silence, stared up at Menkhara.

She held him tight. He put her gently in the chair and left the sunshade.

The next person to poke his head inside was the chief of the Theban Medjay, the local police force. Menkhara had recognized him from the broad blue sash across his chest. They are going to arrest me, he thought.

He glanced at Mutnedjmet as she approached. She flashed him a wicked smile.

A scream came from inside the sunshade. Renehen had found her mate sprawled dead across the floor. The police tore away the front linen panel to reveal the interior. Renehen sat on the floor, holding Pera in her arms, sobbing hysterically. Princess Ankhesenpaaten sat in the chair, her hands covering her bent head.

A Medjay police officer, with the help of the treasurer, Maya, escorted Ankhesenpaaten out of the sunshade. She clung to Maya's arm as they slipped passed the dwarfs.

Mutnedjmet's female servants waited nearby. They took the stunned princess by her arms and walked her back down the path toward the villa. Ankhesenpaaten hesitated. She looked back at Menkhara, fragile and frightened. Menkhara's heart sank at the sight of her.

Menkhara's wrists burned from the rope as they were roughly bound behind his back. Guards ordered him forward, his back burning from the prick of probing javelins. Menkhara took one look back. To Mutnedjmet's right stood a man in the white linen gown of a priest. Moonlight shone on his oiled bald head and fell across his smiling face. Simut.

14

Ay and Mutnedjmet stood at the scene of the crime the morning after Princess Ankhesenpaaten and Menkhara were caught together. Ay had already gone over the story with the treasurer, Maya, as well as other witnesses. From the way her father bit his lip and furrowed his brow, Mutnedjmet could tell that he was not fully convinced. This was not a time to push too hard, she mused. Father must be left to draw his own conclusions. It was her job to lead him gently down the right path.

Ay said, "What makes you think they were making love? No one caught them doing it."

"The guard said that he saw the scribe, Menkhara, with his arm around your granddaughter's waist."

"But the thing is, they were not caught fornicating. Thank the gods for that!"

"Not quite."

"What is that supposed to mean?"

"Nothing, Father."

"Certainly not enough to debar her from sharing the throne with young Tutare."

"She's been with many men. She is talked about in the forecourts."

Ay bristled. "Such slander from the mouth of anyone else, daughter, would be enough to end their lives." He took Mutnedjmet by her shoulders and stared at her sternly. "I've worked too hard to end divisiveness in the kingdoms. I'll not have it thrown away over this dirty affair."

"What about Menkhara?"

"Well, what about him?"

Mutnedjmet was desperate and angry. Her plan had failed, and Pera was dead. "Father, the man killed my pet dwarf. Who would do that?"

Ay laughed. "Any sensible man. Ugly beast, that dwarf! You know, daughter," he began, waving his forefinger at her, "I tolerated those miserable midgets for your sake. I'm glad the ugly runt is dead."

"And so Menkhara is to get away with all this? That's what I'm to expect from my father, the vizier of the Upper Kingdom, the crown regent?"

Ay breathed out a long sigh. "If Menkhara is tried, the entire case will have to be aired at the expense of Princess Ankhesenpaaten. You also know that the Theban priesthood would be looking for any excuse to reject the daughter of Akhenaten.

"You won't give me satisfaction, then?"

Ay smiled. "You better hope that I live a long time, child, because if you played a role in this affair, Ankhesenpaaten will most certainly order your execution the moment I close my eyes to the world. There will be no Father Ay around to protect you."

Mutnedjmet flashed Father an angry sneer. "So you are willing to set a precedent. It's all right for a commoner to destroy the property of a princess, the regent's daughter."

"I said there would be no trial. I don't care what happens to the damned scribe. If you want Menkhara punished, we can arrange something. I simply want Ankhesenpaaten left out of this mess."

Father left her side and poked his head into the sunshade for one last look. "What's that mat doing on the floor? How did it get there?"

Mutnedjmet flushed. "I have no idea."

Ay stared hard at Mutnedjmet, the expression on his face filled with doubt. They left the sunshade and walked back down the garden path toward the villa.

"Isn't it the law, Father, that as owner of Pera, I can decree the fate of the man who killed him?"

Ay studied Mutnedjmet's face and then mumbled. "Yes, that is true. The poor devil. But for now, you leave the princess out of it."

Ankhesenpaaten kept herself closeted in her bedchamber for two days, refusing food and the attention of her handmaidens. She would see no one, not even Tutare. She thought only of Menkhara and feared for his life.

Auntie Mutnedjmet! Her heart raced with anger. How could she have been so foolish as to have believed her. She blamed herself for Menkhara's fate. Her first thought was to appeal to Grandfather Ay, but that would only make things worse. As for Mutnedjmet, why did she do it? *Does she hate me that much*?

The linen on her bed was damp from the tears she had shed during the night. Sleep was next to impossible. She worried for Menkhara's safety. What could she do to help him? Give up her throne? Would that satisfy Mutnedjmet? Grandfather? She would speak to them tomorrow.

❧

Ankhesenpaaten got up at the first hint of light in the Eastern sky, bathed and applied her makeup. She found Grandfather Ay and Auntie Mutnedjmet at their morning meal in the palace garden. Mutnedjmet had been staying in the palace the last several days.

Ay looked up from a plate of ox stew. "Good to see you up so bright and early, child. It's a good sign."

Mutnedjmet cocked an eye at Ankhesenpaaten but said nothing.

Ankhesenpaaten said, "Grandfather, I will not take your time and will come straight to the point."

Ay put down a jar of honey beer and clasped his hands in front of him. "Go on, child."

"Regardless of what you may think, the scribe, Menkhara, was in no way responsible for what seemed to be unseemly conduct.

Think ill of me if you will, but it was my doing, and I don't want him punished on my account."

Ay breathed deep. He pursed his lips and said, "Is that all?"

"No, Grandfather. Spare Menkhara and undo the oath of betrothal that now binds me to marry the future king of Egypt. I do not wish to be his queen."

A small, ill-concealed smile formed on Mutnedjmet's face. She threw a piece of cake-bread she had been gnawing over her shoulder. Two kingfishers darted after it.

Ay smiled. "Menkhara has not been charged with offending you. He's being held for taking the life of my daughter's dwarf. I've judged him guilty, and my daughter has asked that he be given to her in servitude for life. The law is clear: she has that right as a princess at court. And as for you, you will indeed marry the prince and sit beside him as his queen. That is my final word on the matter."

"But what about Menkhara? His punishment is too harsh," Ankhesenpaaten cried.

"It's the law."

Ankhesenpaaten turned to Mutnedjmet, a pleading look on her face. "Auntie Mutnedjmet, you can rescind your request."

Mutnedjmet smiled. "Yes, I could. But I won't." She reached for another piece of cake-bread.

"I beg you!"

"Pera was my pet," Mutnedjmet insisted with a feigned look of anguish. "I have no pity for the scribe. He will serve me all the days of his life. If I had my way, he would be put to death." She flashed Ankhesenpaaten a caustic smile. "One day he may well wish he was dead."

"You set Menkhara up," Ankhesenpaaten shouted. She pointed at Mutnedjmet, her eyes filled with tears of anguish.

"You are lying, dear child," Mutnedjmet purred. "And what is more, you have no proof."

Ankhesenpaaten's face was ashen. She looked coldly at Mutnedjmet. "One day, I shall sit at Pharaoh's side, Auntie. Take care how you address me."

"Enough of this," Ay said, shaking his head. "Both of you, curb your tongues." He turned to Ankhesenpaaten. "And as for you, child, we'll have no talk of revenge. I'm still regent to the crown and intend to remain so for some years to come."

Ankhesenpaaten could take no more. She turned her back to Ay and ran back down the garden path weeping.

15

Ankhesenpaaten sat all night on the cold stone bench by her window and stared into the night sky and the dim outline of the Nile, faintly lit by starlight. She could think of nothing but Menkhara. She thought of going to him, but the palace was heavily guarded, and there were palace guards stationed outside her door. She would have to wait until dawn before leaving the palace grounds, but even then there was no hope of being admitted to the Medjay police station where Menkhara was held.

The sun edged over the Eastern Desert, and she realized she must have dozed off. She bent down over an alabaster bowl of water and splashed water on her face. The water was cold, and it felt good. She went back to the window and squinted out at the eastern horizon, gazing at the shaft of sunlight slanting across her room.

There was only one thing left to do.

She would seek solace and peace, if only for a short while, in her father's old temple of the Aten, the lovely open-roofed edifice he had built when he lived in Thebes and shared the throne with Mighty Bull.

She dressed quickly in a simple skirt and cloak. She wore no makeup and applied only a few strokes of the brush to her long black hair.

She left the palace in the cool dawn and walked down to the small palace harbor at Lake Tiye, where she boarded the state ferry for a ride down the long canal and across the Nile to the East Bank. From the harbor, she hired a sedan chair and left for the extreme eastern end of the precinct of Karnak.

The temple, called the Gempaaten, rose provocatively out of the harsh beginnings of the Eastern Desert. It was a vast rectangle consisting of an open court divided by lateral walls and gates, and around the periphery a roofed colonnade of square piers. Against each pier a gaily painted sandstone colossus of her father faced into the court. Much to her disgust, the temple had fallen into a state of disrepair. Weeds and wild camel-thorn grew among the garden of dried-up shrubs, mud-crusted ponds and mandragora bushes.

She wandered across the court until she came to a wall upon which was incised the orb of the sun with ray-like arms stretching down to its only son, Pharaoh Akhenaten. Sunlight gleamed brilliantly across the Eastern Desert, lighting the courtyard in its golden abundance, and its warmth was comforting on her face and breasts. The hot rays of the Aten entered her, stretched through her, and fell upon the distant voluptuous gold-burnished face of her father, the sun-king. She gazed up at the rising sun, remembering a poem she had written on the eve of her father's death:

Thou dawnest, O Neferkkheperu-ra, Wa-en-ra!
in the golden robes of the living Aten
as he peaks over the rim of the horizon.
O father mine; you are one with the living Aten,

And I shall hearken to thee in death as I would in life.

Ankhesenpaaten left the temple grounds and made her way back across the precinct of Karnak to the quay and the ferry that would bring her across the Nile to the palace city of Malkata.

Leta spotted her mistress as she came silently into her apartment's receiving chamber. "Princess," she blurted excitedly. "Have you heard the news?"

"I seem to be the last to hear of anything," she said with a weary smile. "What fresh gossip have you for me today, Leta?"

"Menkhara!" Leta cried out. "Menkhara is no longer in jail. Your aunt, Princess Mutnedjmet, has claimed her prize. Menkhara has been removed to her house as her servant. You must be pleased that he is no longer a prisoner," said Leta.

Ankhesenpaaten shook her head. "Pleased? He now belongs to the most loathsome woman in the kingdom."

Leta answered with a consoling smile. "You mustn't fret, lady. There are other fish in the sea."

Ankhesenpaaten looked away. Why am I confiding in this foolish girl? she thought.

Leta's face was rounded with a lecherous smile. "We all know what Menkhara's servitude means. It's common knowledge she prefers the company of younger men; and, my lady, you once said—"

Ankhesenpaaten slapped Leta hard across the face. "I did not ask for your opinion!"

Leta whimpered.

Ankhesenpaaten burned with anger. She could not bear the thought of Menkhara in Mutnedjmet's arms. Leta was right, of course. Mutnedjmet's liaisons with men of all classes were matters of common gossip everywhere. She felt faint.

"Mistress?" Leta whimpered.

Ankhesenpaaten turned her back on Leta. “Get out of here, you stupid girl!”

When Leta closed the chamber door behind her, she began to cry.

Tutare stood in the doorway as Leta passed. He held a bag of game pieces. “I’ve been playing Hounds and Jackals with Auti. Will you play with me?” he said in a hopeful voice.

Ankhesenpaaten turned with a sad smile. “I think not.”

Tutare, debarred by age from any understanding of what had happened, knew only that his best friend and betrothed was sad. He walked over to where she stood. Smaller than Ankhesenpaaten by a foot, he put his eel-thin brown arms around her waist and rested his head on her breasts.

“It is going to be all right, Ankhesenpaaten,” Tutare said softly. “I will not let anyone hurt you, for I shall be Pharaoh of the Two Lands. I shall require all my subjects to love and adore you, and pour libations in your honor. But none shall love you more than I.”

Ankhesenpaaten gave the prince a soft smile, then circled his shoulders with sisterly tenderness and rested her chin on his head.

“Dearest Tutare,” she whispered, “my dear friend. You are very good.”

Simut had hoped the affair at Mutnedjmet’s sunshade would finish off Ankhesenpaaten and end the terrible obsession that governed his life. Incredibly, Ankhesenpaaten survived the plot against her. Simut felt doomed and at once sank into the blackest depression. There had to be another way to get rid of the bitch, he thought, over and over. He had sought an audience with

Mutnedjmet. She did not answer his request, and this made him more despondent.

He thought about his once-close friend, Menkhara. He survived the plot against Ankhesenpaaten and would spend his days in the relative safety of Mutnedjmet's villa. Menkhara may have been reduced to the station of a servant, but at least he was near to Mutnedjmet, and perhaps she and the handsome young scribe would become lovers, another sore point that weighed upon his mind. Mutnedjmet had embraced his own crippled, obese body, kissed him deep on the lips, praised his sexual power, made love to him in a way that no woman had before. He thought he had something going for him with the princess, a consolation prize in his failed effort to ruin the daughter of Akhenaten. But even that was not to be. If he could not wreak his vengeance on Ankhesenpaaten, or deal with his jealousy of Menkhara, he would do the next best thing. He was, after all, the second most important priest at Karnak, and in that capacity had control over the Theban tomb builders in the workers' village, and that included Menkhara's parents. He vowed to repay his old friend in a way that would hurt him most.

16

More than a month had passed since Menkhara was released into the custody of Mutnedjmet. He was put to work at menial outdoor chores reserved for the least desirable servants, spending his days cleaning the stables, the grain silos and the kitchen. At the bottom of the chain of command, he was fair game for everyone and his tasks among the most distasteful and repugnant duties required of a servant.

On days when not working for the chamberlain, he spent his long hours repairing the trenches that carried water from Lake

Tiye to the villa gardens and kitchens. Gnats and mosquitoes bit his arms and legs, and the stench from the canal was overpowering.

With his outside tasks completed, there was the incessant call from the kitchen for someone to pluck feathers from fowl, or scrape soot from the ovens. He slept in the outside servant quarters. His room, a sandstone rectangle, was stripped clean of its few amenities by the other servants. He had not so much as a reed mat to lie down upon.

The days, monotonous and hot, seemed endless. Menkhara knew peace only in those quiet moments late at night when the moon's radiance fell across Lake Tiye, and its smooth waters shone like pewter. In the darkness he heard the sound of living things among the reeds, the cooing of a gamecock, the nasal quacking of ducks and the flapping wings of a gray heron rising above the lake.

One day, while working on the canal beneath a pitiless sun, he was summoned by the deputy chamberlain. The interruption of his work was a blessing, for on this day the stench rising out of the canal was enough to paralyze a wild beast.

Menkhara dropped his pick where he stood and followed the deputy chamberlain to a servants' washroom inside the villa, a place reserved for the servants closest to the family. The cool water was like a balm against his skin. He happily applied a thin coat of oil to his bruised body, and when he stepped out of the bath, a serving girl presented him with a fresh kilt and sandals.

The deputy chamberlain watched Menkhara indifferently from a stone bench then rose and motioned him back into the courtyard. Menkhara followed a woman servant through a door into an entrance hall surrounded by a loggia. She motioned him into a room with a glazed tile floor. On the brightly colored walls were paintings of shady papyrus marshes, shimmering water, soaring ducks and a fine tracery of reeds and grasses. At the far end of the empty chamber was a gilded bed, a chair and two massive clothing chests.

Long after the servant left, Menkhara continued to wait in the eerie silence.

A voice, high-pitched and mean: "Come here, boy."

Menkhara stepped around a blue linen screen.

Princess Mutnedjmet sat in a low-back armchair, her gilded sandals resting on a hassock. She wore a filmy white linen gown with wide pleated sleeves. Her hair, glossy black, matched the color of her large eyes. Her neck was adorned with a simple collar of semi-precious stones.

Mutnedjmet's smile was denigrating and unfriendly. Menkhara sensed she was bored, which explained her reputation for turning her household inside out over trifling matters.

Menkhara's eyes shifted to the monkey who appeared from out of nowhere and bounded onto her lap with the familiarity of a family pet. The monkey grinned, showing his yellow teeth, and then nestled up against his mistress, his face and lips pressed against her cheek. Menkhara watched Mutnedjmet run her fingers through her pet's hair.

Mutnedjmet looked at Menkhara steadily for a few moments and then said: "Well now, son of Pawero; how goes it for the once-promising scribe?"

Menkhara's monotone betrayed none of his feelings. "Well enough, Princess."

"Well enough?" she repeated. "Hardly the answer I would have expected from one who has labored in the fields. Here, let me see your hands." She reached out and took his hands in hers, running her fingers across the palms. The monkey studied them with equal interest. Menkhara flushed.

"Blisters. How they must hurt," she purred. "Your soft scholar's hands are not yet hardened to the task of digging ditches and laboring in my gardens. We'll make them hard." She smiled, squeezing his fingers.

Menkhara returned her aristocratic sneer with a look of indifference. "I have voiced no complaints, my lady."

Mutnedjmet frowned. She let go of his hands. "Don't you trifle with me, young man! Your life is in peril, your career all but ended. The last thing you need to show me is pride and indifference."

"I've nothing to show you, my lady, but good service."

"Did you really think that I approved of your intimacy with my niece?"

"You gave me reason to think so, lady."

Feigning indifference, she continued: "Tomorrow you begin your new duties as my fan bearer. You have drunk my wine and mingled by night with the children of the high and the mighty, and now you are my servant."

The monkey chattered as though he shared some private joke with his mistress.

17

Preparations for the coronation of Tutankhamun were in full swing. Thebes made ready to receive dignitaries and guests from every part of Egypt and the kingdoms of the world.

Ankhesenpaaten could not enjoy the festivities that swirled around her. Confined to the grounds at Malkata, she had little news of life outside the palace gates. She worried about Menkhara, and blamed herself for his new life of servitude in Mutnedjmet's villa.

Mutnedjmet and her husband, Tanehes, who had just returned from his summer holiday in the Fayyum, agreed to give a banquet to honor Panakht, the governor of Kawa. Mutnedjmet posted notice of the banquet, and Ay expected the future king and queen of Egypt to attend.

Ankhesenpaaten was reluctant. She had not stopped brooding over Mutnedjmet's treachery. She could not bear to see Menkhara in the capacity of an ordinary servant. She had protested to Grandfather Ay, feigning sickness two days before the banquet. He sent her a terse response by messenger: You will attend the banquet given in honor of the governor of Kawa.

❧

The following evening the palanquin bearing Ankhesenpaaten and Prince Tutare to Mutnedjmet's villa bounced gently upon the shoulders of the carriers, as they made their way down a garden path.

The solar princess wore a filmy white linen robe with wide billowing sleeves, clasped at the waist by a fringed scarlet sash. She gazed over at Tutare, seated across from her, the massive pectoral gleaming across his frail chest. She gave her future husband a benign smile. He smiled back, his large innocent eyes filled with devotion.

Tutare was the beneficiary of her love for Menkhara. The cruel jokes she had played on her young cousin no longer seemed amusing. Love had made her generous. She studied Tutare, feeling his helplessness and his youth. She would have to do something for him. She was not sure what, but she would try. She smiled warmly, and the little prince answered with a flush of pleasure.

The banquet hall was warm and inviting. Lotus-shaped standing lamps sent flickering crimson light across the room. From somewhere in the dark of a far corner came the soft strains of a harp.

The presence of the future Pharaoh and his queen was an unexpected pleasure for Mutnedjmet's guests, the lesser lights of the Theban court. Governor Panakht, the guest of honor, was largely ignored as attention shifted to the royal couple. Mutnedjmet and her husband, Tanehes, sat next to Panakht and his wife. Ankhesenpaaten and the prince sat across from them.

The sight of Tanehes at the low ebony table, with his thin triangular face and derelict eyes, made Ankhesenpaaten uncomfortable. She had managed to put the loathsome Tanehes out of her mind, but his presence brought back ugly memories.

She was eleven, and had come down to Thebes for a visit. She stayed at Grandfather's villa. She remembered the way Tanehes leered at her when they were together, and the too affectionate way he stroked her body when he found her alone in the gardens. Those encounters might have been forgotten were it not for the night he came into her bedchamber and lay beside her on the narrow bed. His breath smelled of wine and beer when he tried to kiss her, and his hands pawed her body. Her sobs were muffled in his chest, and then she screamed as he tried to mount her. It was enough to send Tanehes scurrying from her chamber. She told Auntie Mutnedjmet the following day. Auntie said she must have been dreaming, and that was the end of the matter.

Ankhesenpaaten stared over to the high alabaster table from which the food was being served. The last thing she wanted was to see Menkhara, servile and overworked like the other servants, trotting back and forth in the huge hall. She saw with a sigh of relief that Menkhara was not there.

With each passing hour the formality marking the beginning of the meal faded in proportion to the amount of wine consumed. Stirred on by rhythmic sounds of tambourines, naked dancing girls and too much wine, the guests left their tables and visited with one another.

Ankhesenpaaten was grateful for the whirl of activity. She could now disappear from the room and make her way to the servants' quarters in search of Menkhara. She had visited the villa many times as a child and knew the place like the back of her hand. Her hosts would believe she was in the unction room applying fresh oil to her skin. She slowly worked her way to the darkest corner of the hall, and then, believing her movements unnoticed, slipped through a doorway.

Ankhesenpaaten followed a passageway to an unction room, and then to the villa's west loggia and the door to the backyard and the grain silos, stables and servants' quarters.

As she came into the yard, she heard voices from the kitchens, and the sound of platters and sharp commands. She moved swiftly, avoiding lamp light where possible. There was simply no way to explain her presence here, and she didn't want to create fresh gossip only days before the coronation and wedding.

The yard was empty. The back walls closed off any chance of a breeze, and the air felt dense and warm. Beads of sweat gathered on her brow, and her gown stuck to her body. She went to the servants' hut. The double doors were open.

The interior was dark like a cave, the only light from the stars. She could barely make out the rows of reed mats and the few bundles of private possessions. The place smelled like a cowshed, and the air was heavy and cloying. She had no intention of entering the quarters, but stood on the stoop and called out Menkhara's name. There was no response.

She wandered over to the stables. From that vantage point she could see into the kitchens. Perhaps she would catch a glimpse of Menkhara near a blazing oven. Coming around the stables, she absentmindedly stared through an open door. The first stall was unoccupied, except for a dark form nestled against a sack of grain.

Startled, she heard a voice call out, firm and commanding. It was his voice. "My lady!"

"Menkhara?"

The dark form in the stall unraveled into humanness, rising up tall and masculine. Menkhara peered through the darkness. She rushed into his arms. Menkhara tried to whisper a term of endearment, but she stopped his mouth with a deep kiss.

After a long silence, they drew apart, but only slightly. Menkhara guided her outside the stable, away from its stifling heat. He lifted her hand and kissed it. "As badly as I have wished for you, I wished more for your safety. You should not be here."

"I don't fear for myself."

Menkhara held her tight around her waist.

Her eyes adjusted to the dark, studied his face in the faint starlight. How wonderful he looked, so innocent and decent. She wanted to be with him forever, even as she was queen and wife to Pharaoh Tutankhamun. If she were honest, maybe he would not reject her. She had thought of life as a queen, and all the good things that came with it. It made her feel guilty. She wanted him simply and completely and not by guile or special advantage. She hoped, she prayed he could love her in the same way, though she would be married to Tutare.

She said, "I'm here because I could not bear to let another day pass without seeing you, Menkhara."

"This is more than I could have hoped for."

"I pleaded with my grandfather not to punish you for that awful dwarf's death. It was all my fault. If I had not—"

"You must not blame yourself," Menkhara interrupted.

"When I am queen I will release you from your servitude. I will find high office for you, Menkhara."

"I would be in your debt."

Ankhesenpaaten studied his face. Sensing something wrong, she said softly: "What is it, my love?"

"You are in too much danger. If they find out—"

Ankhesenpaaten placed a finger over his lips. "Without you

there is no life."

They stood in the long silence that followed. She felt helpless. She wanted to hold him and never let go. She was breathing hard and next to tears. No promises could be made and kept.

She stared at him and brushed a lock of hair from his forehead. "Say that you will always love me, Menkhara."

"You make me the happiest person in the world, even when I should despair."

The smile on Menkhara's face vanished. "I have not heard from my parents, Princess. I worry for them. Have you heard anything?"

"No, but I shall inquire and let you know."

Menkhara touched her check with his open hand. "I worry for you, as well. Mutnedjmet is not to be trusted. She will find a way to hurt you if she can."

Ankhesenpaaten laughed. "I'm not afraid of her."

Menkhara did not smile. "There is something else, Princess. When we were in Amarna, on our way home from the Inn of the Two Brothers, your would-be assassin that night was a friend of mine, and he wanted me to participate. It was Simut, the second high prophet of Amun. His family name and rank got me into the Society of the Kap, and through his influence, I received my commission as a royal scribe."

Ankhesenpaaten shook her head and looked away. "Why have you said nothing about this to me?"

"Because he was my friend, and I knew he would die for what he had done."

Ankhesenpaaten's face softened. She reached over and pressed her lips to Menkhara's mouth. "The regent cannot live forever, and when my husband comes into his own, Simut and Mutnedjmet will wish they were never born."

Voices came from the direction of the villa. They turned. Two figures approached down the walkway. Ankhesenpaaten gasped.

Menkhara squinted into the darkness. "Servants!" He took her by the hand and led her on a circuitous path back towards the villa. He pointed to a door. "It will take you into a store room that feeds out into the main hall. You must go, and may the gods bless you, Princess."

Ankhesenpaaten felt cheated. Tears rolled down her face. She wanted more of Menkhara, and had hoped that they could make love in the stable. But that was not to be. She gave him a quick kiss and reluctantly drew away.

Tutare had gotten himself drunk on three goblets of pomegranate wine. Everyone wanted to talk about Tutare. When he fell asleep, his great Aunt Mutnedjmet had him carried upstairs and put to bed.

The guests found the event titillating. Several of them gathered around Ankhesenpaaten to tell the tale of the prince who had too much to drink, as though the event were one deserving universal acclaim.

Ankhesenpaaten was not amused, but she smiled, more as a cover for her own distress.

"I put him to bed. Why don't you let him spend the night here?" said Mutnedjmet.

Ankhesenpaaten went alone to the guest bedroom. Tutare was curled up in a sound sleep. She sat at the edge of the bed and gazed down at her betrothed. A fly settled on his cheek. She brushed it away. The prince looked much younger than his years. His breathing was light, and occasionally he moaned softly. She wondered what fanciful thing occupied his dreams. I am to be married to him, she mused without any feeling of regret or anticipation, or any special feeling other than disbelief. It was as though she too had wandered into a dream.

18

Mutnedjmet sat at her cosmetic table staring into a bronze mirror. She compressed her lips and returned a cake of ochre to her toilet box. More and more, she had ordered Menkhara to attend upon her in her chamber.

Menkhara was shocked when she offered him a smile and said airily: "If I asked you to make love to me, would you oblige me?"

He decided to ignore the question, and hoped beyond all hope that she would grow bored with him and find some new source of amusement. He continued to run the ostrich feather fan in great sweeps above her head.

"I made you my personal fan bearer for good reason," she continued with a wry smile. "You could still be out in the fields digging drainage ditches and swatting mosquitoes."

Menkhara ventured a look at her. She sat at her low table, her forefinger probing her cluttered makeup box for a cake of kohl. Across the room, her pet monkey silently sat on a chest eating figs. Menkhara continued swishing the plumed fan above Mutnedjmet's head.

Mutnedjmet put her hands in her lap, turned and stared hard at the young man. "You think I am too old and ugly for the likes of you. Is that not so?" Mutnedjmet waited in silence, a slow angry smile forming on her face. She made a half-hearted effort to rise from her seat.

Menkhara offered her his hand. She waved it aside, staring dully at him. Then she lifted her head and filled the room with a derisive high-pitched laugh.

"Sota," she called.

The monkey, who had been watching his mistress and Menkhara with indifference, jumped off the chest and scampered over to Mutnedjmet. She reached for his paw. Sota knew what to do. The monkey arched his back and pulled Mutnedjmet to her feet.

Menkhara had been given status no greater than that of her pet monkey. And now that he had refused her offer of love, there would be no chance to improve his position in her household.

"I have a new task for you, Menkhara. If you're good at it, I'll promote you to cleaning piss pots. Beginning this instant, you will be Sota's constant companion and servant. You will attend to his needs, cleanliness and food. And in the heat of the day when he likes to rest, you will fan him. Yes, you will attend upon dear Sota. You will cater to his every need. It is the right kind of job for you."

She stood up, threw a damp cotton towel at Menkhara, and headed for the door. Words spoken in laughter trilled behind her. "Monkey see. Monkey do."

⁂

Menkhara jogged toward the Nile, sweating profusely in the night air. One dead dwarf, and now Sota.

He had killed the monkey and fled Mutnedjmet's villa, darting across the villa forecourt, then slowing to a walk as he exited through the gates, like one taking in the early evening air. The smell of urine from the piss pot Sota had thrown at him brought his thoughts back to the scene of the crime. His kilt was still damp.

A mindless rage had taken hold of him. He'd reached for the bronze lamp stand, then delivered pounding blows to Sota's head. He would never forget the monkey flattened into a hairy, blood-drenched mat, his skull cracked, the walls of the vile-smelling room speckled with blood. He had dropped the lamp stand and fled.

Outside the gates, beyond the view of the gatekeeper, he jogged in the direction of the Nile. He came to a series of river channels and finally the city quay. He slowed to a walk, sucking in the warm night air, his heart pounding hard against his chest.

He did not like visiting his aging parents with problems of his own, but he would need shelter until he decided what to do. There was only one place to go: the workers' village at Deir el-Medina.

A Nile ferryboat cast off its lines. Menkhara reached for his money pouch. The fare was a quarter of a deben of copper. He paid the pilot and climbed aboard.

Arriving on the West Bank, he decided not to take a sedan chair across the floodplain. They were too slow, and he was impatient.

He jogged across the gravelly plain, picking up his pace as he went. By the time he reached the mortuary temple and towering colossi of Mighty Bull and Queen Tiye, he was sprinting.

It was sunset when he entered the workers' village through the south gate. A cool wind blew when he reached his family home. On an evening such as this, Father kept the front door open to let in the breeze. He was surprised that it was shut. No matter, it was his parents' habit to sit in the shade on the back patio beneath a roof overhang that Father had erected for that purpose. He walked around the side of the house.

A man sat in his father's chair, and his mother was nowhere to be seen. Menkhara recognized the man as his parents' neighbor. His name was Wadjmose, a hardworking tomb engraver his father admired and trusted. The man stared up shyly at Menkhara.

"My father is not here?" Menkhara asked.

Wadjmose stood up, his brow wrinkled, a look of confusion on his face. "You have not heard, Menkhara?"

"Heard what?"

Wadjmose wrung his hands. He went pale. "May the gods forgive me, Menkhara, but your father is dead."

Menkhara looked at Wadjmose in disbelief. He shook his head. "What are you saying?"

Wadjmose grasped Menkhara by the shoulder. "The priest, Simut. He was here. He told your father that he was no longer foreman. He did not give a reason."

Wadjmose began to tremble. He had known Menkhara from the day he was born. Tears filled his eyes. "I am sorry I have to tell you, Menkhara, but your mother, Neferabu, has gone with your father to the fields of Yaru. It was grief that killed her. She lost the will to live and died the following day."

Menkhara demanded an explanation. "Tell me at once what happened to my parents."

Wadjmose related the story in careful detail. He had not been present when Simut first appeared with the scribe of the Domain and his soldiers, but Pawero was dismissed as foreman and ordered to surrender his home. He related how neighbors helped them move their possessions out of the house, and that Pawero, believing his wife in danger, was killed as he rushed to help her.

"Blinded by tears, Menkhara looked away. "I must see my father's deputy, Hesunebef."

Wadjmose shook his head. "Hesunebef is no longer deputy, Menkhara. He was replaced. I was forced by Simut to replace your father. Hesunebef is now a worker in the mines with no special advantages. A hovel was found for them, one befitting a common worker, so small that when his daughter, your betrothed, Mayet, received an offer of marriage from an old priest who lives in holy Iunu, they sent her away with him, though I understand she protested to the last."

The two men sat deep in thought, Menkhara with his hands over his face.

Wadjmose trembled and tears gathered in his eyes. "Forgive me, Menkhara. I did not seek this. Your father and I—we were friends."

Menkhara put his arm across Wadjmose's shoulder. "You are blameless in this. Do not grieve. I wish you well."

On hearing these words, Wadjmose wept.

Menkhara turned and walked away, then wheeled around. "Wadjmose, may I believe that my parents are buried in their tomb?"

Wadjmose looked pale. "Simut denied your mother and father burial in their tombs. The gatherer of the dead came down the following morning, and they were taken away without so much as a prayer from a priest of Anubis, much less a proper preparation for burial in the House of Vigor. They were taken into the Eastern Desert for burial in an unmarked grave."

Menkhara left Deir el-Medina sick with guilt. He blamed him-self and his infatuation with Ankhesenpaaten. He cursed himself for getting involved in Simut's wild plan to discredit her. My parents dead, buried in the Eastern Desert, no chance of an afterlife, and poor Mayet in the arms of a husband who means nothing to her.

By the time Menkhara had reached the ferry landing on the Eastern Shore, it was dark. His guilt had hardened into hatred for Simut. He vowed revenge, but for now, he was hungry and alone, a fugitive from the vizier's justice, and with barely enough to pay for his ferry ride across the river.

Desperate, he had no choice but to place himself at the mercy of the only man who could help him, his former teacher and master of the school of the Kap. It was a slim prospect to be sure, but it was all he had.

19

The villa of Kenofer, master of the school of the Kap, was among the grandest residences in Thebes.

Sweating profusely beneath a canopy of brilliant stars, Menkhara waited by the villa's gates while word of his arrival was brought to his old schoolmaster. Finally the gates swung open. He entered the grounds, passing the gatekeeper's lodge and then walked down a path leading at right angles to the main building.

A servant greeted him in the reception hall and guided him into the central room. The servant brought Menkhara to a sunken stone basin at one corner of the room to receive lustrations of water poured over his hands and feet. He was offered a damp towel and an alabaster cup filled with cool water.

Menkhara sat on a stone bench that ran the length of a limestone platform. The ceiling was supported by four columns decorated with plants and animals. Between the columns, he looked up at bright stars shining like jewels through the narrow stone-barred windows.

Menkhara studied the ceiling, with its soaring kingfishers flying and swooping through the fronds of date palms. This was the work of Kenofer himself. He had been a painter long before he rose up through the ranks to manage Pharaoh's estates and become Master of the Kap.

Finally, Menkhara heard the whispered scrape of sandals. He looked up. Kenofer had come out of a loggia above the entrance hall and descended a stairwell. He gave the young scribe a friendly smile, which he held until he reached the bottom step.

Menkhara left the bench and fell to his knees in the manner of a suppliant.

"Get off your knees," Kenofer ordered in a stiff voice. "I am not a god, and you are not a toad."

Menkhara stood in time to receive Kenofer's embrace. "Master, I have been such an utter fool."

Kenofer responded with a gentle smile. "That is what youth is about. But no more of this. You look tired. Perhaps something to eat?"

"I am not hungry, Master."

"Nonsense! All young men are hungry. We'll start with some wine."

He took Menkhara by his arm and guided him across the room to his study. They sat facing one another in two large ebony chairs at the head of Kenofer's writing table. A servant poured wine. Kenofer tried to brighten the young man's face with a humorous story concerning a drunk visiting dignitary.

Menkhara listened patiently, and while goblets were refilled, Kenofer finally said. "Now then, Menkhara, I sense you have had a misadventure, and you wish me to hear of it."

Menkhara lost no time relating all that had happened to him. Kenofer listened with a look of immense gravity. His response was blunt and to the point. "If they find you, you will be put to death."

Menkhara nodded in agreement. He drained his goblet. "The law is not just," he said. "I am nineteen, and I will do what I can to save myself, if only to find and kill Simut." He paused and stared directly at Kenofer. "I am alone in the world and with no more than a deben of copper in my purse. I must beg your help, Master."

A slow caring smile spread across Kenofer's face. He reached over and took Menkhara's hand and nodded. "I can do nothing for you if you are caught. But I can help you get out of here. You must leave Thebes before the coming of Ra's first light."

"Bound for where?"

"For the Divisions of Ptah, my young friend. Your best chance of remaining alive is in the army. I will secure a commission for you as a lieutenant of infantry. General Horemheb owes me a debt, and he'll be glad to repay me with this. No one will think to look for you in the army."

Menkhara stared at Kenofer in disbelief. "I've heard his army is camped somewhere in Palestine or the Lebanon, and it is rumored our forces will cross the Orontes and offer aid to our vassal states now threatened by the Hittites."

Kenofer smiled. "You have an ear for news. Yes, it is all true. We may yet do battle with our ancient foes. I can't promise you gardens of pleasure, my young friend, only the chance for a new life as a military officer, providing you survive long enough to enjoy it. Do well and you'll prosper. And it may even come to pass that, the gods permitting, you'll return to our river valley land."

"The army?" Menkhara repeated. "But how—?"

"A packet ship leaves for Memphis at dawn," Kenofer interrupted. "You'll be on it. You'll make your way across the delta and book passage to Byblos, and then on to Tyre. You'll have on your person a letter of passage as well as my personal letter to Horemheb."

Kenofer rested his hand on Menkhara's knee. "Soldiering is not an easy life, Menkhara. I would not wish it on so brilliant a scholar and scribe as you. But there are no easy answers to the mess you've gotten yourself into. Mutnedjmet's father, Ay, isn't a young man, and when he's dead you'll be able to return without fear of prosecution. I haven't the slightest doubt you will once again use your great talent to good advantage."

"And Simut?"

"Kill him now and you risk losing your own life. Would your parents want that for you?"

Kenofer set down his goblet and both men rose together. "I would say you could do with a bath, a well-deserved meal and a good night's sleep."

20

The night before his coronation, Tutare woke from a terrible dream with a piercing cry of alarm.

Sitamun had him brought to her bedchamber in the arms of the chief steward, where he lay curled up next to her like a babe suckled into contentment.

Tutare knew the rituals would bring forth masked priests with beaky noses. There would be angry gods, and costumed priests who would come forth like creatures from hell, with hollow eyes and pointy ears. He was bound to forget the Sacred Questions, and there would be rituals he would forget to perform. The gods will be angry. He saw himself frail and uninviting in his simple kilt, the object of universal scorn and ridicule.

"Oh mother, I fear tomorrow," he said, dozing off in her arms.

When the sun rose out of the Eastern Desert and glittered on the electrum-tipped obelisks of Karnak, Prince Tutare was awakened and placed in the care of two young priests from Karnak's temple of Amun-Ra. Scrubbed clean in the manner set out in the ancient texts, he was massaged in oil of lily and given a simple kilt. Then his dark hair was combed and braided into a single glossy black strand, which fell across his left shoulder and halfway across his chest.

Outside in the forecourts, Tutare was grateful to find his two friends, the young scribal student Khay and his playmate, Paneb, a happy sight in contrast to the somber priests. The small party walked to the royal ferry tethered to the dock at Lake Tiye.

The eastern shore was a forest of masts belonging to the ships that brought dignitaries from all parts of the world: Babylon,

Kadesh, the cities of Syria and Lebanon; from Nubia, Kush and all the temples of Egypt. There were barges of state, river boats, stately sailing ships with sterns resembling gigantic lotus flowers, sleek war vessels with furled sails, Kefti sailing ships, lighters and ferry boats of every description.

Ay, flanked by the high priest Inmutef and Simut, was the first to greet Tutare when he stepped onto the quay. Behind them ranged the high priests of the temples of Egypt.

Tutare and his party led a procession down a route cordoned off by household guards, red pennants fluttering from their javelins. The shouting of the people pressing in from all sides was deafening. Though it was warm, Tutare felt a chill wind whip across his hollow chest. Clad only in a loincloth, the nine-year-old was lost between the immense figures of his uncle and the priests.

Led into the first courtyard, the procession stopped between the obelisks of his ancestors, Thuthmosis I and Thuthmosis III. From out of the shadows came two figures masked as gods. Tutare's heart raced.

One priest, wearing the falcon mask of Horus, took Tutare's hand and led him toward a chapel-screen in front of the second pylon, while another priest, disguised as the god Atum, took his other hand and pronounced the first words in the rite of enthronement.

For the little prince there was something new and more fearful at every turn, for no sooner had the Horus and Atum priests led him into a hall of the temple, when he was handed over to other priests for the purification of his body.

Stepping out of a shallow pool, he was greeted by the Ibis-beaked Thoth, and the god Seth with his curved muzzle and pointy ears, and two more falcon gods. They poured water from tall golden ewers, thus transforming the boy-king into one who approached godliness.

Tutare hesitated as the procession moved into a special sanctuary. Greeting him were more priests dressed as gods, each looking like a creature from the abyss of hell, things meant to do him harm.

The sanctuary was divided into two pavilions. One contained priests impersonating the ennead of the gods: Nekhbet, Buto, Isis, Neith, Nephthys, Horus, Seth, Osiris and others. The divine creatures loomed large and frightening in aspect, each one blurring into a part of his fellow, so that all seemed arrayed against him, evildoers come to mar his coronation. Tutare shook uncontrollably. Tears rolled down his cheeks. He stood alone, with no assuring adult arm to quiet his fears. Vaguely, from his preparatory lessons he remembered the words of a wise young priest from the scriptorium counseling him on royal conduct: You must find the courage to stand alone before the gods.

Chanting loudly through masks like a herd of thundering water buffalo, the entourage of priests entered the temple's southern chapel.

Tutare, thrust forward by the priests, found himself face to face with Amun's daughter, the snake goddess. Raising her expanded cobra's hood, she rushed to embrace him. She coiled around his head, and lifted her flat serpent face over his.

From somewhere came the faint nauseating sour-smelling breath of decay.

Tutare fainted.

The high priest Inmutef, dressed in his leopard-skin and plaited hair wig, silently approached the fallen prince, bending over him for closer inspection. This was no time to administer medications or kindness. The coronation of the Horus god on earth had to continue uninterrupted.

Protected from view by a knot of priests, Inmutef slapped

Tutare hard across the face, and in an instant the prince opened his eyes. "Stand up, damn you!" Inmutef whispered in his ear. "Don't embarrass yourself!"

Inmutef's voice was grave and commanding. Tutare sprang to his feet. Inmutef placed the leather war crown on his head, then covered the war crown with the red crown of Lower Egypt. Finally, the white mitre crown of Upper Egypt was inserted into the red crown.

Tutare, top heavy with the assortment of crowns, wobbled like a top, and would have spun out of control were it not for the steadying hands of the priests. Fortunately, after a brief ceremony of words spoken quickly by a half dozen priests, all of the crowns were removed except for the blue war crown. Tutare, now clad in a light tunic thrown over his shoulders, and sanctified sandals, left the chapel.

Before crossing the threshold of the fourth pylon, Tutare's entourage turned right. He was led into a side chapel and brought before a shrine of rose granite flanked by huge statues of Osiris. Here he was forced to kneel and endure the long, two-hour ceremony, where Amun would confer upon the prince's head the power of his crowns and the divine authority to rule over all the domains of the sun.

Finally, Simut, decked out in his panther skins, stepped forward and pronounced the names of the new Pharaoh:

Take unto yourself splendid God
Of the Two Lands thy Horus name,
Ka-nakht tut-mesut, Strong Bull
Of created forms.
Take unto yourself the golden
Falcon name, Wetjes-khau Sehetep
Netjeru: He who displays the

regalia.
Take unto yourself thy prenomen,
Nebkheprure, so that all for
Eternity shall know thee by thy
Deeds.
Take unto yourself thy birth nomen:
Sara, Son of Ra Tutankhamun
Heqa Iunu-shema, living image
Of Amun.

With the names of his kingship granted to him, the boy-king Tutankhamun rose unassisted from his knees, the acknowledged son of Amun.

But there was one more matter to attend to. Pharaoh was led into a private chapel. His bride, Ankhesenpaaten, waited for him. She was dressed in a tight fitting gown, tied with a golden sash, and looked as radiant and fresh as the morning sun. She wore no wig; her hair, gathered in a ribbon, fell black and glossy down her back. Stretched across the top of her head was a gold band holding the double uraei, thus establishing her oneness with Pharaoh.

The young Pharaoh had never seen Ankhesenpaaten looking so beautiful. His chest swelled with pride. She is worth more than all the crowns of Egypt, he thought. Grandfather Ay stood close by.

Pharaoh Tutankhamun was brought to her side, boyish and short despite his blue crown and tunic.

The ceremony was brief. The couple was bound together at the wrist by a bright red linen ribbon, and pronounced one with Amun.

And then Simut spoke the queen's new name. It would forever replace the name her father had given her: Ankhesenpaaten. She winced as Simut's voice drilled into her ear.

"Thou art joined as one with Amun-Ra and the company of gods, the Horus god on earth, Tutankhamun and his queen, our lady of the Two Lands, Ankhesenamun."

It was over, and Tutankhamun and his queen left the temple of Karnak. They crossed beyond its spacious forecourt. In the dazzling light of the mid-morning sun, from a specially constructed platform, they greeted a multitude of well-wishers, all chanting praises for their young Pharaoh and his queen.

⁂

Kenofer was true to his word.

At the crack of dawn, Menkhara, in the company of trusted household guards, was brought to the Theban quay where he boarded a packet ship, waiting to begin its voyage downriver to Memphis.

It was the morning of coronation day, and even at such an early hour, ships of every description were tying in at the long stretch of docks. Huge crowds of merrymakers gathered along the quay to catch a glimpse of the wedding party boarding their state ship.

Menkhara stared out across the docks to the gray dawn and the warren of streets, the government buildings, temples, obelisks and the vague outline of Karnak's walls. Thebes was awake with throngs of people, despite the hour.

Menkhara's packet boat cast off its lines and was slowly rowed out to midriver. As he drifted away from Thebes, the gray light of dawn revealed the patient faces of Pharaoh's subjects. It was as though all the eyes of the world were fastened on the quay, awaiting the arrival of the frail prince who would be their king.

BOOK II

1332-1330 BC

1332 BC
Memphis

Seven years later

1

It was Akhet, the season of the flood, and in the Delta the waters of the Nile rose out of its riverbanks, invigorating a network of stagnant tributaries.

Waterfowl, pausing in migrations, filled the wetlands and chattered to their hearts' delight. Fish of every kind were there for the taking, and ibises, herons and cranes stalked them silently among the reeds.

In one large lagoon east of Memphis, the sound of laughter filled the marshes. Waterfowl fell silent as three skiffs rounded a bend in the lagoon.

Pharaoh Tutankhamun, wearing a short unadorned cotton kilt, stood in the prow of the lead skiff, his tawny chest covered in a bright collar strung with beads of gold, carnelian and feldspar. He held a throwstick in his right hand, his eyes fixed on the sky.

Ankhesenamun, his wife and queen, was in the stern. They had been married seven years. She accompanied her now seventeen-year-old husband on many hunts, and knew his limitations. She had a premonition that this throwstick, like so many others, would flutter harmlessly through the air, and the birds sensing little in the way of menace, would stay anchored to the ground, with only the most timid among them taking flight. Her handmaidens, Leta and Auti, trailed alongside her in a second skiff, followed by two household guards in a third.

The throwstick curved in a high arc through the air, far from the lumbering fat goose it was intended for. The bird, as though in contempt of its stalker, lifted lazily into the air and settled down on an open stretch of water.

At that precise moment Leta and Auti let fly a squeal of laughter. Startled waterfowl on the banks and in the water rose up in one sound of flapping wings.

"Now see what you've done," Tutankhamun shouted. He shook his fist at Leta and Auti. "Well, that is the last time I bring you two. Damn your hearts!"

Leta and Auti obliged Pharaoh with looks of contrition, knowing they had nothing to fear.

Tutankhamun shouted a command at his rower, ordering him deeper into the lagoon where the startled birds would once again settle among the banks and the waving tufts of papyrus reeds.

Ankhesenamun broke off her conversation with her handmaidens, nestled down among the bright cushions in the stern, and allowed her hand to languidly play across the top of the water. A white lotus blossom drifted by. She reached into the water and let it nestle in the palm of her hand, and then brought it to her nose.

She glanced up at her husband. He had removed another throwstick from a cotton bag. Standing upright again, he glanced at his wife, shrugged his shoulders and waited for the next opportunity to bring down a bird. Ankhesenamun encouraged him with a serene smile.

Encouragement wasn't enough. Today was his birthday, and she wanted him to have an especially happy day. Something had to be done. And that was why she had paid young Paneb, the shipwright's son, to hide among the reeds. He was muscular and athletic and made money instructing men of wealth and leisure in the art of hunting.

The plan was this: When Tutankhamun let fly his throwstick, Paneb would fling a throwstick that would curve gracefully toward its mark. The chance that the young Pharaoh would see Paneb's throwstick was slim, for he always finished his shot off balance, and as a result, was unable to recover in time to see the trajectory of his own throwstick, much less Paneb's. Tutankhamun would believe he had brought down the bird, and the happy event would be a subject of conversation at the state banquet.

Ankhesenamun imagined Paneb squatting on the spongy wet banks of the lagoon, hidden by a thick stand of reeds, waiting for the skiffs to come into view. Above the chattering of the birds and buzzing of insects, she listened to her husband bark a command to his oarsman in that reedy adolescent voice of his. A bothersome swarm of gnats circled above his head. The queen watched a crocodile slip silently through the water and hoped that Paneb kept an eye on the water as well as the sky.

Tutankhamun stood in the prow as silent as a statue, arms outstretched. Bald geese flew in low over the water. Ankhesenamun saw the vague outline of a human form behind the flowering papyrus tufts, a throwstick clenched in his right hand.

Tutankhamun flexed his arm and let fly the throwstick. Struggling to keep his balance, he was a hair's breadth from falling out of the skiff. At the last moment he reached for the prow pole, his eyes cast downward momentarily to his sandaled feet.

Paneb's throwstick, launched from behind the waving papyrus stalks, whizzed threw the air, and just before arcing back on its return flight caught a gray goose in the gullet. The goose spiraled downward fifty cubits off the port bow of the skiff.

Tutankhamun regained his footing and looked up. A cry went up from the party. Could it be? Yes, Pharaoh had brought down a fine large goose. It fell conveniently on a thatch of dry land. The oarsman, without waiting for a command, was already plying his way toward the downed bird. Pharaoh, stirred by all the shouting and cheers, could scarcely believe his eyes when the oarsman reached over and seized the stunned bird by its neck. Then the oarsman expertly snapped the wings, a procedure that would render the goose helpless when it regained consciousness. He handed it up to his majesty. Tutankhamun beamed with pride.

The handmaidens were still applauding from their skiff when Ankhesenamun leaned back upon her cushions, a smile on her face, thinking all the while that she had never seen her husband looking so good, even desirable, standing erect and proud in the golden sunlight.

2

Ankhesenamun's long cool bath was a welcome relief from the sticky heat of the lagoon. When she left the unction room she glistened in a thin coat of oil of lily. She dismissed Leta and Auti, preferring the solitude of her bedroom before getting dressed for the banquet.

Naked, she lay in bed thinking of the evening ahead. It was to be the first state banquet she and Pharaoh would give since the court had moved to Memphis.

It had been three years since they left Thebes. Ay had argued against the move, but the young couple wanted to live in Memphis. It had been the first time Tutankhamun, with encouragement from Ankhesenamun, rebuffed his regent.

Ankhesenamun never looked back, though she had not stopped thinking of Menkhara. The young royal scribe was her one romance, a memory that gave a touch of melancholia to her quiet moments, when she yearned for the mature companionship of a man. Tutare did not fill that need despite two stillbirths and their shared sadness.

"Oh, Memphis," she had murmured from the prow of her state ship when the city's white double walls had come into view. It had been love at first sight. It was her kind of town—cosmopolitan, fun-loving Memphis—worthy home of Ptah, the creator god. It was a tolerant town, a place of reconciliation, where even Horus and Seth got along, a far cry from the stuffy conservatism of Thebes.

Ankhesenamun dozed off. She was awakened an hour later by Leta. "Your guests have begun to arrive, my lady. May I help you prepare?"

The queen sat up with a contented smile and yawned. It had been a good day. Everything had gone right. Standing at the foot of her bed, she allowed Leta to wrap her in a filmy white linen gown made expressly for the occasion.

The guest of honor was the celebrated young General Horemheb, the Lion of Palestine. His reputation as a war hero had spread across the two kingdoms. His successful campaign against the Libyans had preceded his arrival, and Pharaoh, on advice of his regent, was obliged to take the occasion of the banquet to honor him.

None of this mattered to Ankhesenamun. Despite her domestic contentment, there was still one matter, one piece of news, which could bring her sublime happiness, or plunge her into the depths of despair. Menkhara had communicated with his former master Kenofer, from his army post in Syria, asking the Master of the Kap to convey his compliments to the queen. Now there was only one question she wanted to ask the famous general: the whereabouts of a certain young officer who had joined his army seven years ago. Was he dead or alive?

As the years rolled swiftly by, the memory of Menkhara slipped from the real world into dreams of what might have been. She embellished the dream, pampered it, made a shrine of it, never once thinking anyone could take Menkhara's place in her heart.

Ankhesenamun sat with her cosmetic table and stared into a shiny copper mirror. "And you say you saw the general's party arrive?" she asked Leta.

"Yes, ma'am," Leta continued excitedly. I saw General Horemheb carried in his palanquin from the Memphis quay to the palace doors. He looked so proud and handsome, my lady."

"And was there anyone else in the general's party?"

Leta answered with a girlish smile. "The General's wife, Amenia, and a good dozen or so of the handsomest officers you might imagine."

Ankhesenamun applied kohl to her eyes and brows. A dozen or so officers she thought, her heart filled with hope. *Could my Menkhara be among them?*

She completed her makeup, allowed her handmaidens to finish dressing her, and then joined her husband. Pharaoh Tutankhamun had been waiting patiently in the small chamber outside her suite.

She gave him a broad smile when the doors opened. Pharaoh was dressed in a pleated robe with a blue sash, and seemed too small for the heavy colorful pectoral that draped over his shoulders and chest. He wore his favorite blue war crown banded with the uraeus. Adolescence had improved his looks. At seventeen, he was of average height for his age, and considered good-looking. He had a squared firm jaw and full sensuous lips. His slightly flattened nose and tawny complexion suggested an injection of Nubian blood in his ancestry.

Breaking with tradition, Ankhesenamun walked at her husband's side rather than trailing slightly behind him as was the custom. Exiting the queen's suite of rooms, the royal family ascended a ramp to a high doorway and followed along a descending alabaster balustrade that led into the columned banquet room. They entered the great room to a steady rain of applause from guests crowding up against one another at the entrance.

Ankhesenamun's eyes swept the room. Most of the guests standing in the receiving line were from Thebes and had taken up temporary residence in Memphis. They had come downriver to help celebrate the return of the general whom Ay had called the man of the people. Memphis was definitely the place to be.

Ankhesenamun wished she could have sent all the Thebans packing. They made her feel uncomfortable, even resentful. She distrusted Karnak's priesthood and the politicians from the southland; and the person she distrusted most was her own Grandfather Ay. He had come up to Memphis with his daughter, Mutnedjmet, and his son-in-law, Tanehes.

A way opened up for the royal couple. They moved slowly toward the dais where a table was set up for the royal party.

General Horemheb waited for his hosts at the foot of the dais steps. His wife Amenia stood a few paces behind him in the shadows. Ankhesenamun had never met the great man, but there was no mistaking who he was. This much she knew about him: He was the child of nobodies, peasant-farmer stock from the ancient town of Herakleopolis. But her knowledge of the man contrasted sharply with his military bearing and his rugged good looks. There was about him a zone of authority that reached out from where he stood like an invisible source of energy.

Ankhesenamun glanced at her young husband. He was holding up rather well, but she detected a nervousness about him as they approached the general, a slight twitch of his cheek, and the familiar quick look he gave her when he needed assurance. The general flashed Tutankhamun a generous smile, and he returned the greeting with the happy eager grin of an uncertain youth.

The general bowed low, and Tutankhamun offered his hand in return. "All Egypt welcomes you back from your triumphs abroad, brave sir. You do us honor with your presence."

Well said, thought Ankhesenamun, with the smile of a proud parent.

Horemheb, using the time-honored response one gave to his Pharaoh, expressed his unworthiness at so great a reception. Then he introduced his wife. Amenia stepped forward.

She was a woman of astonishing beauty and presence, a worthy wife for so great a general. Ankhesenamun liked her at once. She had an open, honest face and a frankness that was likeable. This could be a friend, she thought.

There were two long tables set in a v-shape on the dais, allowing the royal couple and their party to observe the guests below them as they dined.

A squad of servants filled the banquet hall for the sole purpose of filling golden goblets with the very best wine from Mareotis and the Fayyum. After the first goblets were poured, the conversation became more robust. Horemheb talked about his campaigns against the Libyans, of a coming conflict with the Hittites, and spoke nothing but praise for the divisions of infantry and chariotry under his command.

Ankhesenamun forced her mind to drift elsewhere. She managed a conversation with Amenia but thought only of Menkhara. Would she be alone with Horemheb long enough to inquire? Had the general heard about the awful scandal years before? Was there a possibility that her Menkhara was somewhere in the banquet hall, one of those handsome officers Leta spoke of? And finally, would she recognize him after so many years? Her heart ached.

The servants served food from large steaming platters resting on alabaster tables. The smell of roasted meats and fowl filled the air. There were baskets piled high with fruit, bread and cakes. Through the sound of laughter, which seemed to grow with every ewer of wine, came a series of pleasant tunes. The gentle swell of harps and lyres mixed with the piping of the flutes.

Horemheb, utterly relaxed by a continuous flow of wine, recounted his defeat of the Libyans as though this triumph had given him the experience needed to talk about Egypt's role in Nubia and Palestine and the Levant. "Well now, upon my word, this Suppil . . . what's his name?"

"Suppiluliumas," Ankhesenamun interjected.

Horemheb's face turned red. "Yes," he managed. "The damned Hittite must at last be taught a lesson for his attacks in Mitanni. Wasukani has been sacked, and our ally Tushratta murdered."

A painful moment of silence swept across the banquet table. Horemheb's warning was a breach of protocol and good manners. This was no place to discuss war and politics.

It was a fine time to change the subject and talk about pleasantries. Ankhesenamun could find no better opportunity to talk about her husband, who until this time had been largely ignored.

"Well, you see the fine gray goose just now laid before you," she said excitedly. "It was brought down by Pharaoh a few short hours ago. Not enough time to fatten it up properly, but I so wanted it made ready in time for tonight."

All eyes fell upon the roasted goose steaming in its clay platter. There was a round of applause and a chorus of compliments.

Tutankhamun beamed proudly and nodded his head in thanks. Now for the first time they were applauding something he truly believed was his own doing. He gazed over at Ankhesenamun, and she could see how happy he was. It was his day, and as a double treat she would let him share her bed that night, provided he did not get himself drunk on pomegranate wine.

The silence was broken by a breathless moan from Mutnedjmet. "That's him!" she cried. "There! There!" She pointed to a young man standing next to a column.

The subject in question was well above average height, with good-looking rugged features and a distinct military bearing. His skin glowed like polished bronze in the flickering lamplight.

Mutnedjmet continued: "Do my eyes deceive me or isn't he my run-away servant decked out in fine linen robes and wearing the red sash of a Lieutenant of Infantry?"

"You must be mistaken, lady," Horemheb said confidently. "That is the most promising junior officer on my staff."

Mutnedjmet was unimpressed. "I tell you he is my servant, Menkhara. Why, the man's a felon. He killed my beloved Pera, an offense he should have died for. He showed his response to our mercy by killing my precious Sota and fleeing."

Ankhesenamun's heart raced at the mention of Menkhara's name. She stared across the room searching vainly for him. *Was Mutnedjmet mistaken*?

Horemheb shook his head. "And who may I ask is Sota?"

"My pet monkey."

Horemheb flashed Mutnedjmet a flat impatient smile. "I should tell you this so-called felon of yours, this monkey-killer, has also killed many enemies of Pharaoh, and has been awarded the gold of valor by my own hand."

Mutnedjmet was at her cranky worst. "Nevertheless, I want him arrested."

Ankhesenamun stared at Mutnedjmet with a commanding smile. "That's not going to happen, Auntie. Some years back the warrant was withdrawn. Menkhara was granted a royal pardon."

Mutnedjmet paled, looked to her father as though for help, and then stared down angrily at her plate.

Ay broke into the conversation with a look of astonishment. "It is the first I've heard of it." He glared at Ankhesenamun. "I thought royal pardons were the business of Pharaoh, with the advice and counsel of his vizier."

Ankhesenamun smiled. "You're quite right, Grandfather. It is the business of Pharaoh. The warrant was lifted only hours after my husband's coronation. Perhaps you have forgotten."

She could tell from his brooding look what was going on in Grandfather's head. She had expected to incur his wrath when she thrust Menkhara's pardon under Tutankhamun's nose and watched him sign it.

Grandfather and Horemheb exchanged glances. The general put his hand to his chin and shifted his gaze to Ankhesenamun. His kohl-black eyes were as steady as a bird of prey. A cold shiver ran up Ankhesenamun's back.

As the banquet progressed, noisy guests drowned out the strumming of the great harps. Ankhesenamun circulated among the guests, but whenever she could she searched the crowded room for Menkhara. Occasionally she got a glimpse of him, only to be interrupted by a guest.

Someone tapped her on the shoulder. It was Pharaoh. He wanted her to meet his friend, Huy, the viceroy of Kush. "Yes, of course," she answered with a smile. "I'd love to meet the viceroy." She glanced back over her shoulder. Menkhara stood with his back to her, talking to a Memphite architect; and later, from the corner of her eye, she saw him leave the banquet hall.

Her heart beat against her ribs.

3

"I would kill the bitch if I could," said Mutnedjmet.

She sat in her father's study. It had a dry musty smell, like all the other rooms of his seldom-used Memphis villa.

"To think that Queen Ankhesenamun had pardoned Menkhara, a fugitive from justice." Mutnedjmet wagged a forefinger at her father who sat across from her, a tankard of sweet beer raised to his lips. "After all, you are the vizier, and he was condemned in the house of Maat. Can you abide the thought of it? You must put an end to this, Father."

Ay shrugged. "If only it were that easy."

Mutnedjmet gave her father a crafty smile. She wanted to call him a crusty old fool and chastise him for his stupidity. Instead she said calmly, "Is there anything you cannot do father? You were the companion of three Pharaohs, the army's Master of Horse, vizier of Upper Egypt. Your voice was the voice of Egypt in all the courts of the world. Our young king admires you. You've more influence with him than you give yourself credit for. Tell me you cannot silence Ankhesenamun, and I will tell you the world is turned upside down."

Ay said carefully, "Ankhesenamun has already made two trips to the birthing stool and has yet to produce an heir. She might even try for the crown should Tutankhamun die."

"She is a woman."

"So was Hatshepsut, and she reigned for twenty-two years."

Mutnedjmet got up, sat beside her father and placed her arm on his shoulder. "You're the brother of Queen Tiye, and loved as much for your military skills and your daring as for your statesmanship. The people are tired of weak kings. They want a warrior-king, a real leader." She leaned over and kissed his cheek. "Father," she whispered near his ear, "you are that man."

Ay laughed and shook his head. “You’ve a scheming mind, daughter. You’re thinking that if I were Pharaoh, there would be something in it for you as daughter of a Horus god. I know what you’re getting at, and may the gods forgive you for hoping the worst for our young Pharaoh and his queen. Besides, any reign of mine would be a short one.”

“What if something did happen to Pharaoh? Would you refuse the crown?”

“I would have to think on it. I’m an old man, short on years. Besides, my right to the throne would be challenged.”

Mutnedjmet smiled, “But if the crown were promised to a younger man after you have quit this life, Father? What if he were a strong man that no one would dare challenge? Such a man could well afford to wait you out if promised the crook and flail.”

Ay smiled. “You’ve filled your idle time with thoughts of kingship. And this successor, I suppose, would have to be a man of the people, a fresh face who could lead Egypt, and one whom you could trust. Is there such a man, daughter?”

Mutnedjmet flushed. “General Horemheb.”

Ay nodded, an amused smile on his face. “I might have guessed. I saw the scandalous way you stared at him at the banquet.”

Now it was Mutnedjmet’s time to smile. “He has everything, and he’s your friend.”

“And enough pride to fill the Nile.”

“You can’t fault him on that account.”

Ay shook his head and looked sternly at Mutnedjmet. “The king is not going to die, and I don’t want him dead. I’m no fool. I know what you’re hinting at. I’ve done some terrible things in my life, daughter, but regicide won’t be one of them. You lure me into these stupid conversations, these fatuous dreams.” He pointed an accusatory forefinger at his daughter. “If you want Horemheb, all’s well and good. But he’s married to a beautiful woman, and you’re married to a spineless idiot. Enough of your scheming, woman. If you embark upon intrigues, I'll have you sent from court."

Mutnedjmet burned with embarrassment. It had been some time since he'd talked to her that way. "I know my shortcomings," she stammered.

"I'm glad to hear it. But no more of this kind of talk. Tomorrow I begin my holiday with General Horemheb and our young Pharaoh. We're spending it in the Fayyum. It's high time young Tutankhamun spent more time in the company of men. We will get to know him better, and will help undo any undue influence Ankhesenamun may have on him."

"General Horemheb! Father, take me with you."

Ay laughed. "Don't be silly. It's not the sort of thing one does. Besides, we're gong to a special place to relax. It's not for women. Or I should say, the kind of women you would care to know."

"When my sister Nefertiti was alive, nothing was too good for her. You were always in attendance."

Ay grunted. "She was queen. She could do what she wanted. And besides, she wasn't a scheming troublemaker."

"And when you breathe your last, what will become of me?"

"If you schemed less and attended to your own business, you'd have little to worry about."

Mutnedjmet accepted the goblet of wine her father handed her, the small smile on her face masking years of resentment and malice. As Father grew older, she stopped taking him seriously. Perhaps the old man didn't know what was best for him or his daughter. But it didn't matter. She would set things right.

4

Mutnedjmet could not get General Horemheb out of her mind. And that is why she invited her husband, Tanehes, to her bedroom.

Tanehes, she thought with an ironic inner smile. That pig of a man will yet be the key to my own happiness.

Tanehes was late as usual. While Mutnedjmet waited, her thoughts drifted back to Horemheb. He was everything she wanted in a man. He was strong, proud, handsome and respected, and he answered to no one but Pharaoh. He was going places, and she would be swept along with his success. More important, the general and her father were the best of friends. The whole thing seemed so easy.

Tanehes came into her bedchamber unannounced. Normally he would have been chastised for the discourtesy. But not today.

He slouched deep into a chair, stretching his thin brown mottled legs across the floor. His eyes were cast upward, as though searching for something among the painted date palms.

Mutnedjmet watched Tanehes pour himself a goblet of wine. They had not made love for more than a year, though he tried often enough. His arrogance no longer bothered her. Tanehes was a fool, and he would dig his own grave. She would have little to do but hand him the pick and the shovel.

"You and I have had an understanding since the early days of our marriage," Mutnedjmet began. Tanehes nodded in agreement. "We've both enjoyed lovers from time to time, and in this regard have cooperated in avoiding scandal."

Tanehes smiled. "What's all this leading up to? You've a new lover, dear wife?"

Mutnedjmet smiled back. "No, but presently you will."

Tanehes perked up, his eyes riveted on Mutnedjmet.

"General Horemheb's wife, Amenia, has asked about you. She need hardly have inquired, for I could tell from the looks she's been casting in your direction."

"You think this could lead to something?" said Tanehes, sitting up straight, his voice pitched high with excitement.

"That depends on the kind of man you are. She would take you as her lover."

Tanehes sank back into his chair. "Don't play me for a fool, Mutnedjmet. What would the wife of a powerful general have with me?"

Mutnedjmet laughed. "You are indeed a fool to think that way. Amenia has confided in me. She wants you. She understands I would harbor no jealousy. I told her about our understanding." She smiled seductively at Tanehes to make the point. "Amenia and I have become fast friends, and I would be pleased if you took her for your mistress. The gods only know, I could never satisfy your needs."

Tanehes stared up at the ceiling, and Mutnedjmet knew him well enough to realize that he was attempting to conceal his excitement.

"If Horemheb found out," Tanehes mused half aloud, drawing an invisible line across his throat with his finger.

Mutnedjmet gave him a brittle little laugh. "He would probably reward you for taking her off his hands. You know, it was common knowledge among the officers' wives that she was seeing a young lieutenant of chariotry during her husband's campaign in Lebanon and Syria."

Tanehes sat up again. The look on his thin face, and the glare in his beady black eyes showed interest. "Can you bring this about?"

Mutnedjmet pursed her lips. "Tonight the general leaves for the Fayyum. I've invited Amenia to spend several days here at our villa. She was excited at the prospect."

"What did she say?"

"Let me say she would not be surprised if you paid her a visit. Your chamber is only a few steps from hers."

Tanehes gave her a crafty smile. "I'm in your debt."

Mutnedjmet returned his smile and nodded. "Your happiness is mine, dear husband."

⁂

The following day Mutnedjmet greeted Amenia with a hug and a kiss. They were standing in a guest bedchamber, as bare-chested servants staggered forward, arms filled with chests of Amenia's clothes.

"Dearest Amenia," said Mutnedjmet. "I'm so glad you have consented to stay with us."

Amenia gave Mutnedjmet a broad smile. "The honor is mine. It's never easy with my husband gone, but I've made so many friends since coming to Memphis, I think I would like to remain here the rest of my life."

"I wish I could share your view," Mutnedjmet answered. "We have a much larger family villa in Thebes. I have it to myself, and Father lives in the palace at Malkata. I always feel a little cramped here in Memphis. If you visit me in Thebes, you will have a bedchamber twice as large."

Amenia looked around the bedchamber, her long dark hair swirling with her head. She looked young, almost a girl, and there was a playful innocent smile on her face. "Oh, Mutnedjmet, it's as grand as anything I could imagine."

Mutnedjmet laughed lightly. "Then I am glad you're pleased. And when you have bathed and freshened up, I'll show you our gardens. We'll sip pomegranate wine in the sunshade and learn as much as we can about one another."

Amenia took Mutnedjmet's hand. "Between your friendship and the graciousness of our queen, I could not have wished for more."

Mutnedjmet said gently: "You are like a new sister, and you fill our home with the joy of your company. And before you know it, your husband will be back in your arms." The two women embraced.

Later, the women sat in the shade of a weeping willow on the edge of a pond. For the occasion Mutnedjmet had unplugged a small amphora of her father's most prized wine, marked with a vintage year dating back to the reign of Mighty Bull.

Amenia could not stop talking about her husband.

"And he treats you well in all respects?" Mutnedjmet said with a smile.

Amenia knew what her hostess was getting at. She flashed her a schoolgirl smile. "His lovemaking is both volcanic and gentle, and I could not imagine that he has ever offered himself in such a way to any other woman.

Mutnedjmet felt a twinge of envy. "You are the most fortunate of women."

5

Mutnedjmet had selected Amenia's bedchamber. It was next to hers, separated by a thin sandstone wall. The hole she had bored in the wall was discreetly hidden behind a small meruwood chest. Lying down and peering through, her eyes could range from one end of Amenia's bedchamber to the other. The workman who drilled the hole was Utan, a strapping young man from Tyre who regularly serviced the princess in more ways than one. His loyalty to Mutnedjmet was won with a single threat: one indiscretion and he would be sent back to Tyre to beg for food in the town streets.

Mutnedjmet was grateful for the shaft of moonlight that penetrated the clerestory window in Amenia's bedchamber. She had waited for Amenia to retire, then, pushing the chest aside, she lay next to the borehole and watched her beautiful guest, restless in the strange bed. Amenia sat up and slipped from under the covers.

She stood up. Sweat glistened on her youthful breasts. It was a warm, still night, with no cooling wind for the roof vents to capture. Amenia let her gown fall to the floor and sat naked by the window, her eyes fastened upon the ships' canal linking the palace to the Nile.

But what was keeping Tanehes? Mutnedjmet cocked her ear, listening for the sound of his sandals in the hall as he made his way to Amenia's chamber. She had seen to it that the servants were alerted to possible problems that night, and asked them to remain awake with their chamber doors ajar.

A scuffing sound. It had to be Tanehes. In the distance was the intermittent baying of a dog and an occasional laugh from young partygoers on the road outside the courtyard. The scuffing sound grew louder, and then a silence. Tanehes was at Amenia's door.

Finally the door to Amenia's chamber slowly opened with a creaking sound and the flickering light of a hall wall torch. Tanehes walked slowly forward, peering cautiously around the screen.

He held a wine ewer. Amenia sat nude on a window bench, her oiled lustrous body parallel to the window. Her long bare legs were drawn up, and her cheek rested on her knees.

She slowly turned her head, the serene smile phasing into shock. She recognized Tanehes immediately.

"At last we are alone," Tanehes said with an anxious smile.

Amenia's mouth fell open.

Mutnedjmet adjusted her aching body on the floor. Was this to be Amenia's first adventure outside the marriage bed?

"I have brought some wine from Pharaoh's own stock," said Tanehes. "If there are cups ..." He looked around the chamber.

"You do not belong here," Amenia managed in a soft but firm

voice.

Tanehes broadened his smile. "Modesty becomes you, my dear. But I know your desire matches my own, sweet woman."

Amenia, not within reach of her gown, drew her legs up as close to her chin as she could. She said hurriedly, her voice trembling, "I don't know what you are talking about. You had better leave."

Tanehes saw two cups resting on a nearby cosmetic box. He motioned to them.

The fool expects her to retrieve the cups, Mutnedjmet thought. Perhaps he wants her standing to see her in all her naked radiance. It was all she could do to keep from laughing.

"Please leave at once," Amenia insisted in a demanding voice.

Mutnedjmet, an eye pressed against the borehole, recognized the look on Tanehes's face. He was clearly annoyed.

Tanehes fetched the cups and stepped toward Amenia. In an instant he was at her side. "The wine will warm your heart," he said.

"I do not want your wine. You are making a mistake, sir. Please leave my chamber. I will say nothing of the matter."

"I'm sure of that!" Tanehes said impatiently. He filled the cups with wine, set the ewer down on the ledge and offered her a cup. She shook her head.

He set down the cups, reached out and placed his hands on Amenia's bare shoulders. He twisted her body gently toward him. She resisted. He scowled.

An expression of terror came over Amenia's face. "Please," she said with a choking sob.

Tanehes let his hands drop from her shoulders to her breasts. He squeezed. She pulled back.

Mutnedjmet, her hipbone hurting from the floor, stretched her body, but fearing that she might have missed something, thrust her head back to the borehole. Amenia's large bright eyes were dazzling, and the moonlight glistened on her moist lips. Tanehes had his gown off, and his cock thrust forward unashamedly. Mutnedjmet felt desire in her belly, and without thinking, she slipped her hand under the hem of her nightdress and ran it up her thigh.

Tanehes rested his face against Amenia's cheek. Her lips stretched away from his in disgust.

Mutnedjmet knew from experience that Amenia's refusal would only inflame Tanehes even more. The fool thinks she is being coy, she thought. Now it seemed that Tanehes no longer cared how she felt.

He forced a hand between Amenia's legs. She cried out: "No! Please, no!" The ewer and cup crashed to the floor.

It was an awkward affair. Amenia was pressed back against the narrow window niche, her long legs drawn up at the knees. Tanehes paused long enough to consider his next move.

Mutnedjmet watched, her forefinger busy beneath her gown.

Tanehes brought his left arm around Amenia's back, and his right arm under her knees. He lifted her up as though she were a sack of grain. Amenia kicked her legs with such force Mutnedjmet thought the woman would slip out of his arms. He clamped his arms hard around her waist and carried her across the room to the bed, throwing her down on the covers.

He stared down and positioned himself over her. He forced her legs down and kissed her hard upon the mouth, content with merely lying on top of her. He was in no hurry now. But her thighs remained locked tight. No amount of prying with his fingers could part them.

Tanehes whispered in her ear. "Open your legs or I will kill you." To back up the threat he placed his thumb and fingers around her slender neck and squeezed. She gasped for air. Suffocating, she shook her head in agreement. He released his hand. Amenia slowly relaxed her legs.

Tanehes bullied his body between her legs and entered her. She screamed.

Mutnedjmet watched wide-eyed, her body stretched at the point of orgasm.

~

Mutnedjmet, out of breath, flung open Amenia's bedchamber door. Behind her, the shapeless faces of two servants. Tanehes blinked, rubbed his eyes and sat up.

"Loving Hathor!" Mutnedjmet cried out. "What is this? My husband bedded with Amenia!"

"By the beard of Ra!" Tanehes cursed. "What are you doing here?"

Mutnedjmet turned to the servant she had summoned. "Bring my father at once!" The servant, wide-eyed, ran from the room. Mutnedjmet, looking dazed, stumbled back toward the door, all the while pulling at her long black hair like a crazy woman.

Tanehes sprang from the bed. He stared at Mutnedjmet in disbelief. He drew back like a caged animal with no place to run. "Oh, you bitch!" he cried. He moved toward Mutnedjmet, hand cocked, ready to strike.

Ay appeared in the doorway in his nightgown, flanked by two household guards. "I wouldn't do that if I were you."

Tanehes froze.

Ay pushed Tanehes back into the room and entered, followed by the guards. One of the guards carried a torch. Ay motioned to him, and in an instant a wall sconce was lit, filling the room with an orange glow. By now several household servants, aroused by the noise, stood by the entrance, peering in with wondering looks.

Mutnedjmet's screams softened into sobs. "My husband!" she cried. "And you, Amenia, my friend!"

Amenia sat naked at the edge of the bed, hands crossed over her crotch. Her eyes were set wide in disbelief.

Ay stared hard at Amenia. "What does the wife of General Horemheb have to say in her defense?"

"Defense?" she sobbed. "Am I on trial?"

"No, but you will be." Ay shook his head sorrowfully. "I regret I did not arrive sooner. Poor General Horemheb," he said softly. "Who will tell him?"

"I was raped!" Amenia cried. "I did not invite that man to my chamber." She turned to Mutnedjmet. "Tell them, Mutnedjmet!"

Mutnedjmet threw up her arms in a show of disgust.

"Oh my God!"Amenia cried, placing a hand over her face. She reached for a linen sheet and covered herself and then looked around the chamber with pleading eyes. "Please ... please. What are you all thinking?"

In desperation, Tanehes turned to Ay, but the regent was soothing Mutnedjmet, who sobbed hysterically.

Ay looked up, his hand still resting comfortingly on the crown of his daughter's head. "Arrest this man," he said, pointing at Tanehes..

"What is this?" Tanehes cried out, drawing back.

The guards drew their swords.

Tanehes whitened. "This is a setup!" he screamed. "I was invited to Amenia's chamber. I swear to it. Ask my wife." The guards prodded him with their swords. Tanehes began to shake. "You just ask her. Ask Mutnedjmet!"

Mutnedjmet ran from the room with a cry of despair. Opening the door to her bedchamber, she looked back. Tanehes, hands bound behind his back, was led away. Ay called after him. "You may plead your case in the temple of Maat."

Tanehes's screams echoed down the hall. "This is not right. I was put up to this. You are all mistaken! This is my wife's doing. Oh, the bitch! The bitch!"

⁂

Snuggled comfortably in bed under a light linen sheet, Mutnedjmet could still hear her husband's curses sounding in her ear. She wondered whether or not Father believed her story. No matter. She was his daughter and Father had no choice but to accept the accusations, at least in public. A slow smile played across her face. Then she yawned, snuffed out the flickering lamp and slid into a deep sleep.

6

Tutankhamun loved to sign important documents. He didn't always understand what he was signing, but that wasn't important. Making something official with a few scratch marks made him feel good.

He would not forget signing his first royal warrants. They were warrants of execution that would send two convicted criminals to their deaths. He would not forget the day a scribe from the Hall of Maat brought the warrants to his chamber.

The vizier had convicted and sentenced Tanehes and Amenia to death. Young Tutankhamun didn't question the sentence. He was vaguely aware of the court gossip about the case, but was sure his regent, Ay, had made the right decision. Refusing to sign the warrants was unthinkable.

Tutankhamun, propped up in bed, opened his old school writing box and took out a reed pen. Ankhesenamun sat at the edge of his bed. The scribe handed him Tanehes's warrant. He signed it without hesitation, and then looked up at Ankhesenamun. She gave him an approving smile. Then the scribe presented him with Amenia's warrant of execution.

Ankhesenamun rested her hand on her husband's arm. "Leave us, scribe," said Ankhesenamun. "Please wait in the hall."

The scribe backed away, bowing as he went.

"Listen, husband," said Ankhesenamun. "You mustn't sign Amenia's death sentence. She was raped."

"I've heard that Aunt Mutnedjmet testified that Amenia was seen embracing Tanehes, and offered no resistance."

"It's a lie. A damnable lie!"

"Why would she lie?"

"Oh, for the sake of the Aten!" Ankhesenamun fired back. "Are you so blind as to what is going on, husband?" She stood up and stared down at Tutankhamun with a bitter grin. "I don't want to disturb your happy world with things called intrigue and ambition. I would not want to confuse you."

Tutankhamun went pale. He stared down at the warrant, pointing to it with his reed brush. "What am I to do with this? What will uncle Ay think?"

Ankhesenamun sighed and sank back to the bed's edge. "Trust me, Tutare. You know Amenia. She is a sweet person. You must know that Auntie Mutnedjmet is jealous of her. Do not send her to her death. She is young like you, and so innocent. Do not stain your hands with innocent blood. In the end uncle Ay will be proud of you." She swept her hand gently across his cheeks, then reached over and kissed him on the lips. "I know that I will be proud of my husband."

Tutankhamun colored at her touch. "I must do something."

"Write this: Writ of execution denied. Then write that she shall remain under the protection of Pharaoh until such time as he deems fit to remove her from court. "

Ankhesenamun watched Tutankhamun scratch out instructions to the vizier and sign his name. "Horemheb will be angry," he said, laying the reed pen aside. "If he regards her as an adulterer, he will not take kindly to our granting her the protection of our royal court."

"Dearest husband. You are Pharaoh, the Horus god on earth. You can do whatever you want to do."

Later, when the scribe of the domain left with the warrants, one signed and the other denied, Tutankhamun saw a sparkle of pride in his wife's eyes. He had done the right thing, and he knew from experience that she would give him something special. He smiled and said, "Would you like to play Hounds and Jackals?"

"I have a better idea," Ankhesenamun said. In an instant she pulled off her gown and crouched naked over him. She reached for the corner of her husband's gown and raised it back across his belly. She could feel him grow in her hand. She smiled down at him. "You're a very good man, my Pharaoh."

One week later, Tanehes was taken from his prison cell and brought out into the northern desert, near the ancient village of Abu Rawash. He rode on a donkey, his hands free.

Ankhesenamun followed Tanehes in her palanquin, no more than thirty cubits behind him. It was not the custom for a woman, much less the queen, to witness an execution, but Ankhesenamun insisted, and that was the end of the matter.

Officials, including Ay, Usermont and royal scribes, followed in sedan chairs. Horemheb never doubted Amenia's guilt, and was angry that Pharaoh had not approved her sentence of death. He declared himself divorced from his wife, and refused an invitation to witness Tanehes's punishment. In the vanguard was a column of the queen's household guards.

From time to time Tanehes twisted around on his donkey and stared at the queen with pleading eyes, hoping for a last-minute pardon. She did not look away, but stared indifferently back at him.

Beyond a line of bleak umber hillocks they came upon a jumble of flat stones partly obscured by windblown sand. The palanquins and sedan chairs of the royal party were lowered onto the sand. Tanehes was helped from his donkey. Medjay guards bound his hands and led him to a nearby abandoned tomb. Ankhesenamun exercised her royal prerogative and followed the condemned man. Behind her were the royal scribes and the Memphite chief of police. She had planned everything, including Ay's final words to Tanehes, which he had written down with care.

The place was a single chamber tomb, abandoned before its completion. Between two upturned slabs, stone steps led down about ten meters into a chamber that had not escaped destruction over the years. Inside the musty room were several oil lamps, their light casting flickering shadows on the faded and cracked painted walls. In a far corner was a bench and a large leather flask of water.

Ay waited until everyone gathered around the entrance of the tomb. The prisoner stood facing Ay, hands bound. Ay spoke in a loud but solemn voice. "This tomb has been prepared for you, Tanehes. We would not have you die quickly, and so it has been furnished with enough water to last several days. Nor will you be deprived of air, for we want your death to be a slow one, time enough for you to contemplate the horrible thing you have done."

Tanehes glanced at Ankhesenamun, a look of disbelief on his face. She stared back at him, unflinching.

The rope binding Tanehes's hands was cut from him. He was

prodded down the steps. Along the way he lost his balance, and fell to the dirt floor. Slowly he picked himself up, looked around the tomb, and then in the flickering light looked up.

Ay and Ankhesenamun stared down into the tomb. There was silence. Ay continued: "You will not be alone, Tanehes. Rats will be your companions in death. They are waiting for you in the dark corners of your tomb. Look carefully and you will see their eyes shining in the flickering light of the lamps.

"One rat, I am told, is called Gluttonous Glah, the burrower. He's a chubby fellow with a small body and a large head full of teeth. He loves soft flesh, and when the lamplights flicker their last, he will seek you out and find the tenderness of your groin.

"The second rat has been named Reamenhet, the ravenous rodent. He has teeth as sharp as a razor. An ill-mannered rodent he is, for he tears at his meat, and is very fond of human flesh. Finally, there is Tabat, the snapper. You will like Tabat. He is your kind of rat, Tanehes. He is rabid and frothy at the mouth. He's a hard-biting rat with the quickness of a striking snake. Now you see him, now you don't. He will torment your bones long after you have been stripped of all flesh.

"These three companions and their family of one hundred hungry children will share your final hours. When the lamps spend their oil they will come for you, Tanehes. You see, they have not eaten in days."

Tanehes fell to his knees, and with his hands now untied, lifted his head and cried up to Ankhesenamun, hoping that she would listen to his plea. "Mighty and good queen, I have abused your friend. Take my weakness for what it is and show mercy. Cast me out, exile me. But if that is not to be, then send down a knife so I can do quick work upon myself."

Ankhesenamun, showing no emotion, looked away, her eyes fixed on the rim of the horizon. Ay had spoken the words she had written. Surely Tanehes could not fail to understand that his punishment was also repayment for what he had done to her when she was a child, as well as his assault on the unfortunate Amenia.

Servants strung ropes across a stone slab and pulled it over the entrance, leaving a thin opening for air. The grating sound of the moving stone mixed with the sobbing of the entombed prisoner.

The party formed and began a slow trek back across the desert to Memphis. No more than fifty meters from the tomb, Ankhesenamun ordered her palanquin lowered to the ground. She called to one of her household guards and asked for a dagger. Ay and Usermont immediately ordered their sedan chairs lowered. Ankhesenamun waved them back, took the dagger and walked alone back to the prison tomb where she paused by the stone cover. The sunlight shone through her fine white linen gown as though she burned with an inner light. The shadow of a knife dropped from her hand and fell into the darkness of the tomb.

There was a scrambling sound. Tanehes looked up into the thin shaft of sunlight. "May the gods bless your mercy, my lady," he cried.

Ankhesenamun spoke to Tanehes in a soft, but firm voice. "Hear this, Tanehes. I am your final judge. You and I share a secret. We both know the punishment meted out to you this day is as much for your attempted rape of a princess royal when she was a child, as it is for your rape of Amenia. Oh, that you had shown poor Amenia and myself a fraction of the mercy I grant you with a dagger. You will suffer only a brief period in hell. A child can outgrow a memory, but poor Amenia will suffer more, for you have plundered a married woman and left upon her soul a loathsome memory time will not erase. But now, fly to your death, evil man. I'll think no more of you." Ankhesenamun walked alone back to her palanquin. Around her danced a spray of sand stirred up by the hot desert wind.

7

The talk now in Memphis was of war. Ay and Horemheb's planned offensive against the Hittite hordes sweeping across Egypt's vassal kingdoms in Syria was set in motion. The details had been worked out during their holiday in the Fayyum, plans which the young Pharaoh Tutankhamun readily approved.

Troops came daily from the north and south, crammed aboard barges and boats of every description. The divisions of Amun-Ra were camped at Dahshur in the south. The divisions of Ptah built a city of tents in Saqqara. Units from allied lands, Libya, Kush and Wawat, awaited marching orders from their camps at Giza and Abusir.

Ankhesenamun watched the military formations from her palace window. On the road below, a battalion of infantry spread out along the Royal Way, the main street from the palace gates to the temple of Ptah. The soldiers, dressed in kilts and sandals, wore short swords and carried javelins that glittered in the noonday sun.

The huge army gathering beneath the queen's window was a constant reminder of her fading influence at court. It was for this reason that she allowed her husband the pleasures of her bed. There was still the chance she would conceive an heir to the throne. She had been twice to the birthing stool, and each time her child was stillborn. She gave oblations to the Aten and prayed to her father, Akhenaten, for the penetration of his light upon her womb, and the quickening life that would endure beyond its delivery. But all to no avail. The stillbirths meant that anyone in a position of power could ascend to the throne if something happened to her Tutare.

Tutare loved Ankhesenamun. As the army prepared for war he was almost slavish in his attentions and devotion. When he curled close to her like a child, she gave him the protection of her arms and the promise of a good night's sleep.

She understood how much his Uncle Ay and General Horemheb dominated his life. They had drawn him into their council, made him feel good, worthy and masculine, and shared women and wine in the brothels of the Fayyum. In the delirium of such comradeship, they pronounced him worthy of waging war and enthralled him with the promise of adventure. With no more thought than that of a dung beetle at his daily chore, Tutankhamun had signed an order directing the register of recruits to call into formation one of the great armies of his day. How could she compete or blame the too young Pharaoh for bending to their will?

Ankhesenamun had hoped that Horemheb would keep Menkhara at home and at work on his tomb at Saqqara, but she had received word from Kenofer that Menkhara would ship out with the divisions of Ptah. She had not spoken to him for more than seven years, and got only a glimpse of him at the banquet given in honor of Horemheb several months before. She burned to see and talk to him, but she could not afford fresh scandal. She was satisfied to worship her one love from afar, knowing he was safe and improving his life with every passing day. She wondered if he had married. There were rumors of that kind, but she did not probe too hard to find out. She didn't want to know. It was the dream of him that she could not let go of.

She waited as the days slipped by and the waters of the Nile spilled out of its banks. The first gentle cool winds of late Akhet blew out of the north, carrying with them the steady sounds of drums and trumpets that spoke to her more of hopelessness than of war. She began to think that Menkhara would not come back alive, and how she would regret not sending for him. Finally, in desperation, she ordered the commander of her household guard to seek him out and command him to attend upon his queen.

The following morning Ankhesenamun could hardly contain her excitement when Leta escorted Menkhara into the chamber, bowed and promptly left her mistress alone with the handsome Captain of Infantry.

Menkhara looked thin, and had more the bearing of a soldier than the scribe she remembered. But there was self-assurance in the way he conducted himself. His improved rank was proof enough of his skills as an officer.

He gave her a warm smile. "My lady," he began, "you honor me with your invitation."

Ankhesenamun answered with a playful admonishing smile. "You don't have to stand on ceremony with me, Captain. We're friends, with nothing to hide from one another."

"I hope you will continue to honor me with your confidence. I hope that your husband, great Pharaoh, is in good health."

"Well enough to go off to the wars. How are your parents doing, Menkhara?"

Menkhara's face lengthened, and his brow furrowed. "Then … you have not heard?"

"What are you saying?"

"My parents are dead."

Ankhesenamun struggled for words. "Oh, Menkhara, what happened?" she finally managed in a voice that was barely audible.

Menkhara bit his lower lip, reluctant to go over the details. "Simut removed my father from his position as foreman, and ordered him into the tombs as a common workman. My parents were ordered from their home. The neighbors helped them move, but there was a scuffle with the temple guards. I'm not sure what happened next, but when it was over my father lay dead from a wound. My mother died of grief a few days later. Their village tombs had been confiscated, and when I asked after their bodies, I was told that they were buried, unprepared for the afterlife, in some unknown place in the Eastern Desert."

"Simut had no authority," Anhesenamun shouted. "Only Grandfather, as vizier, could authorize such a thing, and only after proof of some wrongdoing certified by the scribe of the domain."

Menkhara shook his head. "He must have slipped something under the vizier's nose."

She stood up and came to Menkhara's side. He rose to his feet, towering over her. She took his hand. It was warm. Her heart beat with love and anger. She wanted desperately to hold him. "Oh, I am so sorry, Menkhara. Had I known."

For one brief moment it seemed to Ankhesenamun that the years of separation had vanished, and they were lovers again. "I will speak to Grandfather about Simut, and Mutnedjmet too. If he does not act, I will have Tutare order their arrest."

Menkhara gave her a cautionary smile. "No, Ankhesenamun," he said, addressing her for the first time by her court name. "The pleasure of revenge must be mine. I will handle this when I return from Syria."

"Your betrothed … I've forgotten her name. What has become of her?"

"Mayet's father was deputy foreman. He was dismissed from his job as well, and sent to the tombs as an ordinary gang worker. Her parents had no choice but to accept the proposal of a priest from holy Iunu, on behalf of their daughter. He was a distant relative and getting on in years. I would like to think that she is happily married."

"Then you are not married?"

"No."

Ankhesenamun gave him a sad smile. "There was a time when

such news would have thrilled me, if only for my selfishness. But no longer is that so. I would sacrifice anything to bring Mayet back to you."

Without realizing it, she found herself in Menkhara's arms. She was not sure whether she sought the warmth of his arms, or if he acted first. It simply happened. They kissed.

Menkhara said softly in her ear: "This can no longer be justified, my lady. Grant me permission to withdraw."

There were too few people in her life she cared about, too few who would defend her. When his strong arms released her, she felt empty, deprived. With a tremor in her voice, she said, "Must you go so soon?"

"We leave tomorrow, and I must be with my men."

"When will I see you again?"

"The gods willing, when we have defeated Egypt's enemies."

She nodded. "Come back as soon as you are able. Promise me, Menkhara. Please promise me."

Menkhara lifted her face under the chin and kissed her on the lips. "I promise."

Long after he had gone, the warmth of his kiss and the protective feel of his arms around her lingered. She ran to the window, hoping to catch a glimpse of him on the Great Royal Way, but the road was crowded with soldiers and vendors hawking their wares. A blare of trumpets, and another roll of those infernal drums. She began to cry.

The following morning the Divisions of Ptah, regimental strength Libyan archers, Sherden troops and chariot corps, three chariots abreast, joined up with the Divisions of Amun-Ra. Forming along the Royal Way, the ranks extended far into the suburbs south of the city, each with its colorful standards flapping in the wind.

In the late afternoon came the sound of trumpets and the beat of drums. The army marched out of the city and headed toward the desert plateau between Memphis and Suez. It was only after the last of the supply carts rumbled by her window that Queen Ankhesenamun turned away.

8

1331 BC
One year later

The second month of Peret, the season of the coming forth.

Mutnedjmet's large black eyes were fixed on Simut. They sat on pillows, facing a low table in Simut's villa study. They had just finishing eating, and Mutnedjmet had mentioned General Horemheb's triumphant return to Memphis with news that his army had destroyed the Hittite stronghold at Kadesh.

Simut listened to her half-heartedly. His thoughts were elsewhere. He enjoyed basking in Mutnedjmet's company, especially since her visit to his villa had taken him by surprise.

"We would all be better if a Hittite arrow found our Pharaoh's heart."

"For what purpose, Princess?"

"For one thing, Ankhesenamun would not be allowed to rule in her own right. Secondly, I know my father's secret ambitions, though he has tried to hide them from the world. He would take the Horus crown for himself if Tutankhamun should die. He's the most logical choice, is he not? He was the father of two queens, and has been honored with the title, Divine Father. There's no one in all of Egypt with a greater claim."

Simut did not take Mutnedjmet seriously. "The material fact, cousin, is that young Pharaoh is back on the black soil of Egypt, safe and sound."

Mutnedjmet smiled. "That doesn't undo the wish, and sometimes it takes more than hope for something desirable to come about."

Simut studied Mutnedjmet's face. That flat dangerous smile of hers. She wanted something from him. He clasped his hands together, unconsciously rubbing one thumb over the other. "If you're thinking of sending our Pharaoh from this earth, lady, I will not be a willing participant."

Mutnedjmet breathed out an angry sigh of impatience. "So long as my father lives, we are safe. When he is dead, cousin, the queen will turn on us. By all the gods of Egypt, she would have good reason. Father is not a young man; his beating heart stands between death and us. Time is running out. We need each other."

"So what are you thinking? Regicide? You want to involve me?" Simut eyed Mutnedjmet suspiciously. "No … no," he insisted. There was a note of hysteria in his voice. "I won't do it."

Mutnedjmet smiled seductively. "Listen to me. With Tutankhamun out of the way, my father would have to accept the sekem of power; and then, my darling, he would need a strong successor, a man who would defend his right to the crown."

Mutnedjmet smiled. "Cousin, you are that person. Were you and I united in marriage, Father would look to you as his successor; he would offer you the crown upon his death, and I would be your queen."

"You're dreaming."

"It would insure the continuation of his blood, and at the same time please the Theban clergy at Karnak. Imagine, the second prophet of Amun as their new Pharaoh."

Had he heard her correctly? He, Simut, a Horus god, Pharaoh of the Two Lands? The idea, so remote and unimaginable, excited him. "Me?" He trembled.

Mutnedjmet grinned from ear to ear. "Who else, my love?"

"You would marry me, Mutnedjmet?"

"My heart would be yours."

No sooner were the words out of her mouth that she rested her head on Simut's bare chest. She kissed his chest and ran her tongue in circles across the tiny nipples, nearly hidden beneath a thin coat of oily black hair. Simut's face flushed red as she slid her head down the rolls of his pudgy torso, her hand raising his white gown above his thighs as she went.

Simut's body buckled with pleasure at the feel of her head between his legs, and then the unbearable strain of her relentless mouth. He thought he would burst.

When it was over, Mutnedjmet sat up abruptly and drank deep from a flask of wine. She began at once to lay out her plan, and Simut, still relishing the moment, had to sit up and bring his thoughts into focus.

Mutnedjmet said, "My father has invited Pharaoh and the queen to attend the festival of Amun-Min here in Thebes. They cannot refuse him." Mutnedjmet became excited as she spoke, and her eyes flashed. "Now, my dearest cousin," she continued, "an opportunity to end a weakling's reign presents itself. The plan is so easy, so fortunate, the gods must have devised it. When we are done with it, the queen we most despise will be sent into retirement, and we'll have a new Pharaoh. And then begin the happiest days of our lives."

Simut listened, his heart thumping wildly at the enormity of the crime proposed by his beloved, and wondering at the same time if he was up to it.

"Now then," Mutnedjmet continued, "this is what we must

do."

9

Large-breasted Hapi, god of the Nile, lavished the land with water from his woman's breast. And when the cool winds drove down from the distant Great Green Sea, all that remained of the inundation were small pools of water glowing like a thousand eyes in the midday sun. Great Geb, god of the flowering earth, brought forth his sheaves of rippling wheat. It was the season of the coming forth, and the people of Egypt prepared to celebrate the festival of Amun-Min and the success of Egyptian arms.

According to all reports, Egyptian troops had restored the honor of Pharaoh and country by laying siege to Kadesh and driving back in disarray a small contingent of Hittite regulars and Kadesh tribesmen.

Pharaoh and his queen accepted Ay's invitation to attend a banquet honoring the success of Egyptian arms. As the royal couple traveled the Nile toward Thebes, the cities and villages along the route celebrated the army's victory. But no celebration would be so great as the one awaiting them at Thebes. Every Theban who could walk waited excitedly at the quays to watch the docking of Pharaoh's golden falconship, Userhat.

The royal couple took up residence in the west bank palace at Malkata. Even Ankhesenamun allowed herself to believe in the greatness of Tutankhamun, and felt less threatened by the Theban clergy. She saw that her young husband was flushed with happiness and was even beginning to show signs of leadership. Nothing in his brief reign had given him so much joy as praise from his uncle Ay and General Horemheb. Sculptors were already at work on his mortuary temple, planning scenes that showed him leading troops into battle.

Ay hosted the banquet for Pharaoh and his queen. Those in attendance had also been invited to participate in the hunt the following day.

The guests arrived in festal garments and dined on roast duck, oxen and venison, vegetables and fruit. Pharaoh went among the guests and gave necklaces and flowers in garlands and wreaths to the ladies. In the warmth of the torch-lit hall, warm bodies shed the scent of perfumes and oil of lily. Musicians played pipes and flutes as Tutankhamun made his rounds of the tables, followed by servants carrying gifts for each guest.

Ay gave a toast to the warrior-king, again praising him for his military prowess. He placed the chain of valor around Tutankhamun's neck. Ay was in a jovial mood, attentive and courteous to the royal couple. Tutankhamun remarked that he could not remember seeing Uncle Ay so happy.

It was the night before the planned assassination, and Mutnedjmet was nervous. As the banquet wore on, Mutnedjmet worried about Simut. The fat priest had his work cut out for him early the next morning. He was to ride with Pharaoh and arrange for an accident that would end Tutankhamun's reign. The plan was simple, but from the way Simut was drinking, there was some question as to whether he would be able to pull it off.

Mutnedjmet had another reason for getting Simut to retire for the night. Horemheb had cast his eyes in her direction more than once. She wanted to be with him.

She found Simut coming into the banquet hall. He had gone outside to pee. His limp was exaggerated by the large quantity of wine he had drunk. She had never seen him that way. She caught up with him before he reached his table.

"For shame, cousin. You're half-drunk, and it's the night before the most important day of our lives. Off to bed with you."

Simut gave her a silly smile. "Why so, lady love?" he mumbled.

Mutnedjmet looked around nervously for anyone who might have overheard Simut, and she whispered in his ear. "Don't be so familiar with me in public, you fool. Now hear me well: tomorrow at the crack of dawn we meet in the stables. You know what you must do."

The words had an immediate sobering effect on Simut. He held a forefinger up to her face. "Yes," he said, "I know it is the right thing to do."

Mutnedjmet sensed uncertainty in the priest's voice, despite his assurances. She needed Simut. This was no time to chastise the fat fool. She smiled prettily. "Listen, my darling: there are two things we both want, a long life and each other. Neither will be possible unless you do the deed. Now go to bed, my love. Tomorrow you will have to give the best of yourself."

Simut nodded with bleary eyes and a drunken smile. "All right," he slobbered. "But first you must come back outside with me, so that I might feel the warmth of your lips upon mine."

Mutnedjmet forced a smile to her face and lied with as much conviction as she could muster. "Yes, I also hunger for your lips."

They turned and left the hall, hurried through a side door, and stood on the palace pavilion near the steps leading down to the courtyard below.

Simut flung his thick arms around Mutnedjmet. He planted several kisses on her face, and covered her lips with his mouth. His breath stank of vomit.

Mutnedjmet felt sick, but managed to smile through her revulsion. "Now go, my sweet. Go to your bed, and dream only of your loving Mutnedjmet."

Back inside the banquet hall, Mutnedjmet could not get to a goblet of wine fast enough. This she did easily enough, but just in the nick of time. General Horemheb stood behind her.

"I've been hoping for the honor of your company all night, Princess," he said with a soft smile.

Mutnedjmet thought her heart would burst. General Horemheb, the scourge of Syria, Father's dearest friend, handsome, ambitious Horemheb. She loved everything about him.

"I am glad that you found me, General," she said in a voice that left no doubt of her interest. "I congratulate you on your success in Syria."

Horemheb gave her a modest smile. "The gods favored our army."

Mutnedjmet laughed. "The gods favor Horemheb."

"Princess, would you share the night air and take a turn around the courtyard with me?"

Mutnedjmet gave him her hand.

Outside, the air held the day's heat, and it was humid. The couple walked across the courtyard. Horemheb suggested that it would be cooler along Lake Tiye. The palace gates swung open for them as they headed toward the lake.

Horemheb carried with him a flask of wine. They sat on the wharf drinking from the flask and listening to the ferryboat groan softly on its moorings. Mutnedjmet allowed the general to hold her hand. He had strong, sure fingers, and suddenly she felt a surge of desire in her loins. She wondered when the general had last taken pleasure with a woman. Did he miss his divorced wife, Amenia? She laughed to herself, thinking that she was responsible for the divorce. And now, if everything worked out as planned, and Father became Pharaoh, this handsome general would one day rank high at court.

Horemheb studied her face in the waning moonlight, and she

communicated her desire with her eyes. They stood up together, as though on cue, left the wharf, and strolled into a small garden, out of sight of the ferryboat and the ferryman asleep on deck.

Mutnedjmet was in Horemheb's arms, precisely where she wanted to be. Gently the general lowered her to the ground and lay down beside her beneath a weeping willow. A gentle wind set the willow's limbs rustling with a silky seductiveness.

She helped him raise her gown, aware of a splendid firmness sliding across her belly. And then she lay back with a sigh of joy.

10

The banquet was over and the guests safely back in their villas. It was early morning, and a chill hung in the air.

Simut stood straight as an arrow outside the doors of the chariot barn, his head tilted up to the star-filled sky. A light wind trilled across the flood plain, sending fine sprays of sand onto the sandstone stable walls with a ticking sound.

His offer to ride with the young king was a novel idea since priests did not often partake in the hunt. Despite his infirmity, he was a skilled charioteer. Simut was delighted when Ay approved of him as Pharaoh's riding partner. The regent would one day be his father-in-law, and it was good that they were getting on so well. When he married Mutnedjmet, Ay would secure the happiness of his daughter and make him the next Horus god on earth. Simut smiled. Things were looking up.

A second figure came out of the darkness wearing a bright white cloak whipped up by the wind and fluttering ghostlike in the darkness. It made straight for Simut. A voice low and feminine called out to him.

Simut answered back. "Mutnedjmet, thank the gods. Did you bring the pin?"

"Yes."

"Good."

They entered the barn. The door swung shut behind them. Inside, Simut lit a lamp, and by its dull flickering light they made their way down a row of chariots. Above the sound of sandled feet on straw was the distant whinny of a horse from the nearby stables.

Near the end of the line, an unadorned chariot stood like a poor cousin among its wealthy relatives. Lacking side panels, it had a dragonfly lightness, the ideal hunting chariot, stripped down for speed and maneuverability. The bridlery was unadorned, and the yoke's bare wood stood in sharp contrast to its gilded neighbors. The chariot was Tutankhamun's favorite.

Mutnedjmet handed the slimmed down linch-pin to Simut. "The craftsman told me it is a perfect match," she said.

"How did you come by it?"

"Don't ask."

Simut held it close to the lamplight. The linch-pin had been pared down at the center according to his directions. It would not survive a hard jolt but would snap, and with the leather thong at its base left untied, the wheel would separate from the axle. He had seen such a thing happen to chariots when he practiced at the school of the Kap. The carriage, if handled right, would flip and throw the charioteer to the ground, often with fatal results. If that was not enough, Simut could make use of his strong arms and hands, and hasten the young Pharaoh along his way westward to his afterlife in the fields of Yaru. He rubbed his hands down the pin's smooth shaft. "Perfect," he whispered. "Absolutely perfect."

"Any doubts about the outcome, cousin?" Mutnedjmet said nervously.

Simut gave her a boasting smile in the candlelight. "Taking priestly vows does not debar a priest from hunting and mastering the chariot. I can ride with the best of them."

He lowered himself until he was eye level with the axle. Mutnedjmet held the candle low.

Simut replaced the pin. "It's done," he said, raising himself up.

Mutnedjmet blew out the candle and put her hands around his waist. "My darling man," she intoned. "I can already hear the trumpets blow at our marriage, and then we need only wait for your coronation, when dear Father is laid to rest in his tomb. She gave him a sweet smile. "My Pharaoh, my husband and my lover," she said, encouraging Simut to lower his head and receive her kiss.

Simut's heart exploded with excitement.

Still giddy from Mutnedjmet's words, he returned to his villa but did not retire immediately. Despite his show of confidence, he was afraid, and what he feared most were nightmares.

Helped along by wine, he sat in his study, imagining himself as Pharaoh. He was now as close to the throne as any man could be, and soon he would be married to the aging Pharaoh's daughter. So close to kingship. It was almost too good to be true. He, who only wanted to save Egypt for Amun-Ra, would become the Horus god on earth. And now his sweet Mutnedjmet's own ambition nudged him gently to the deed. He would do it as much for her as for himself. He was ready.

He lay down and closed his eyes. All that remained was a few hours of badly needed sleep.

11

Simut dressed by the gray light of dawn. His servant had brought the King's favorite hunting chariot around to the villa's front gate.

He stood next to the chariot, facing the villa, guessing that his darling Mutnedjmet slept like a baby, without a thought or concern in her heart. He would not let her down.

Smiling to himself, he climbed into the chariot and took the reins. Looking around, he spotted Pharaoh in a sedan chair, in the center of a retinue of servants. Simut politely climbed down from the chariot as Pharaoh's sedan chair was lowered. Tutankhamun shivered in the cool morning air. Simut offered him his cloak. Tutankhamun refused it and climbed into the chariot.

The hunting party rode their chariots in a single file across the Eastern Desert. Simut looked back over his shoulder. All of the hunting chariots had formed into squadrons. Lagging behind were weapon tenders, scouts sitting bareback on fleet horses, and bullock-carts filled with food, beer and water.

Ay was designated master of the hunt, although he would not actually participate. Riding alone in his chariot, he came up beside Simut. "You give Pharaoh a good hunt, nephew," he called out.

"With all my heart, uncle."

Ay winked and then pulled back and came around to the passenger side of the chariot.

"A good morning to you, my Pharaoh," Ay said.

Tutankhamun, so excited at the prospect of the hunt, could hardly talk. He smiled at Ay and nodded.

Ay bowed politely. "The oryx and the lion will quiver in fear at your approach, Majesty. I wish you a joyous day."

A horn sounded, and the chariot drivers snapped reins.

Tutankhamun and Simut had been on the desert for nearly an hour, and had paused twice to drink water and rest the horses. Simut remained silent, dutifully taking orders from Pharaoh, who seemed sure of himself on directions.

Tutankhamun had brought down two hares, but had not yet spied large game. To return to Thebes with nothing more than a brace of hares would be an embarrassment. Simut watched the look of determination on the frail young king's face.

The relentless sun was beginning to take its toll. The dry wind parched Tutankhamun's lips, and from the slouch in his posture, it was clear to Simut that Pharaoh's strength was waning.

Tutankhamun spotted a distant herd of ibexes. Excited, he pointed at them, commanding Simut to go faster.

The terrain was rocky, the kind of surface Simut would need. His heart beat in his chest. The chariot clattered across a glassy bed of rock, near the base of broken hills.

Simut looked back over his shoulder. The rest of the squadrons had split up, going their own way. There would be none close enough to witness what was to follow.

Simut waited. On his right, the low hills raced by; dead ahead, an outcropping of jagged rocks. There was enough room for him to jump free of the chariot. One large smooth rock caught his eye. He inched closer to it.

Simut braced himself. Years of experience as a charioteer taught him what to expect. The wheel would collide with the rock, shattering the linch-pin, and he would be thrown forward and out of the chariot. If lucky, he would escape with a bruised body, or at worst, a broken limb. He reached back and grasped the back of the chariot's wooden frame, anticipating the rising right side of the chariot and then the collapse as the shattered wheel broke away. He would try to brake the horses if he could, and at the same time jump free of the carriage.

He glanced over at Tutankhamun. Pharaoh stood erect, a bow in his left hand, his right hand grasping an arrow. He squinted at the distant ibexes. The chariot moved closer to the rocks on his right.

A hard jolt, and a snapping sound.

Simut had the sensation of flying effortlessly in a soundless world, his head tilted downward. He was unaware of hitting the ground, but felt his body tumbling out of control across the abrasive sand.

Blackness momentarily surrounded him. He fought the darkness, but to no avail. Moments later, when he regained his sight, he lay face down. Ahead, the smashed remains of the light chariot lay on its side, its one good wheel still spinning. Farther ahead, the horses raced across the desert, leaving a cloud of dust behind them.

Pharaoh lay in silence among the rocks. Simut shuffled over to him. Tutankhamun was face down on a small flat bar of sand between two outcroppings of rock. With a sinking heart he watched the young king try to raise himself up.

"Help me," Tutankhamun cried out, struggling to his knees.

Simut was paralyzed with uncertainty. The king's injuries were apparently mild. No head wound. He gazed back across the Eastern Desert. The scouts had seen the accident and pushed their horses into a gallop. If Pharaoh lived and testified against him, he would be tried in the House of Maat for his negligence, and most certainly sentenced to an ugly death. Ay, the man who might have been his father-in-law, would have no reason to show mercy.

Tutankhamun was on both knees, staring blindly into the desert. Simut reached down and grasped a large jagged rock in his hand. Using his good leg, he sprang forward, ignoring a sharp pain in his ankle.

Simut aimed for the back of Tutankhamun's head. He moved as Simut brought the rock down with murderous force. The blow landed slightly to the left of where the neck joined the skull.

Tutankhamun fell forward with a grunt and lay still.

Simut dropped the rock and fell to the ground next to the fallen king. The muffled sound of the scouts' horses grow louder as they raced across the desert.

Simut, helped by a scout, shaded Pharaoh as best he could. "Our Divine Lord is dead," said Simut in a mournful voice.

The scout took Tutankhamun's pulse. "He lives!"

Simut's heart sank, pounding against his ribs. Summoning all his strength, he managed a nervous smile. "May Hathor protect and shield him from pain."

The two men waited in the hot sun. Tutankhamun moaned incessantly. Simut cursed himself angrily under his breath. He had failed.

Pharaoh was taken off the desert in a traveling carriage drawn by oxen. At the dock he was brought aboard a ferryboat on a stretcher. The ferry cast off and headed toward the west bank and the palace at Malkata.

Ay and the court physician Pentu wanted Pharaoh brought to the House of Life in the precinct of Karnak, but Ankhesenamun, informed of the tragedy by messenger, insisted on having her husband brought home. Ay honored her request.

The king was brought to his chamber and laid upon his bed. Ankhesenamun was hysterical, and when told that Simut had ridden with her husband, hysteria turned to anger. She guessed at once that Simut was responsible for Pharaoh's injury. She wanted to rip his eyes out, but there was nothing to be done—not now. She remained at her husband's bedside throughout the remainder of the day and long into night, until finally, in the dawn hours of the following day, she allowed her handmaidens, Leta and Auti, to escort her back to her palace apartment.

12

Tutankhamun remained unconscious for several days, and then one week after his injury, opened his eyes.

Ankhesenamun, keeping a vigilant watch at her husband's side, had dozed in a chair near the bed. She heard a soft sigh and sat up. She looked over at Tutankhamun. His large doe-like eyes were open and staring at her, a dazed look upon his face.

"My dear husband," she cried out, rushing to his side. "Praise to Thoth, to the falcon god, Horus, to loving Hathor, and praise to the Aten for your return."

"What has happened to me?" Tutankhamun said softly.

"An accident, dearest Tutare. Your chariot overturned."

"And now I am going to die."

"Don't talk such nonsense!"

"I am going to die," Tutankhamun persisted. "I see it in your grief, your eyes."

Ankhesenamun clasped her husband's hands in hers. "You must not even think that, my lord. You have nothing to fear."

"My head feels as though it will burst. I'm so tired."

"You must rest."

"How long have I been here?"

"Not long."

"By all the gods, wife. Tell me!"

Ankhesenamun was taken aback by the command. Tutare had never talked to her that way. "A little more than seven days," she answered.

Tutankhamun looked at Ankhesenamun as though she stood at a distance. "Every mortal should fear his own death. Say what you will about my godliness, wife, I fear for my life." A tear rolled down his cheek, and then he gave her a tired smile. "Some confession for a Horus god."

Ankhesenamun could not hold back her tears. "All will be well, dear husband."

Tutankhamun winced. "I'm in pain," he cried out in his reedy voice. It is my leg. The throbbing is without end. Where are my physicians? Where is Pentu?"

"I am here, my lord," said Pentu, who had been keeping vigil in a chair positioned in a corner of the chamber.

"Give him something for his pain," Ankhesenamun demanded.

"I've prepared a compound," said Pentu, producing a small wooden box. "I've only to add it to a goblet of wine."

The concoction was immediately prepared. Tutankhamun, with the help of two servants propping him up, drank from the goblet and then lay back upon his headrest. "Am I going to die?" he said softly, grasping Ankhesenamun's hand.

Ankhesenamun held back her tears. "No, my dear husband. You will not die."

"I should not have to. I'm too young." He thought for a while, and then added softly: "If I am Pharaoh, the Horus god on earth, why do I fear death so?"

"You must not speak that way," Ankhesenamun scolded. She sat at the edge of the bed, holding her husband's hand. "I love you," she said.

Tutankhamun spoke in a weak voice, scarcely aware of the queen's presence. "I paid scant attention to the building of my tomb," he continued. "I pretended indifference; but I'll tell you, I feared that tomb and took no joy in thoughts of an afterlife. I fear more than anything else the blackness when it closes down around me."

"No more of this," Ankhesenamun insisted.

"You see how unworthy I am of kingship," he droned on, his eyes fastened on the ceiling. "I cannot mount the throne of Osiris with the courage of a god. There is no strength in me, not in my heart or limbs, Ankhesenamun. I die unworthy of what I was meant to be. The years shall roll by, and one day some miscreant in search of treasure will say: 'Here is the tomb of Tutankhamun, a king with very little to his credit.' "

"No more talk of death, husband," Ankhesenamun pleaded.

"Ankhesenamun!" Pharaoh cried out. "Promise me this. Promise me you will set lamps in my tomb, lamps with deep wells of sesame oil. You will do this when I'm set in my tomb. Promise me this!"

Ankhesenamun clasped his hand tightly to her breast. "I swear, my husband."

At this point, Pentu, who had been conferring with two physician-priests, came back into the chamber. "How goes it, my lord?" he asked with all the cheerfulness he could muster.

Tutankhamun's eyes, wide and glassy, stared through Pentu, as though unaware of his presence.

"When my tomb is sealed, have them store a bit of sunlight within," he mumbled. "One golden shaft—a gift of the Aten."

"No more, husband," Ankhesenamun cried, staring down at him in sad frustration. In her mind's eye, he seemed older, manlier in his sorrow, and she felt strangely helpless. Ruined eye makeup formed a kohl-blackened riverbed for her tears.

"Send for Ay," Tutankhamun said weakly.

"You must rest."

"Send for him I say," Tutankhamun demanded.

Their eyes met. Ankhesenamun saw that his familiar pleading look was gone. Stunned by the command, she turned to Leta. "Send for the vizier at once."

Pharaoh had dozed off when Ay came quietly into the chamber.

Ay had bathed, and his short hunting kilt was replaced with a red linen robe.

He glanced at the queen, paused long enough to read the suspicion in her eyes, and then went to Pharaoh's bed, knelt down and kissed his face.

Tutankhamun opened his eyes. "I'm not getting the truth from the queen, dear uncle. Speak the truth. Am I going to die?"

Ay looked up at Ankhesenamun, as though to leave the decision to her. She looked away.

"My liege lord, my Pharaoh … my good friend," Ay began haltingly, brushing a lock of hair from Tutankhamun's forehead. "I have spoken with all the physicians assembled here. Your head wound is of no concern, but rather the fracture to your thigh. It cannot be repaired, and decay has set in. The poison is spreading. There is little that can be done."

Pharaoh's face relaxed. "I thought as much."

Except for the drilling whine of a fly, the chamber was silent. Tutankhamun turned to Ay. "Protect my widow from harm, and preserve me well for all eternity."

"I shall, my lord Pharaoh."

"You know how quickly tombs are robbed. Not even the pyramids of the Giza plateau are immune."

"Yes, my lord."

"Protect me even to the edge of time, uncle, and the gods will reward your loyalty."

"Doing my duty is reward enough, my Pharaoh."

Tutankhamun squeezed Ay's hand. "Oh, uncle, I'm not cut out for this."

Ankhesenamun paled as she listened to Tutare and Grandfather Ay. Death was for old men, like Grandfather, not her Tutare. She had nurtured the boy king, encouraged him, and now he was dying. She could not let him see her so distraught. She turned and raced from the room, hands over her face, sobbing as she went. Auti and Leta followed dutifully behind.

13

Tutankhamun died quietly in his sleep. Word of his death spread like wildfire up and down the Nile. City officials and village elders, one after another, announced to stunned assemblages: "The falcon has flown up to heaven."

Ankhesenamun was at Tutankhamun's side when he took his last breath. The passage from life to death was not heralded with a change in appearance. Her Tutare seemed as he always did when asleep. His glossy black hair lay tousled over his forehead, the hint of a smile on his full lips. In death, there was about him an aura of disarming innocence he was unable to outgrow in life.

She did not immediately call for Leta and Auti, or break into the kind of piercing wail expected of Egyptian women in moments of grief. Instead she rested her head next to his. Their cheeks touched. His cheek was still warm.

She clasped his hand in hers, and she whispered softly: "My dear good friend, my Tutare, my lord, my childhood friend. You were as close as any brother could be. I love you so."

She cried, softly at first, then from deep within her came an overwhelming sense of loss so great, her sobbing segued to a plaintive wail, not unlike the howl of a desert fox hovering above the body of her dead cub.

⁂

The following morning Tutankhamun's body was taken to Karnak's House of Vigor for transfiguring to incorruptible matter, the ritual of mummification and purification, rebirth and godliness, the beginning of a long process that would take seventy days. Women, poor and rich alike, poured out of their villas and their hovels shrieking a discord of grief behind the donkey-drawn bullock cart holding the body of the dead king.

Ay lost no time paying a call on the grieving widow.

"I know the depths of your grief, Granddaughter," he began, "but let me assure you I stand ready to assist in any way I can. The transition will go smoothly, and when it's done, you'll be honored and adored by your people as though your Tutare were still alive and at your side."

Ankhesenamun, who had received Ay in her drawing room, stood up. "Transition, Grandfather?" she said after a long silence. "What is this transition?"

Ay gave her an avuncular smile. "Surely you cannot be in doubt, child. You and your husband had no heirs. Egypt must have a Pharaoh."

"You?"

Ay breathed deep. Grandfather was about to play his hand.

Ay said, "I am by birth and position, by title and by deed, the next lord of the Two Lands. Were I an ambitious man, I would have sought the throne of Horus upon your father's death. But now I have no choice but to assert my right, which is absolute. I have the sanction and support of the priesthoods of Amun-Ra and the temple of Ptah. My right of accession was never in doubt, and I am surprised at your ignorance of it."

Ay put his hand around her waist. "You've been under a strain. I should not have disturbed you." Her body tightened. He released his grip and stood back.

Ankhesenamun looked directly into Ay's eyes. "You come here to offer your condolences, and even before my husband is entombed, ask for his two crowns and his sekhem scepter?"

Ay smiled weakly. "All things will be as they were. We shall be united in marriage, and by such a union you will continue to breathe the divine afflatus. In short you shall remain the lady of the Two Lands, queen of Egypt. My queen."

Ankhesenamun's reaction to the proposal was spontaneous. "Married to you, Grandfather? Never!"

Ay gave her a tight smile. "It's the custom, a right reserved by royalty to preserve the purity of divine blood. Such marriages have been sanctioned by the temples of all the gods since the beginning of time." He stopped short, and cocked his head to one side. "But hold on! I see what you are getting at. You think that I would lie with you!" He snickered beneath his breath. "Ah, so there's your fear!"

Ankhesenamun remained silent, her eyes fixed on him.

"The marriage need not be consummated," he continued. "Though I will say I could bring more to the marriage bed than anything you could imagine."

"Old man!" Ankhesenamun shouted.

Ay smiled. "Old Pharaoh, if you don't mind. And by that logic, your Pharaoh, and your liege lord! How you lie abed is your choice, lady, but my queen you shall be."

⁂

Angry and feeling abandoned, Ankhesenamun turned inward, finding resources and comfort in her active mind. Smarting from Grandfather Ay's arrogant assumption of power, coupled with his belittling smile, she began an earnest search for a way to preserve her status as a solar queen, short of becoming the wife of an aging warrior. Grandfather was right. There were precedents for such a marriage, and to preserve the purity of the line, the priesthood often insisted upon it. And where there was no male heir, the temple priests sometimes insisted upon father-daughter marriages. Her own father had married her two deceased sisters, Mayati and Meketaten, and afterwards she too had shared his throne and bed. But regardless of precedent, the thought of lying with Grandfather Ay was repugnant to her. "I've no stomach for this," she cried.

She made a short list of men of influence who could help her. It came down to the ever-loyal master of the treasury, Maya; Tutare's dear friend, Huy, the Viceroy of Kush; the scholar-priests of holy Iunu and Kenofer, the Master of the Kap.

Then she thought of Menkhara. He was in Memphis and had no authority, no influence. But she wanted him close by, and caution be damned.

As important as these influential men were, they were nothing compared to Ay's allies, notably the army. Ankhesenamun would soon be in danger, her every move watched by spies in the service of Ay. With each passing day, Grandfather would gain more and more control. He was already planning the funeral rites for her husband, beginning with the embalming ritual in the House of Vigor. He would select family furniture and choice of funerary equipment for Tutare's tomb. She would not be consulted. Even the scribes would soon know more about court affairs than Pharaoh's widow.

Out of desperation she sat down to write a letter to her father's dearest friend and confidant, the beloved Master of the Kap, Kenofer. She asked to see him, and Menkhara as well.

14

Ankhesenamun sat in Kenofer's study, facing the old master of the Kap and Menkhara. Several days had passed since Ay offered to take her in marriage. Fear of her life and a future with her aging grandfather had driven her into a state of despair. Not even the sight of her beloved quieted her fears.

She drank deep from a goblet of wine, and then told them of Ay's pretensions to the throne as her husband's successor, and that she was little more than a prisoner in her own palace.

Kenofer and Menkhara listened carefully, both concealing their thoughts until she came to Ay's offer of marriage. "Upon my life, this is something I cannot do." She stared expectantly at Kenofer, and then at Menkhara, as though they would immediately produce some magical way out of her dilemma.

Kenofer said, "My lady, how important is the vulture-goddess crown upon your head? Would you consider surrendering it and learn to live in peace upon your estates, independent of Ay?"

"Never!" Ankhesenamun cried out contemptuously. "I am the daughter of the only true servitor of the Aten, Akhenaten. I am a solar queen and shall remain so until the day I die."

"My lady," Kenofer answered with a pensive smile, "if you wish to hold the sekhem of power, then you must wear the false beard of kingship and rule as king. Tradition and the laws of Egypt forbid you absolutely from ruling alone as a sovereign queen. But I must tell you even if you choose this course, the longevity of your reign will be in doubt. Too much power is arrayed against you. You do not have the support of the priesthood of Amun-Ra, and your husband died too young to earn the protection and trust of powerful men."

It was the answer Ankhesenamun did not want to hear. She sat in silence, pondering her options.

"Consider what would be required, my lady," said Menkhara.

Ankhesenamun turned to face the young captain of Infantry. Their eyes locked.

Menkhara began cautiously: "You would have to abandon your sheath dress and wear instead the regalia of a king, and, like Hatshepsut, the one queen who became Pharaoh, your body would be weighted with broad collars and your beauty effaced by a black beard no amount of pampering would hide. All who love you, friends and servants alike, would think it a crime that Egypt had been deprived of its most beautiful ornament."

After a long silence, Menkhara left his chair and knelt at Ankhesenamun's feet. "Great lady, listen: the widow of Tutankhamun could lead a happy life among her friends and loyal servants. If your grandfather means to wear the crown, surrender it you must. There is nothing to be done. The material fact is this: you do not have an heir. We are your friends, not workers of magic."

The queen of Egypt looked pensively at Menkhara, at his upturned face and deep brown eyes. She reached over and took his face in her hands, and smiled bitterly. "You once offered me your sword, brave Menkhara. Yet all I hear from you and the Master of the Kap are terms of surrender. Is that what you are made of? Are you cowards after all?"

Ankhesenamun stood, signifying that the meeting was at an end.

Kenofer motioned to Menkhara to follow her from the room.

Menkhara followed Ankhesenamun down the villa steps to her waiting palanquin. As she climbed into her palanquin, Menkhara's hands rested on the edge of the cab. She smiled and covered his hands with hers.

"Dearest Menkhara, I know what is in your heart, but you cannot know what is in mine. I am the daughter of Akhenaten. I will not surrender the crowns of Egypt to Grandfather, nor will I sit at his side as queen. I shall rule as queen or I shall be nothing."

"Great lady," Menkhara cried out. "Think what you do. The people of Egypt love and adore you."

Ankhesenamun smiled. "And you, my darling Menkhara?"

"More than life itself, my lady."

Ankhesenamun's eyes filled with tears. "If I could make myself a commoner, I would fly to your arms. But I'm the daughter of Akhenaten, and I can't undo what my god has made of me."

She motioned to the carriers, and in an instant the palanquin rose up into the air and moved silently away, the only sound coming from the soft scraping of the carriers' sandaled feet on the granite surface of the courtyard.

15

Three days after the meeting at Kenofer's villa, Ankhesenamun summoned Menkhara to the palace at Malkata. She sat at her cosmetic table putting the finishing touches of makeup on her face. She applied red ochre to her lips with a reed brush, gazed approvingly at herself in the mirror, and then ran a brush down the length of her lustrous blue-black hair. When Menkhara entered the chamber she turned to him, smiled and pointed to a comfortable chair directly across from the cosmetic table.

"Your mood is much improved," Menkhara said.

"I've done some soul-searching these past few days," she said casually. "Let me tell you quickly that I've decided never to surrender the two crowns of Egypt to Grandfather. He is a former captain of chariots, at his best an old soldier who served Pharaoh well, and at his worst, just another court fixture and collector of titles. In any event, he is a commoner. His sister, the late queen and widow of Mighty Bull, and his brother Anen, were the children of good and worthy parents, but they were not of royal stock. I'm the daughter of Akhenaten, son of the third Amunhotep, Mighty

Bull. My claim to the throne is above reproach. Grandfather is not worthy of kingship. Since I have not produced an heir to the throne, I'm free to offer the throne of Egypt to a young man of royal blood worthy of that honor."

"Is there is such a prince worthy of the throne, my lady? Your father sired none, and Mighty Bull's seed died with your husband."

"It's not to my father's line I look, Menkhara. I'll take a husband from our foe's own family. Suppiluliumas, king of the Hittites, has many sons, five in all, and all proud and bright and daring like their father. Great Suppiluliumas, vicar of the storm god, has put our army on the run. He is the scourge of Mesopotamia, a sacker of cities, the new voice of the world."

Menkhara shook his head. "You're prepared to surrender the sovereignty of Egypt to a foreign prince?"

"Surrender? I don't think so. I shall have a young man who will give me sons; and they shall be raised as any true-born Egyptian prince."

"I can only advise against it," Menkhara said wearily. "The army, the priesthoods of all the gods will challenge your right to seat a foreigner upon the throne."

Ankhesenamun's voice softened. "I did not ask for your approval, but for your friendship and your love."

"I have only your safety in mind."

Ankhesenamun smiled. "Think now of your own safety, Menkhara. Mutnedjmet has long wanted you arrested and executed for the murder of her dwarf and her monkey. Don't think for a moment she's forgotten you. With her father on the throne, how long do you think you would last? Not even General Horemheb would save you, especially if he hopes to secure his position at court and take Mutnedjmet as his wife."

Menkhara did not answer right away, but then said softly: "If there were another way to end this threat I would—"

"There are also reasons of state which force me to importune the Hittite king for a son in marriage," Ankhesenamun interrupted. "Reports have reached me that King Suppiluliumas is planning to lay siege to the fortress at Carchemish and take Aleppo. This he will do in response to Horemheb's adventures in Syria, and the attack on Kadesh. Carchemish and Aleppo will fall, and then Suppiluliumas will cross the Orontes and wrest all of Syria from us. The Hittite king will be less inclined to wreak his vengeance upon us if his son sits upon the thrones of the Two Lands."

She paused and looked Menkhara squarely in the eye. He looked so handsome; her heart was breaking from desire. She said haltingly, "We can't be lovers, Menkhara, though I love you as much as any woman can love a man. You promised me your sword, your loyalty. Do I have it?"

Menkhara came to his feet and knelt before the queen. "I am your servant."

Ankhesenamun breathed an inner sigh of relief. "I'll dictate a letter to the king of the Hittite people. You'll deliver it as my personal emissary. It will be no easy task, for Ay has his spies everywhere. You must slip out of Egypt, and make your way across hostile territory between Gaza and the Euphrates."

"With your permission, lady, I would like to take my friend Critias with me, if he's willing."

"The Greek scribe?"

"There is no better man to travel with. He's strong, resourceful, and experienced in travel abroad. He would serve you well."

Ankhesenamun smiled. "Good, then take your Greek friend."

"When do you propose to write your letter?"

"Now."

"Shall I send for your scribe?"

"No. They are not to be trusted, especially while we visit here in Thebes. I will dictate the letter to you."

"In Hittite glyphs?"

"In Akkadian, the language of nations. None write it so well as you, Menkhara. There are many at the Hittite court who can read and translate it for the king." She stood up and gave her hand to Menkhara. They walked to her desk on the far side of the room.

Blank scrolls of papyrus, an inkpot and reed brushes were laid out neatly on her writing table. She waited until Menkhara sat down, adjusted himself, unrolled a sheet of papyrus and took up a reed brush laden with ink. Then she strolled over to a small window just behind Menkhara's right shoulder and stared out across the western desert. After a moment of silence, she began in a steady voice:

My Lord:

> *Word has reached you by now of the death of my husband, beloved Pharaoh. Egypt mourns his death. I find myself very much alone at court. Our marriage was not favored with a child, and therefore I have no heirs to offer my people.*
>
> *There are many at court who would propose marriage, but I will not have any of them. I cannot take a husband from among my servants no matter how esteemed they are for good service to the crown.*
>
> *The widow of Tutankhamun is afraid, my gracious lord. She fears for her very life. In these fearful times, I turn to you with humility and beseech you to come to my aid. Send me a son that I may cleave to in marriage. Yes, a proud, strong son of the great Suppiluliumas who would share the throne of the Two Kingdoms. You have many sons to choose from, and surely can spare one.*
>
> *I beg you hearken to my plea, my lord.*

Ankhesenamun
King's wife
By this seal known[1]

A long silence filled the chamber, then the queen gave Menkhara a gentle smile and removed a signet ring from her hand. "Set my seal upon it, and keep the ring lest your authority be questioned."

Menkhara rolled the papyrus and sealed it with a layer of resin. He pressed the ring to the resin, producing a high relief cartouche bearing Ankhesenamun's name, and then he placed the papyrus in an oxhide tube.

Ankhesenamun walked Menkhara to her chamber door. "My minister of foreign affairs is Hania," she said. "He served two Pharaohs with distinction. My father loved him. He is waiting for you now in the antechamber, and will further instruct you on your trip and provisions. The king of the Hittites maintains his palace at Hattusas. It is, I have heard, a cold, wind-swept land lying in the midst of the mountains of the northlands. Your task will not be easy, but there is so much at stake, and you are the only person on Earth I can turn to with confidence."

"But my work on General Horemheb's Saqqara tomb? I am due back in Memphis."

"I will put it out that you are on state business in Nubia."

They stood facing each other by the postern. Her arms went around his shoulders, and she pressed close to him. Menkhara looked deep into her eyes. She felt small and vulnerable in his arms. She said softly in his ear, "I've loved my Pharaoh as I might have loved a brother, and I suppose, in time, I shall learn to love

[1] Letter discovered in the archives of the royal palace, Hattusas/Bogazköy, the Hittite capital of Asia Minor. Hans Güterbock, *Journal of Cuneiform Studies* 10(1965):47.

the man who will become my lord; but darling Menkhara, know that no one shall ever replace you in my heart."

Her lips brushed his at the very moment her eyes caught a glimpse of a familiar figure through the open door to the receiving room. It was the foreign minister, Hania. He looked away, pretending not to see her. Ankhesenamun stepped back and said in a hurried whisper, "I will remain in Thebes until after Pharaoh's funeral, and then I will return to Memphis. My husband's body will remain with the priests of Anubis in the House of Vigor for seventy days. Undoubtedly I will be here upon your return."

She took his hand and continued softly. "I beg you and Critias to take care. Use every artifice and disguise to avoid discovery. Our friendship has not gone unnoticed, and my grandfather's agents may have followed you here. When you return to Thebes, go to Kenofer's villa. I will speak to him. That is where you will stay. Trust no one and keep your own counsel."

She managed a weak smile. "I wish you a safe and swift journey, Menkhara, and give my grateful thanks to Critias."

Ankhesenamun looked away before Menkhara could see her eyes once again fill with tears. He excused himself, bowed low and left her chamber. She listened to the whispered tread of his sandals on the tile floor, and then there was silence. She stood facing the window, feeling as isolated as any castaway. She was thinking there was still something to be said to Menkhara, some words and thoughts waiting for a voice, though she was not quite sure what those words might be.

She turned. The chamber and the receiving room were as silent as a tomb. She went to her desk and sat down. She picked up the reed pen Menkhara had used to compose the letter, cast it aside and rested her head in her hands.

Generous tears filled her eyes. She thought of her husband, the magnificently innocent young man so full of life, prematurely delivered into the hands of the priests of Anubis.

And there was Menkhara, her true love, and one who would gladly march into hell and back for her sake. Two men who loved her in different ways, one dead, the other slipping away. She imagined, with an inner sigh, the bareness of that cold, wind-swept land of the Hatti, where the young Hittite son of a proud king would be called upon to transform her fear and her loneliness into a lifetime of happiness. She pondered the possibilities, her hopes too vague and ill-formed to quiet the fear in her heart.

16

Three weeks on the Nile.

Menkhara could never have imagined himself weighted with so much responsibility. The young man who grew up in the village of the workers would soon face one of the great rulers of the earth, Suppiluliumas, to whom he would present himself as an emissary of the queen. Aboard ship, he had time to think of the various possible outcomes of his journey, one of which included his own death.

The captain of the ship was a merchant from Abydos. He regularly brought goods up the Nile to Tanis, and then to ports along the Phoenician coast. Though the ship's ultimate destination was the Phoenician port of Sidon, Hania had urged Menkhara to transfer to another ship at Tanis for travel up the coast, anything to shake off a would-be assassin.

Tanis looked like a great mound rising out of a flat lowland with the brackish waters of Lake Menzalah glistening in the distance. On its seaward side, a broad lagoon protected the town. Its landward side opened to exposed flats often submerged by high water.

The captain sailed into the harbor, passing hundreds of ships of every description. The fetid smell of the quay was immediately apparent as they inched closer to the docks. Menkhara and Critias heard the shouting of fishmongers and watched the streams of stevedores come down barge gangplanks, straining beneath huge sacks of grain.

Slowly, expertly, the captain steered his boat into a narrow slip. The oarsmen raised oars as dock workers fastened the ship's ropes to the mooring rings.

The quay was packed with merchants, sailors and suspicious looking military police. Shouts in a dozen languages assailed his ears. Reluctant to become a part of the scene, Menkhara looked over at his best friend. The Greek flashed him a reassuring smile. He would not be alone.

Menkhara and Critias said goodbye to the ship's captain, and without looking back, descended the gangplank onto the busy quay.

The port district of Tanis seemed as foreign as any faraway land. The commercial heart of town was a rough-and-tumble place, and the two emissaries of the queen sensed immediately upon disembarking that they had better have their wits about them or at very least a tight grip on their purses.

Menkhara decided to put all his trust in Critias. He was wise in the ways of foreigners, knew many languages, and would know how to find a ship that would take them up the Phoenician coast to Ugarit.

The two men set off down a narrow street parallel to the quay. They passed the shops given over to the needs of the seafaring trade: sailmakers, carpenters, hull repair and blacksmith shops. Turning a corner at the end of the street, they stopped to eat at a bustling tavern.

All the tables were taken, but Critias found one occupied by only two men, whose russet skin was a sure sign of race. They spoke a dialect of Greek resulting from the Mycenaean conquest of Crete.

Critias knew pure Cretan, the seldom used but much-admired language surviving the Mycenaean conquest. In that same language he asked the men if they could share their table. It was a courtesy not expected in a wide-open seafaring town. One sat where he chose, and if his presence didn't precipitate a fight, there he would remain.

The Cretans, taken aback by Critias's eloquent manner of address, took him to be a fellow countryman, and invited the strangers to join them.

The Cretans could speak Egyptian. One man called himself Theas and the other introduced himself as Lasos. They were members of a ship's crew whose destination was Ugarit. They had sailed from Crete with a cargo of pottery and olives, which they traded at Tanis for Egyptian linens, papyrus and gold. These items would be traded in Ugarit at a handsome profit before returning home to Crete with dyed cloth, gold rings and oil flasks.

Menkhara expressed an interest in booking passage to Ugarit. The Cretans agreed to introduce them to their ship's merchant-captain.

The four men shared a platter of beef, cakes, figs and good sweet beer. As they progressed through the meal, half a dozen noisy Mycenaean sailors took an adjacent table. Their swearing and laughter soon drowned out the conversations of those seated nearby.

"Argolid Mycenaeans from the mainland," Lasos explained with a sneer. "It's been more than one hundred years since the Mycenaeans invaded Crete and stormed the gates of Cnossos. Despite the passage of time, we Cretans continue to hate the very name of those who destroyed and pillaged our land." Lasos clenched his fists. "I would like to shut their faces."

The last thing Menkhara and Critias needed was a fight. Critias clasped Lasos's arm, holding it in check. "But let us save our strength for some serious drinking, my friend. Drinks on me."

The idea appealed to Lasos. The frown on the mariner's face dissolved into a silly smile. "For your sake, and the sake of your purse, my friend, we'll allow the Mycenaean pigs to live another day."

The four men laughed, and Critias ordered four more jars of beer.

Lasos and Theas, their sea legs made uncertain by too much Egyptian beer, escorted Menkhara and Critias back down the noisy quay to the slip where their vessel was docked.

It was a handsome, slender, symmetrical ship about thirty meters in length, with a spoon-shaped hull and a bluff stern. It had a raised mast, and beneath the boom was a spacious deckhouse. The ship was equipped with only eight rower stations, more than adequate for a sea-going vessel since the oars were used mainly for maneuvering.

The ship's crew, including the captain, consisted of fourteen men. Cargo-filled boxes ran the length of the center deck. The vessel was defiantly called the *Mallia*, in honor of a Cretan town and palace destroyed by the Mycenaeans.

Lasos and Theas were late returning to the ship. The captain, quick to give them a good tongue-lashing, held back when he learned his errant seamen had brought two fare-paying passengers with them.

The Cretan sailors spoke briefly with their captain, whose name was Pasias. He stared at the two men with an air of suspicion, and then climbed down the gangplank.

After introductions, Menkhara produced a purse full of silver and gold rings, enough to pay for passage to Ugarit ten times over. Pasias's eyes lit up. Smiling, he waved Menkhara and Critias on board.

Menkhara and Critias sat at the stern, eagerly awaiting the ship's departure. Menkhara watched the crew stow newly purchased sacks of salted fish, meat pickled in brine, huge amphorae of fresh water and flasks of Fayyum wine. The look of the crew appealed to him. The mariners had bronzed bodies and dressed in simple cloth kilts. Many were blue-eyed with hair the color of the sun, or a deep bronze. They were a muscular, good-looking people, and as Menkhara later learned, a mix of Cretans and Achaean and Dorian Greeks.

Pasias gave the order to cast off. The oarsmen rowed the ship out to mid-river. A sailor untied the gaskets holding the furled sail to the mast. Some of the crew took hold of the halyards and hoisted away until they tightened around the masthead rings. The broad sail blossomed in the brisk wind. With a crewman sitting at the starboard steering oar and tiller, the *Mallia* was brought about to the wind. The vessel shivered and lurched forward.

In less than an hour, the *Mallia* passed through the narrow straits at the northern edge of Lake Menzalah, where the water transitioned to a deep green.

Menkhara and Critias, standing at the bow, gazed across an endless stretch of water. The ship groaned and creaked with a human anxiety, as though some hand had seized control of its destiny. Menkhara braced his legs on the rolling deck. For the first time in his life, he felt utterly helpless, and the thought of a watery grave was too horrible to contemplate. In those unfathomable depths there was no afterlife he could imagine.

17

Menkhara and Critias settled into a routine aboard the sailing ship.

By the time the *Mallia* reached the Gaza coast, they had acquired sailors' legs and could move about on deck with the agility of a seasoned mariner, no matter how bad the pitch and roll of the vessel. They shared meals with Pasias in the deckhouse, but preferred the open deck with only a cotton blanket for their night's sleep. Much of the time, Menkhara and Critias sat at the stern passing the time with Captain Pasias, when he was not busy. Pasias was from Khania, a busy seaport town on the northern coast of Crete.

"Why is it we sail so far from shore, while most ships hug the coast?" Menkhara asked, squinting at the distant coast of Palestine.

Pasias answered with a knowing smile. "For the same reason a child hugs his mother, the fearful sailor hugs the shore. Egyptians are the worst. They're not true mariners, only river paddlers."

Pasias pointed a finger at the green swell rolling toward the ship's prow. "The floor of the ocean-sea is littered with the bones of brave seafarers as well as fools. The sea shapes the life of the men who ride upon her in ships. They know they may never return to their land and their wives and children."

"Isn't that reason enough to hug the shore?" said Menkhara, pressing the point with a smile.

Pasias laughed. "You've much to learn, Egypt. The experienced mariner knows too well that a gale can blow his hull hard upon the shoals, smashing his ship to pieces. Besides, pirates lie in wait in coves, inlets and harbors. Many an Egyptian cargo ship has been taken and boarded by stealth in the night. It's not the Greek or the Cretan way! Out here, few mortals dare take us on. Only the gods may work their will upon us."

Menkhara was interested. "Who might those gods be?"

"Poseidon, Zeus and Hera, whose help we cannot expect unless they're propitiated with burnt offerings."

"It's good you have gods to watch over you."

Pasias shook his head. "They're like anyone else, especially Poseidon. He's not always available when you need him, even when the sacrifice has been made."

Menkhara shook his head. "What good is a god if you can't count on him in time of danger?"

Pasias looked at Menkhara, his blue eyes twinkling with amusement. "Our gods do not always do the right thing, Egypt. In times of danger we must sometimes look to ourselves."

With each passing day the distant coastline changed from flat desert land to low-lying hills, and then to mountainous terrain. Even at a distance, Menkhara pondered with awe the sound and fury of the water smashing against the distant cliffs.

The *Mallia* ran a course parallel to the Phoenician coast, stopping only briefly at Sidon, Byblos and the Syrian trade port of Ugarit. From Ugarit, Menkhara and Critias would make their way across the Syrian plain to the foothills of the Taurus Mountains.

The ship put in at Sidon and Byblos, but for no more than a few hours at each port. The entire region was alive with rumors of war, and Pasias had no desire to see his goods seized at Ugarit by an army in search of booty.

At each port, Pasias returned to the *Mallia* with rumors of war. Kadesh had fallen to a Hittite army that had advanced across the frontier. And now the troops of Suppiluliumas were arrayed before the gates of Carchemish.

Day passed into night, and the passing hours turned the aquamarine water to a creamy blue, and then, at dusk, to the color of wine. The highlights of Menkhara's day were sunrise and sunset. With the morning light the sea became the color of amethyst, but sunset provided a more unsettling beauty, when the sun, a swollen orange orb, disappeared in a dazzling display of pinks and yellows splashed across the western sky.

They stayed their course for four uneventful days, sailing parallel to Syria's sandy beaches and coves. Finally the *Mallia* came within sight of Ugarit. The first ship to cross their bow was a Cypriot vessel, her deck loaded with ingots of copper. The crew of the *Mallia* raised right arms as a show of respect. The Cypriots returned the salute.

Slowly, the *Mallia*, as though it had surrendered to some watery lodestone, drew toward the harbor, lost among the bobbing hulls. Sail furled, she waited her turn outside the natural breakwater, long ridges of rock that forked into the bay. Finally, with the signal from the harbormaster's ship, the rowers took up oars and sailed slowly toward the docks and the steady hum of commerce that rose like a distant swarm of bees from the crowded quay.

Pasias, who had many friends among the merchant class of Ugarit, was greeted by a friend who boarded the *Mallia*. The man was a Phoenician who brokered trade arrangements between foreign traders and local merchants. He informed Pasias that word had reached Ugarit that a Hittite army had laid siege to Carchemish, the Hurrian fortress town, twenty-three hours of march to the west. The Phoenician's appearance was not merely a friendly greeting or a desire to acquaint arriving merchants with news of the day. A threat of war and turmoil so close to Ugarit deflated the value of goods brought into port. It was the Phoenician's way of softening up Pasias for the hard trade negotiations to follow.

The news of king Suppiluliumas's success at Carchemish

meant a quick change of plans for Menkhara and his party. They would no longer face the hard overland journey to the land of the Hatti. They decided to set out at once for Carchemish.

Alone with Pasias, Menkhara said, "We're anxious to leave, captain, but will need transportation and directions to our destination."

"You've been vague about that, Egypt, and I've figured that a man's business is his own."

"We are going to Carchemish."

Pasias pursed his lips and nodded. For the first time in the long voyage, he sensed his two passengers carried serious business of state. "The city is under siege," he said looking at them darkly.

"Yes, we couldn't help overhearing the Phoenician. That is our destination."

"It's a long hard ride. You'll need a brace of good horses." Pasias motioned to Theas. "Take our friends to the stables of Ramilil."

Pasias turned back to Menkhara. "Perhaps you'll join me in a goblet of wine before leaving? You two are among the few passengers I've enjoyed having aboard."

"Very kind, but we must regretfully decline," said Menkhara.

"Be on your way then, and may the gods go with you."

The three men and Theas stood at the gangplank. Theas started down followed by Critias.

"Egypt!" Pasias cried out.

Menkhara turned.

"Listen, Egypt. From our long conversations at sea you will remember that I live in Khania, on Crete's north coast. The door of my home is always open to you, both of you."

Menkhara reached over and clasped Pasias's hand in the Greek fashion, by the wrist, and smiled. "Egyptians are loath to leave their land along the Nile. Should I ever stand beneath the mantel of your door, Pasias, know it will be for good reason. I couldn't have wished for a better friend."

18

Ankhesenamun stared at Grandfather Ay with murderous eyes.

He sat in her late husband's favorite chair, his feet stretched out comfortably across a hassock. She was all too familiar with the way he had of throwing his head back with a derisive laugh.

The queen did not like Grandfather's familiarity with her, or the way he entered her apartment without first applying for permission with her chamberlain.

Ay did not immediately give a reason for his visit, and Ankhesenamun decided that she would not inquire. She sat across from him and waited.

After a long silence, Ay sat straight up in his chair and looked hard at her. "Your Menkhara and Critias have long since been absent from court, lady. Their mission must be of some importance."

"A matter of state," Ankhesenamun answered indifferently.

Ay persisted. "They were last seen in Tanis. You've business there?"

Ankhesenamun arched her brow. "You had my royal envoys followed, Grandfather?"

Ay smiled. "I didn't say that. But I know they boarded a Cretan vessel, which according to the harbormaster, was bound for the ports of Byblos, Sidon and Ugarit."

At first, Ankhesenamun was too paralyzed with worry to think. Then, by sheer force of will, she looked Ay straight in the face. With an outward calm that must have been exasperating to Ay, she shook her shoulders with an air of indifference and said, "There was a matter you wished to discuss with me?"

She sensed from Ay's demeanor that he was going to make an outrageous demand. She would refuse him, of course, whatever his proposal. There would be a confrontation. Ugly words would be exchanged. She braced herself.

"No Horus god sits upon the throne of Egypt," he said in a measured voice. "Something must be done." He nodded his head as he spoke, as though to lend truth to his every word.

"But I'm Egypt's anointed queen, Grandfather. I hold the sekhem of power. I'll wear the beard if need be."

"The priesthood of Karnak is in no mood to offer the crowns to a woman made over as a man."

"What are you saying?"

"You've no heirs. I'm father of the late queen, Nefertiti, father-in-law to one Pharaoh, brother-in-law to another, and uncle to a third. I've been the close companion to all three, and have held every major office in the Two Lands, including the vizierate of the Upper Kingdom, commander of chariots and regent and lord protector during the childhood of your late husband. There is no Egyptian living who can boast these credentials, child. I rightfully should take up the sekhem of power. It's my will, and the will of the people."

Ankhesenamun's knuckles were white from her hard hold on her chair's armrests. Grandfather Ay made very few mistakes in his career. He would not be reaching for the kingdom of a god had he not felt it within his reach.

She would not show her anger. "Your ascension to the throne will not be sanctioned so long as I am queen. How would you become Pharaoh, Grandfather, with poison or the assassin's knife?"

Ay's face erupted into a huge smile, as though he were offering a present to the undeserving. "No, my child. I will not kill you. To the contrary: I intend to marry you!"

"You have made that offer once before and received your answer accordingly."

"And as you can see, I have put my pride to one side and again renew the offer. It is made with the blessings of the priesthood at Karnak."

Ankhesenamun stared at Ay, her thoughts in a whirl of confusion.

Ay said, "You would be queen so long as I reign, and for that time on will enjoy every royal prerogative."

Ankhesenamun threw back her head with a disdainful laugh. "Don't ask me why I find the idea so repugnant, Grandfather. It would wound you to the quick. I'll say what I felt the first time you asked. I'd rather be dead."

Ay flashed her a contemptuous smile. "Do you suppose I would anticipate pleasure from the union? Our marriage would never be consummated."

Ankhesenamun looked away and said softly, "My answer remains unchanged."

"You forget I did everything within my power to bring about your marriage to Tutankhamun. You owe me!"

"For your own selfish motives, Grandfather." She gave him a crafty smile. "I have disappointed you. Things didn't work out as you planned. Now you would have me dead!"

"You should stay out of politics."

"And you, dear Grandfather, should be content to find pleasure in your gardens and wait out an honorable death from old age."

Ay shot her an angry grin and thumped his fist against his chest. "This old man, madam, is arranging the funeral of your beloved husband, and not dwelling upon his own."

"I didn't appoint you to the task."

Ay laughed. "Your power begins and ends at the door of your palace chamber." He got up, turned on his heels and left without excusing himself.

Ankhesenamun rested her head back against the tufted softness of her chair and watched the sun's rays slant through the windows, down upon her thighs like the fingers of a warm outstretched hand. She smiled confidently at the fractured prism of an ankle bracelet jewel caught in the shower of light. And she thought hungrily of a stunning revenge.

Grandfather, you will pay dearly for your ambitions.

❧

Leta entered Ankhesenamun's dressing room and announced Mayet's appearance at court. Ankhesenamun, freshly bathed, sat naked at the edge of her bed, brow wrinkled. "Mayet? Who is she?"

"Of no importance that I can tell, my lady. But she managed to get past the palace guards. I wouldn't have disturbed you but for the fact that she mentioned Menkhara's name."

Ankhesenamun cocked her head. The woman's name, brought together with Menkhara, gave it fresh meaning. Yes! The young lady betrothed to Menkhara—the same lady married off to a priest.

"Your instructions, my lady? Leta asked softly.

The queen looked up as though coming out of a trance. "Oh, for God's sake, Leta; don't just stand there like a tree. Send her in!"

The young woman timidly entered the queen's chamber. Ankhesenamun studied her face. She was young but seemed to lack the freshness of youth. Still, she was Menkhara's childhood love, and that alone made her special in a strange sort of way. That fact alone gave Mayet credentials deserving of respect.

"Mayet?" said Ankhesenamun.

"Yes, great lady."

"Don't be shy. You're welcome here."

Mayet fell at Ankhesenamun's feet. "Great lady, thank you for receiving me."

Ankhesenamun reached down and took Mayet by her arms and raised her up. "My dear woman, I'm glad you are here. Tell me about yourself."

"We share the same sad state, my lady. We're both widows, you see."

"Then I am sorry for you, Mayet."

"It's a state that could be borne, my lady, were I not made destitute. I confess that is why I've come here from holy Iunu. I had hoped to find the man who was once betrothed to me, a royal scribe now serving in the army. His name is Menkhara, and when I found that he has marched to the wars, I had no one to turn to, and so came here."

Ankhesenamun smiled. "Menkhara has spoken to me about you. He related the misfortunes of your family, and that your parents arranged your marriage to an old priest from holy Iunu.

"My parents insisted. They had nothing to offer me when my father was made to work in the tombs."

"Am I to believe that you are now alone?"

"My husband is dead, great lady. The day after he was set in his tomb, his surviving son and daughter by a previous marriage asked me to leave. No provision was made for me, either by writing or declaration before the vizier. Everything was left to the surviving children. I was cast aside like so much baggage, given a few deben of copper and made to fend for myself. My parents are dead, and I am alone." Mayet put her hand to her face and began to cry.

Ankhesenamun listened carefully to Mayet's story. She could not resist enveloping the bereaved woman in her arms. "You'll stay here with me, and you'll not want for anything."

"I can't impose, my lady."

"Impose?" Ankhesenamun laughed. "If I knew you better, I would say you've a silly nature."

She clapped her hands. Leta and two handmaidens came into the room. "Make up a spacious chamber for my friend," she ordered. "Set out for her pleasure a good wardrobe of clothes, and provide her with gowns from my own closets. Draw a bath for our dear guest, and anoint her body in my finest oils." She stared critically at Mayet's thin body. "And ladies, lay before our guest a tray of nourishing food and drink, and tend upon her every need."

Ankhesenamun turned to Mayet and took her by the hands. "We will grieve for our men together, each in our own way. And we shall be friends, and share each other's company."

19

Menkhara and Critias reached the Orontes River near Ugarit. They watched travelers ford it, and decided that the chariot and two strong Mitanni stallions Theas helped them purchase at Ugarit were up to the task. The cold waters rose high up on the wheels of their chariot, then, midway across, poured into the floor of the cab.

They spent the first night in an open field at the edge of a stand of date palm trees. They watered the horses at a nearby stream, tethered them to tree trunks and cut into a cotton bag of grain, which they laid out within reach of the tethers.

They lay down wrapped in blankets. The only sound came from the rustling fronds of the date palm. Menkhara reached down to feel the hard leather correspondence tube strapped to his thigh, and he wondered whether they would gain an audience with the

Hittite king. Finally, he settled back and stared up into the deep blue starlit sky and fell asleep.

In the early afternoon hours of the following day, Menkhara and Critias reached the outskirts of Aleppo. At a public well they heard rumors of a battle waged at Carchemish. There were conflicting reports. Some believed the city had fallen to the Hittites, and others disputed the claim, believing the Hurrian defenders successful.

They spent the night at an inn five hours of march northeast of Aleppo. Menkhara couldn't sleep. He worried about Suppiluliumas. The dread king would be looking for retribution. The Egyptians had broken their treaty with the Hatti when they attacked Kadesh. How could Suppiluliumas think kindly of an Egyptian? The death of the queen's emissaries could be ordered with a flick of the hand.

Menkhara and Critias set out on the last leg of their journey at sunrise. With directions from the innkeeper, they found the road leading northeast to Carchemish.

Almost immediately the terrain changed, and the land rolled with low burnished hills studded with short trees with thick-stunted branches. The once-green abundant cloak of alluvial soil opened wide enough to show limestone ribs of earth.

Beyond Aleppo there were few people, mainly shepherds, and a few hardy souls who scratched out a living growing corn on the dull russet hills.

In the early afternoon they descended onto a long cultivated valley that led them east to the Euphrates river and Carchemish. A light rain fell as they passed extensive lemon and apricot orchards and furrowed fields of leeks, cucumbers and melons. Following a narrow pathway that led behind a hillock, they came upon a field filled with the rubble of war.

The torn bodies of men lay in an eerie silence. The number of dead grew as the two men slowly maneuvered their way across the field. The dead lay mostly in pairs, but on occasion several Hurrian corpses lay in twisted piles. Everywhere were shattered swords, broken spears and wrecked chariots lying on their sides. Menkhara had experienced war in the service of Horemheb on the plains of Kadesh, but he had never seen a field so thick with dead and mangled bodies. The dreaded Hittite chariots rumbling toward the Hurrians must have been a terrifying sight.

The scene of battle produced an unexpected impression on Menkhara, a spiritual wound. Despite his experience at Kadesh, he felt as new to war as any civilian. He looked at his companion. Critias stared incredulously at the field. The best he could do was utter a low soft cry of disbelief.

They came at last to the Euphrates River and the fortress town of Carchemish. It was built on the west bank, its citadel overlooking the river. The river at this point was a narrow defile that could be easily forded. The rain had stopped, though the mist remained when they reached the town's outer gates. Out of the mist, shadowy forms materialized into men on horseback, and they were coming straight for them.

Three Hittites, an officer flanked by two men, approached. Menkhara stopped and waited. The officer looked at them critically.

Critias began in broken Hittite: "We are emissaries of the queen of Egypt. Our sovereign lady desires to communicate with your king."

Critias turned to Menkhara who had immediately produced the oxhide cylinder and the signet ring of Ankhesenamun dangling down its side from a thin strap of leather.

The Hittite officer studied the cylinder and ring without taking hold of it. After a long silence he motioned to his men. The soldiers took up positions on each side of the chariot. The officer wheeled around and led them between flanking towers and up a long ramp.

Carchemish was defended by thick double mud-brick walls. Menkhara's eye was immediately drawn to the rich series of stone slabs set at the bottom of the walls. The slab reliefs were beautifully carved in a style he had seen at Ugarit, and depicted a Hurrian king and warriors celebrating a great victory. But now the fortress town, pride of the Hurrian-Mitanni empire, had been lost to the Hittites and their conqueror, Suppiluliumas.

They passed the city gate, a massive work with a portal figure of the city's patron goddess, Kubaba, represented as a woman wearing a long robe, seated and holding a mirror. They rode through a second portal to a larger court with long open colonnades, and then up another ramp to the citadel. Here, the only evidence of a fallen city was a column of hand-bound prisoners being led away. Menkhara guessed they were city officials and perhaps captured Hurrian royalty. He wondered about their fate, and the fate of the ordinary people who lived in the small stone dwellings in the city's commercial section below the base of the towering citadel.

20

Suppiluliumas, Hittite warrior general, son of Tudhaliyas, king of Hatti-land, slayer of Arzawa, destroyer of the Mitanni, sacker of Wassukanni, scourge of the Hurrian and favored one of the thousand gods of Hatti, sat in an ordinary chair behind a broad table set in a modest chamber. It was here Suppiluliumas began at once to administer Carchemish, punish its defenders and regulate its thriving commerce.

Suppiluliumas's simple knee-length tunic was covered in dust and stained in blood. His plumed war helmet rested on the table. He had a massive bearded face, thick sensuous lips and coarse black curls that covered his broad brow. His nose had the telltale hook of a Hittite. His chamberlain, Hattusaziti, stood at his side.

The king stared hard at the two foreigners for a long time before he spoke. Finally he said, "I am told you are emissaries of Ankhesenamun, the widowed queen of Egypt."

Menkhara was incredulous, surprised the Hittite king could speak the Egyptian tongue. "Yes, great king," he answered. "We've come bearing a letter from our queen."

"Word has reached me of her lord's death. She must be full of grief."

"Yes, my lord. Our queen's loss is Egypt's loss."

Suppiluliumas thought for a while, his puffy lower lip thrust forward. "Your timing has been nothing short of perfect. This has been the eighth and final day of our siege. All Hurrian resistance came to an end only a matter of hours ago."

Menkhara nodded. "We've seen the carnage, my lord. Congratulations on a splendid victory."

Suppiluliumas laughed loudly, all the while shaking his head. "Well, lad, you sound as though Egypt is still an ally of the Hatti. And of course, your country is not. That was made clear when your General Horemheb, in violation of our treaty, crossed the recognized frontier on the upper Orontes River and attacked Kadesh, a loyal vassal state of mine."

"Majesty, I—"

"It's all right," the king interrupted with a wave of his hand. "Your congratulations were intended only as a courtesy. I don't quarrel with messengers." His gaze shifted to Critias. "You are far too fair to be Egyptian."

"True, my lord," Critias answered, "but I have lived so long in Egypt, and have served the majesties of the Two Lands most of my life. If I'm not an Egyptian by birth, I am one in spirit. I am the queen's scribe in her House of Correspondence."

"Yes," Suppiluliumas muttered under his breath. "Your queen has not seen fit to send her foreign minister. I am asked to receive scribes."

"My lord," Menkhara answered, "the queen's foreign minister is getting on in years, and it was thought that travel would be too much an undertaking. Besides, sire, there are other things afoot in Egypt. Energy and speed were all that figured in our lady's calculation."

Suppiluliumas cocked his head to one side and stroked his beard. Finally his face softened. "Very well then; let's hear the words of your queen."

Menkhara held up the oxhide case. Ankhesenamun's signet ring dangled from the side. The chamberlain Hattusaziti came around from the king's side and took the tube. Hattusaziti was small and wiry, with a cynical smile that never seemed to leave his face. He removed the papyrus and unrolled it. Whether or not the king could read Akkadian was uncertain. But when Hattusaziti began to translate the letter into Hittite, it was clear Suppiluliumas wanted to be sure he understood every subtle reference, every nuance of meaning.

The chamberlain's low steady voice filled the small, sparsely furnished room. When he finished there was a long silence. The king sat behind his desk, his hands flat on the table, his face set straight ahead, as immobile as Giza's sphinx. There was no way for Menkhara to read the great king's mind, but a glance at Hattusaziti was disquieting. The chamberlain, haughty and proud by nature, nervously bit his lip. Finally, the king slowly raised his right hand and slammed it down on the table with all his might, producing a sound a sharp as thunder.

"What is the meaning of this?" he roared, his eyes feasting on Critias and Menkhara like a hungry lion. He reached up, snatched the papyrus from the chamberlain's hand and glanced at it, his eyes full of bewilderment. “I cannot believe this madness. Is this a hoax?” He shook an accusing finger at Menkhara and Critias. “You had better explain yourselves.”

Critias immediately spoke up. “My lord, we know of our own knowledge that our queen spoke the letter you now hold. We have no reason to deceive.”

Suppiluliumas gave Critias a suspicious sneer, his large scar-seamed hand enveloping his chin and mouth. For what seemed a long time only the faint sound of breathing came from the vicinity of the king. Then he put his hand and the crumpled papyrus on the table and stared at Menkhara and Critias as though he were looking through them.

Finally, Suppiluliumas raised himself half out of his seat and leaned across the table, his black eyes fastened on Menkhara. Shaking his head, he roared: “How can this be? Does she think me a fool? Your queen offering one of my sons the sovereign throne of Egypt in return for a husband? No! The letter is a fraud, sir! Your lives are in peril.”

Menkhara said, “My lord. I was present when the letter was composed. Critias is right. It was spoken by my queen and written down in my own hand. Were this a subterfuge, my lord, there would be nothing gained from it.”

Suppiluliumas pressed his hands to his cheeks and weaved his head from side to side. “My son would be lured to his death. What your queen cannot win at war, she will take by stealth.”

“Such an insult to my sovereign lady is unworthy of your majesty,” Menkhara shot back, the blood rushing to his face.

Suppiluliumas stared angrily at Menkhara, then, unexpectedly, he breathed a deep sigh and said in a softer voice, “We will talk more on this proposal later. In the meantime, you must be attended to. You’re no doubt exhausted from your journey. You must be fed and bathed.” He turned to the chamberlain, and with a barely perceptible nod of his head brought the meeting to an end.

❦

Menkhara and Critias were allowed the use of a bath house deep in the bowels of the citadel. Afterwards they were fed a hot meal of lamb, leeks and honeyed pears, and then returned to a different palace chamber to await the king.

The room was sparsely furnished with low benches, chairs and tables. Critias guessed it was here where minor officials gathered to take meals. They were made to wait for several hours. Finally, the doors flew open. Suppiluliumas entered flanked by two of his five sons. Menkhara and Critias stood and waited for the three men to seat themselves. They were not waved back to the benches, and it was clear the king preferred that they remain standing.

Suppiluliumas introduced his sons, Piyassils and Telipinos. They were taller than their father, though less muscular, and wore small, thin beards.

"Piyassils will remain on as king of Carchemish," he said with a boasting smile. "And Telipinos will reign over Aleppo. Your country has no friends in all of Syria," Suppiluliumas continued. "Soon my army of invincibles will cross the Orontes near Kadesh and continue on until I have reached the Egyptian border. You should have your queen take care lest a Hittite king and a Hittite queen yet sit upon the throne of the Two Lands." He smiled broadly, showing a row of black broken teeth."

The king waited for his words to soak in and then continued in a somber voice. "It has come down to this: I've consulted with ministers and sought guidance from the weather-god, Teshub. We choose not to cloak our suspicions in diplomatic niceties. It isn't every day a sovereign queen asks for a Hittite king's son to share her throne. I've decided to send my chamberlain, Hattusaziti, to your queen. He will speak to her on my behalf. And if she speaks as she has spoken on the papyrus, I'll again meet with my councilors and seek divine wisdom from my gods. Then, and only then, will she have my answer."

Suppiluliumas stood up, and, flanked by his sons, started to leave. Then he paused, his eyes fixed on Menkhara. "You'll leave tomorrow at dawn. Your companion will remain here. Three of my scouts will accompany you and Hattusaziti as far as Ugarit. Hattusaziti will carry my seal, and present himself to your illustrious queen. In due course he will report back to me."

"Is there any reason, my lord, why I should not return to Egypt with Menkhara?" said Gritas.

Suppiluliumas smiled. "Yes, a very good reason. I'm putting my chamberlain in harm's way. Moreover, should this offer by your queen be not what it seems, you'll pay with your life. When I've finished my business in Aleppo, I'll return to my palace at Hattusas. You'll accompany me, and there remain until Hattusaziti returns from Egypt."

The king was about to leave but turned back, his eyes on Menkhara. "I have a parting gift for you, Egyptian. No one leaves my court empty-handed."

A servant placed a sword in the king's hand. It had a straight blade cast from a light blue-white metal Menkhara had never seen before. The blade and hilt were cast as one piece, the hilt made with an inlay of bone and held in position on either side by rivets and flanged edges.

"It's stronger than any weapon cast in bronze," the king boasted. "If you can fight with a sword, it will serve you well."

Menkhara accepted the gift. "You do me great honor, my lord," he said with a polite bow.

The following morning, when the sun first broke across the

barren hills, Menkhara climbed into a Hittite chariot. He took Critias's hand. "I'm not certain who's gotten the best deal," he said with a smile. "You'll live a life of leisure in Hattusas, and no doubt grow fat and lazy as the king's honored guest."

Critias answered with a shrug of his shoulders and a tight smile. The long trip from Egypt had brought the two men close, though only now did they both realize the depth of their companionship. Critias removed a faience ring from his finger. "Give this to our queen as a token of my love and my loyalty."

Hattusaziti, wrapped in a blue cloak, was helped into a chariot. He nodded to Menkhara. It was time to go.

The party pulled slowly out of the courtyard and through the main gate. In a short time, only a cloud of dust signaled their way across the low-lying hills.

21

Menkhara and the Hittite chamberlain, Hattusaziti, entered Thebes under cover of darkness. Thirty days had passed since Pharaoh's death, and the city was still in mourning. Tutankhamun's body, cleansed of all impurities, would rest in a bath of natron for another forty days before being set in his tomb. Out of respect for Pharaoh, the taverns and beer houses of Thebes were closed. Hattusaziti was struck by the eerie silence as they made their way down the dark streets.

For Menkhara, Kenofer's lovely east bank estate was a joy to behold. The master of the Kap did not keep the party waiting long in the reception hall. Smiling warmly in his linen gown, he greeted them and embraced Menkhara, then bowed low in the courtly tradition when introduced to Suppiluliumas's lord chamberlain.

The tired travelers were shown to their chambers and allowed to bathe, rest up and drink many jars of cooling watered-down pomegranate wine before eating.

During the evening meal, Kenofer steered the conversation away from matters of state. Menkhara was beginning to relax.

Toward the end of the meal, Kenofer grew serious. "It's been arranged for both of you to meet with the queen tomorrow night. There will be three others present, the queen's minister of foreign affairs, Hania, the queen's captain of household guards, Siptah, and the state treasurer, Maya."

"You've not included yourself, Master," said Menkhara.

"There's is no need for me to be there. I've conferred with the queen during your absence. The meeting will not take place at Malkata. It is too dangerous. I've arranged for everyone to gather at a small studio and workshop of the sculptor Aapahte. The old man is away on business, and we appropriated his place for our use. I wouldn't describe it as comfortable, but it's the least likely place for a queen to meet with her subject, which makes it ideal. You can meet in the workshop or the adjoining studio."

❧

Two hours before dawn of the following day, Menkhara and Hattusaziti were the first to arrive at Aapahte's small cramped studio. Siptah, Maya and Hania arrived in sedan chairs. Hattusaziti and the others waited in a nearby workshop where they would wait until the queen had a chance to speak with Menkhara alone.

The queen was the last to arrive, and when she entered the studio, Menkhara fell to his knees and remained in that position until she ordered him to his feet with a warm smile. "Where's Critias?" she asked.

Menkhara presented the queen with Critias's ring. "He was required to remain with the Hittite king, madam. When the king returns to the capital city of Hattusas, he'll take Critias with him.

He asked me to give you his ring."

Ankhesenamun took the ring and studied it. "My father gave Critias this ring as a token of his good work." She turned to Menkhara. "And so my envoy has been taken hostage?"

"Yes, my lady. You could say that."

"I've heard Carchemish has fallen. Can you confirm this?"

"The king received us only hours after the city fell. Aleppo, not wishing to engage the Hittite army, declared itself a vassal state of the Hittites, thus sparing themselves the same fate suffered by Carchemish."

A wry smile spread across the queen's face. "Most of Syria has fallen into the hands of the Hatti."

Menkhara nodded. "All but a small area between the Khabur and the Euphrates, lady."

The queen turned and sat upon a delicately carved chair. Menkhara studied her face. It was easy to see she was tired. The black kohl outlining her eyes had faded, and the red ochre on her lips had been applied indifferently. She wore a plain linen gown and no jewelry except for a simple gold pendant and bracelets.

"Now to the most important matter at hand," she said. "Menkhara, how does the Hittite king respond to my proposal?"

"Intrigued, madam, and also bewildered. He had trouble comprehending your willingness to entrust the sovereignty of Egypt to a foreign prince. That's why he sent his chamberlain. He wants clarification from your lips to his most trusted servant before sending a beloved son to our distant land."

Ankhesenamun sighed impatiently. Menkhara could tell that it was not the answer she was hoping for. "Very well then, take me to this Hittite envoy," she said.

"The workshop is not a pleasant place, and I hope you will not be offended, but we have placed secrecy above comfort."

"I've no use for comfort now. It will serve our purposes."

❧

When the queen entered the workshop, the men stood up. Ankhesenamun allowed her eyes to rove around the room. The shelves sagged with unfinished and broken pieces of sculpture in need of reworking. On the scattering of small tables were the tools of the sculptor's craft: chisels, mallets, drills, adzes and pots filled with reed brushes. Her eyes moved from one man to the next as they stood respectfully next to the large workbench that dominated the room. She recognized the emissary of Suppiluliumas by his dress.

Hattusaziti wore a tunic down to his knees, a red cloak and sandals curved up at the toes. His thick black beard, beaky nose and large glaring black eyes could not be disguised. This was the queen's first sight of a living Hittite, since all the others she had seen were depicted on tomb and stela drawings as bound slaves quaking at the feet of a conquering Pharaoh. But this Hittite looked as fierce as any charioteer who rumbled across the plains of Mesopotamia.

Hattusaziti bowed low.

Ankhesenamun did not wait for an introduction. "Lord Chamberlain," she said, "welcome to Egypt. I trust you bring us good tidings from your gracious king of the Hatti?"

"His majesty conveys his warmest greeting and respect, madam. He was, as you know, the friend of Amunhotep, the legendary Mighty Bull. He prays our two countries will renew their friendship."

Menkhara offered the queen a place at the workbench, but she insisted on standing. Ankhesenamun stared hard at Hattusaziti and said, "My letter has been conveyed to your king. What says he to this?"

"His majesty was honored with the offer, madam, and surprised as well. It's not every day the sovereignty of Egypt is offered to a

Hittite prince. My lord king doesn't doubt a word of your letter, but wanted me to understand the full breadth of your feeling on the matter so he might better understand the urgency of your request."

Ankhesenamun smiled. "Then I'll speak plainly. I've been twice to the birthing stool and am still without child and heir. My husband is dead, and I need a husband who shall rule at my side and give me a child. I'm a solar queen, and must mate with my equal. Our gods would look with favor upon a future heir sprung from the loins of the son of Suppiluliumas, ruler of the Hatti, sacker of cities."

"The king could not be certain of your intentions without first hearing them from your lips, great lady. That's my purpose here."

Menkhara gazed across at Ankhesenamun. She was doing a bad job at hiding her disappointment.

"I had wished for more, Lord Chamberlain," she continued. "I had wished for an answer, but am no closer to knowing now what's in your sovereign's heart. Much time has been lost, and that's the one thing I cannot afford to lose. I'll write again. If he's willing, then let him pick a son for me to wed and send him here at once. There is no more to be said on the matter. I see that you look tired, my Lord Chamberlain. You will, of course, enjoy the amenities of my court. But for now, you may be excused."

Siptah, commander of the household guards, moved forward to escort Hattusaziti out of the workshop. Hattusaziti bowed low.

The queen turned to Menkhara. "You'll tend to the emissary's needs during his stay here, Menkhara?"

"We are staying at Kenofer's villa, madam. He has been generous and kind."

Siptah quietly returned to the workroom. "The lord chamberlain is comfortably situated in the studio, madam."

The queen turned to Maya. "Well, what do you think, Lord Treasurer?"

Maya mopped his pudgy face. "I wouldn't presume to second guess you, great lady, though I'm concerned about the sovereignty of Egypt in the hands of a foreign-born prince."

"I'll be sent a young man who will rule in the midst of a court entirely foreign to him, far from his father's palace city. How could he exercise sovereignty under those conditions? His issue will be as Egyptian as you or I."

Ankhesenamun, without waiting for a reply, turned to her commander of the household guards. "My grandfather Ay and his protégé General Horemheb cannot be trusted. Are we strong enough to withstand an assault upon the palace, Siptah?"

Siptah answered with a smile brimming with confidence. "Great lady, the palace guard is loyal and resourceful. Any one guardsman is worth twenty from the divisions of Amun-Ra. Also, don't forget that the viceroy of Kush was your husband's most trusted friend. He can be counted on to send troops if need be."

The queen turned to her foreign minister. "Hania, you will return with Menkhara to the court of Suppiluliumas. I'll write another letter, and if your health permits, dear friend, I would be pleased if you presented it to him."

Menkhara looked at Hania. The old man was not up to making the difficult journey. He had not left the black lands of Egypt for twenty years. Hania smiled at the queen. "It's only fitting that your lady's foreign minister engage the king of the Hatti. I am your man, madam. It's my right and my honor. And I should be pleased to take dictation of your letter and translate it myself."

Queen Ankhesenamun acknowledged Hania with a slight nod. The matter was settled.

Menkhara escorted Ankhesenamun to her palanquin. It was dark, and there was a chill in the air. She curled her hand around his arm and allowed him to lead her down a narrow path.

"Mayet is here," she said.

Menkhara was dumbstruck.

"Her husband is dead," Ankhesenamun continued. "She presented herself at court, destitute, and with no place to turn. She sought you out, but learned that you were not in Memphis. Having no place else to turn, she came to me. I've taken her in, Menkhara. We have become friends."

Menkhara half expected Ankhesenamun to be angry, even jealous. "I am always in your debt, great lady. Thank you for your kindness toward Mayet."

"Well, would you like to see her? After all, she was your betrothed, and surely the feelings are still there."

"Why, yes, certainly," Menkhara managed.

"I've arranged for you to see her this very night. You'll meet at the home of a wine merchant. The man owes me a favor. I have arranged for him to be away. There will be food, wine, and a freshly made bed."

Menkhara flushed. He missed Mayet, but had gotten used to the idea that she was married to someone else. "I thank you for your kindness, lady," he said.

"Then why the dour look on your face? You're acting like an old stick-in-the-mud."

"You must know I am not the same person you knew seven years ago."

"Nevertheless, you owe this night to Mayet. I'll have Siptah post some of his best guardsmen at the cottage. Do not worry. They will be discreet and respect your privacy."

Menkhara helped Ankhesenamun into her palanquin. He studied her face, softened by starlight. So much was at stake for her. He wondered at her thoughts and admired her for her courage. This was no ordinary lady. The golden throne of Egypt was hers, and she would fight to keep it.

She said, "I need to know something."

"What, my lady?"

"Menkhara, did you love me once?"

"I have never stopped loving you."

She smiled and Menkhara sensed that in her smile she was gathering up all that remained of her youth and giving it to him as an outgrown thing, a memento of better days. She raised her hands and the carriers responded, hoisting her into the star-filled sky. Her voice trailed off in the night: "Goodbye, Menkhara," and for a long while, he stood alone in the silence.

22

Simut had decided to put the girl called Tarina to good use.

She was one of the queen's many handmaidens, a new arrival from Sidon, homesick and lonely. Simut had met her on the pavilion of the main palace. It was the night of one of Pharaoh's many banquets, and he had left the hall to catch some fresh air on the palace pavilion. Simut was not surprised by the girl's willingness to talk to him. What lowborn serving girl from the sewers of Sidon would not want to talk to a high-ranking priest? Tarina was attractive, but in a foreign sort of way. He found her agreeable enough and deigned to engage her in conversation, though he hated her Phoenician accent. All of the negatives quickly vanished when it dawned on him that the girl had something that few young ladies possessed.

She had access to the queen.

Tarina came along at the right time. She could serve him well, and getting her to spy for him would be easy. In the days following their chance meeting, he invited her to his villa. Giving her hopes of a better life, he made love to her and even suggested a more permanent arrangement.

Things had not been going well for Simut. He knew about Ay's proposal of marriage to Ankhesenamun. That's not the way it was supposed to be. Mutnedjmet had painted a very different picture, promising that he would be the new Pharaoh's son-in-law. He had killed Tutankhamun, the Horus god on Earth. But for what purpose? He had been excluded from so much of court life, he had no idea what was going on. But now he had Tarina, and she would be his eyes and ears.

In the days that followed, Tarina reported Ankhesenamun's every word and action to Simut. She filled his ears with gossip fed to her by the queen's unsuspecting senior handmaidens, Leta and Auti. She showered him with bits and pieces of information, and Simut received them with a grateful smile, offering her still more gifts, and even a hint of marriage.

One morning Simut broke off his early oblations to Amun-Ra, a sacred rite that took place every morning in the god's sacred sanctuary at Karnak.

He found Tarina in his villa study.

"I've wonderful news, Holiness," she said in her breathless way. Simut poured her a goblet of pomegranate wine, and then sat on his bed and silently watched her raise the goblet to her lips. Her Phoenician accent was especially strong when she was excited, and Simut hoped that the wine would calm her nerves.

"Menkhara is in Thebes!" she said "The queen and her most trusted allies have met with him."

"At the palace?"

"I don't know, Holiness. But this very night the queen has arranged for a woman to meet with her long lost lover, Menkhara. They've not set eyes on one another for seven years." Tears filled Tarina's eyes. "Isn't it wonderful!"

"Who is this woman?"

"She has been staying in the queen's apartment for some time now. She was at one time betrothed to Menkhara. I've heard that the queen means to bring the two together. Her name is Mayet."

Simut was puzzled at first, then he remembered. Mayet was the daughter of the deputy foreman at Deir el-Medina. Was this the same woman? He had fired Mayet's father and ordered his family out of their house.

Simut gave Tarina a tight smile. He stood up and removed a leather pouch from a chest at the head of his bed. "Twenty-five kite of silver for you, my sweet, dear girl."

The astonished look on Tarina's face came as no surprise to Simut. She could not make so much money in a lifetime.

She put her arms around his neck. "I'll make delicious love to you," she said.

Simut gently removed her arms. His heart raced, but not from thoughts of making love. The information Tarina gave him was invaluable. He was one of the few that knew Menkhara was in Thebes, and that anyone following Mayet after dark would find Menkhara. Horemheb and Ay would want to know about Menkhara's work for the queen, the secret meeting alluded to by Tarina. Menkhara would be grilled and tortured until the truth flew from his lips. Simut wasn't sure what all this would lead to, but it was more than he had now.

He looked into Tarina's face. She smiled, holding the pouch of silver to her cheek. "You put that thing away, and tell no one how you came by it."

"Yes, Holiness."

"You may call me Simut when we are alone."

"Yes, Holiness."

Simut gave her a friendly smile. "I want you to go back to Malkata before you're missed. I'll send for you."

❧

Horemheb and Ay listened carefully as Simut related to the two men all that Tarina had told him. The meeting was held at the House of Maat, north of the precinct of Karnak.

"Menkhara's first duty is to me, to the army," Horemheb said in a tone of dismay. "Now he's the queen's emissary, and may even be in communication with the Hittites, a treasonable offense."

Ay said, "He's an envoy of the queen, and whether you like it or not, General, her right to solicit his service is beyond question. It would be difficult to prove treason. A request made by the wife of the Horus god must be respected and carried out. I am speaking to you now as vizier."

"By all the gods, man!" Horemheb roared. "Speak to me as one who is but a step away from the throne of the Two Lands. I'm not interested in fine points of law. And that bitch granddaughter of yours is not Pharaoh. She does not wear the beard. She cannot be tamed by marriage to you, since she has rejected such an alliance. It's time to take matters into our own hands. Remember your promises to me?"

Simut listen intently. What had Ay promised Horemheb?

Ay looked at Simut: "When did you say Menkhara is to meet with the woman called Mayet?"

"Two hours after the setting of Ra, my lord."

"Very good. We'll follow her. If what you say is true, she'll lead us to Menkhara."

Horemheb breathed a sigh of relief. "Now we're getting somewhere. I'll have a squad of my best men follow the woman."

"Take care no harm comes to Menkhara, General. I want the truth wrung from him first. If my granddaughter has been dealing with the enemies of Egypt, I'll want his confession."

Horemheb said, "Many courtesans come and go from the palace. How do we recognize this Mayet?"

"I can identify her," Simut broke in eagerly.

"Good," Horemheb nodded. "You'll come with me. We'll assemble at the armory tonight at sunset."

Simut's chest swelled. A delicious sense of reckoning burned in his heart.

23

Menkhara stood with one of Siptah's household guardsmen outside the wine merchant's cottage. Very soon his eyes would fall upon Mayet. The girl of his youth had become a woman. He loved her once, but how would he feel about her now. It had been eight years. Did she still love him? What feelings would come into his heart when he set eyes on her?

A lone figure came walking down the path. Menkhara's heart began to race. Moonlight bathing the walkway fell upon a woman; it shone upon her sweet face, pooled down over the contours of her youth and gleamed in her hair. Feeling as though he had tumbled out of a dream, Menkhara was reminded of the way Mayet walked, the smile on her face, denying, almost in defiance of all that she had beeen through, the sorrow and the suffering.

She stared at him now, and Menkhara saw the sudden look of recognition phase into a smile of joy. She left the pathway and, dodging date palm trees, called out his name as she ran.

Menkhara moved forward to greet her, all the while thinking that perhaps he could love her, but in a different way, a way lit by past memories. This much he knew: she was alive, and he was alive, and there had been a separation neither had asked for. But by the grace of the queen, they would soon be in one another's arms.

As Menkhara started toward Mayet, two armed men stepped out of the shadows cast by the date palms, swords drawn.

Menkhara cried out to Mayet, motioning her to go back. She did not understand, and even picked up her pace. He drew his sword from his waste cord, the light blue metal weapon Suppiluliumas had given him.

The gesture was enough to stop Mayet in her tracks, a puzzled look on her face.

An arrow in flight pierced the night air with the ripping sound of cloth, and then a faint, sickening thud. Mayet cried out, teetered backward and fell to the ground.

Menkhara charged across the field toward Mayet. Two household guards stationed up on the path had already challenged three of Horemheb's men. Siptah joined Menkhara, followed by a squad of guards.

More of Horemheb's soldiers emerged from the dense stand of trees and blocked their way. There were six swordsmen and the archer who felled Mayet.

Menkhara ignored the odds against him. Enraged by Mayet's piercing cry, he rushed at the swordsmen.

One man, rather than holding his ground with a companion at his side, made the mistake of meeting Menkhara head on. He lunged with his sword. Menkhara parried a slash. His opponent's bronze sword snapped at the haft. Before the disarmed soldier could consider his predicament, Menkhara ran his sword point into the man's throat.

Menkhara faced another swordsman. The blue sword sang in its arc. Another opponent fell with a gash running from his shoulder to his chest.

The household guards engaged the remaining soldiers. Menkhara wanted desperately to get to Mayet, but could not abandon the guardsmen. He squared off against one more opponent. A household guard came to Menkhara's side. "I'll take him, Captain," he shouted.

Menkhara raced up the path to where Mayet lay. Some guardsmen knelt next to her. Menkhara dropped his sword and brushed in between them.

Mayet was conscious, but in pain. The arrow had penetrated her body from behind, below her right shoulder. The shaft had snapped when she fell to the ground, leaving the bronze head and a small part of the shaft inside her.

The pretty gown she had chosen for the occasion was drenched in blood. Menkhara stared down at her, his heart filled with a helpless rage. He looked around, hoping to see the man carrying the bow and quiver.

"We've got to get her to the House of Life, to Pentu, the court physician," Menkhara cried out, gasping for breath.

"No, Menkhara," said an officer. "I wouldn't send a wounded dog to Karnak. Let's take her back to Malkata. There's one physician, a young respected doctor who practices his medicine wholly unconnected to the House of Life. He's in residence at the palace."

Menkhara, with the help of a guardsman, removed Mayet's gown sash and stanched the flow of blood as best they could. Some of the household guard improvised a stretcher from a meruwood bench found inside the cottage. They covered it with cotton cloth and brought it to where Mayet lay.

Mayet's face was pale in the moonlight. For one brief moment she regained consciousness and raised her hand to Menkhara's face. She whispered, "I love you."

Menkhara choked back a sob. He reached down and kissed her lips. "You will live, Mayet, and I swear before all the gods, when this is over, I will never leave you again."

The guardsmen and Menkhara placed Mayet on the stretcher and carried her down to the quay and aboard a ferry that would take them across the Nile to Malkata.

Siptah decided to run ahead of the stretcher, stole a lighter at the docks, crossed the river and had already brought word of the ambush back to Malkata before Menkhara and the guardsmen appeared at the main gate. He was waiting there with a palace physician and household servants when Menkhara and the stretcher bearers arrived.

"The queen has ordered you to return immediately to Kenofer's villa," Siptah said.

"Mayet's life hangs in the balance," Menkhara protested. "I can't leave her."

"More than her life hangs in the balance. When you get back to Kenofer's villa, you'll best understand why the queen wants you to leave at once. One of my men will accompany you."

Menkhara knelt over Mayet. Her face had the pallor of death. He kissed her and slowly stood up, staring helplessly at Siptah.

"Everything that can be done will be done, my friend," Siptah said.

The palace gates opened. The guardsmen, now relieved of their charge, stood aside while servants bore Mayet into the forecourt and disappeared among the shadows cast from the papyrus-shaped columns.

A party had assembled in the villa courtyard. Kenofer greeted Menkhara at the gate. Behind him was the Hittite chamberlain, Hattusaziti, and the queen's foreign minister, Hania. Outside the gates were three chariots, each harnessed to a brace of horses.

Kenofer took Menkhara aside. "Things are heating up my friend. The attack upon you and Mayet signals the beginning of bad times ahead. It's imperative you leave at once for Hatti-land to present Suppiluliumas with our queen's response. A king seated at Ankhesenamun's side is our only hope of thwarting the ambitions of Ay and Horemheb."

"So much urgency!" Menkhara protested. "Why so quick a departure?"

"The harbor police of every province along the Nile are being alerted to check departing ships. Here in Thebes vessels will be checked by the harbormaster. So you see why you must leave at once. A state ship has been provided, and Hania has letters of transit from the queen. Once you reach Hittite-occupied lands, the presence of the royal chamberlain will assure your safe passage."

Menkhara said, "By the time we return home, Horemheb and Ay will have the harbor police in every port looking for us."

Kenofer nodded. "And that's why you'll have to return by a land route. He handed Menkhara an oxhide cylinder case. "Here is a map I've prepared, showing your return to Egypt. The route home is difficult and includes some of the most uninviting places on Earth."

"And the queen's letter?" Menkhara asked.

"Hania has it."

Menkhara smiled. "There is nothing more to be said."

Kenofer returned the smile. "There are ample provisions stored in your vessel. It's best suited for Nile waters, but will serve you on the Green Sea."

24

The ship was unmistakably Egyptian with its squat design and the telltale lotus blossom carved into its stern.

Menkhara was no mariner, but he could see the vessel was not as sleek in appearance or as well-balanced as the Kefti ships of

Crete. The only question that remained: was it good enough to get his party up the Phoenician coast?

Their two weeks on the Nile passed without incident. Finally, they reached the sea, and almost at once the conspicuously wide sail was filled with a good wind. Thanks more to nature than the mariner's skill, the unlikely Egyptian river ship raced up the coast with good speed. In eight days they reached the harbor at Ugarit.

Hania, Hattusaziti and Menkhara said farewell to the crew, but only after offering them a good meal at a Syrian tavern. The following day they set out in chariots for Carchemish, fording the Orontes in a day and reaching the walled city in three.

Suppiluliumas had given his son Piyassils the kingdom of Carchemish. A mild-mannered, affable man, Piyassils greeted the three men as equals and insisted they spend a full day resting in comfort before setting off for Hattusas. The young king provided his guests with ample provisions, including food, fresh water and two able guides.

On the morning of the second day after their arrival, the two envoys of the queen and the Hittite chamberlain climbed into chariots, and with backs to Carchemish and the Euphrates River, set out for the high plateau country of the Hatti. Between them and the capital city of Hattusas lay a threat no less fearsome than an assassin's sword: the rugged barrier mountains of Anatolia called the Taurus.

The first day out of Carchemish was an uneventful, easy trek across a broad valley with cultivated fields and shallow rivers. On the second day, the party reached golden stretches of dry grass and pebbly brooks.

By the beginning of the third day, the region sloped up to hill country. Yew, lime and fir trees replaced the stunted trees of the valley and the foothills. A bracing wind blew down the slopes. Menkhara was grateful for the warm woolly cloaks king Piyassils had given them.

By the fifth day the Egyptians were marveling at the towering conifers and the lengthy troughlike valleys and basins. Menkhara had heard of snow, but had trouble imagining it. Freezing water seemed an impossibility to an Egyptian, but on the sixth day of their climb, he became a believer. Throughout the day he shivered beneath heavy robes, an eye on the rocky turf crusted in a milk-white frost. Hania suffered so much from the cold that everyone insisted he ride in the bullock cart.

In the afternoon the weather drew down and the wind came barreling out of the north. Between the tops of the high ranging fir trees, wisps of fleecy clouds flew by like sea foam. Even the hardened Hittite guards suffered under the sting of the cold winds. The Hittites issued boots made of leather and lined with wool, as well as heavy woollen gloves. For a time they would dismount and lead their horses through gorges and over ravines, the wind tearing at their faces. The Egyptians, thrust into this strange wintry world, watched in fascination as long funnels of white escaped through the horses' nostrils.

Toward dusk it began to snow. The flakes whirled down from the treetops in gossamer white medallions, attacking their exposed skin like millions of enraged insects. Menkhara's fingers and toes were so cold they had lost all feeling.

The following day the party stopped at two Hittite villages, where they were received in warm wood cabins and given hot food and mulled wine. This kind of generosity toward strangers was not common in Egypt, where newcomers were viewed with suspicion and deeply distrusted.

After passing through a mountain valley, the trees began to

thin out, and the countryside quickly became barren. The ground was spotted with frost, and the bare surface criss-crossed with long sills of eroded sandstone cut by an occasional watercourse. A thin icy wind continued blowing down from the mountains. The Egyptians were informed they were two days from the capital city.

They reached Hattusas on a fine sunny morning. The weather had moderated, and there was a hint of warmth in the light wind. Hattusas towered above the northern slope of a ridge where the plateau began to break down toward the sea. Two torrents that flowed northward from this range in steep rock beds united at the foot of the slope near the city.

Some of the formidable fortifications of Hattusas were provided by nature herself, for on the eastern and northern sides, the city was protected by cliffs so sheer, no invading army could surmount them. The entire city was protected by what seemed an impregnable wall less than one hour of march long. At its base the wall was a full seventy meters wide and narrowed as it rose. Above the rampart was the main city wall with rectangular towers projecting from it.

Word of their arrival had preceded them. Even as their horses trotted up the long narrow ramp leading to the citadel's gates and its flanking towers, servants with sedan chairs waited to take them into the palace.

Menkhara and Hattusaziti climbed out of their chariots, stretched their legs briefly, and then climbed into the chairs. The aged Hania was not so supple and had to be helped out of the bullock cart and led to one of several sedan chairs.

Menkhara turned to thank the Hittite guides who had guided them from Carchemish to Hattusas. It was too late. Anxious to dismount, they had swung their chariots around and were already heading back down the ramp to the well-deserved comforts of a

Hittite inn.

A man who looked vaguely familiar to Menkhara greeted them inside the entrance hall. Dressed like every other Hittite in attendance at court, he wore a knee-length shirt-like tunic with long sleeves, over which was draped an animal skin, almost a requirement on the dry cold plateau. The toes of his shoes curved up. The man smiled.

"Critias!" Menkhara cried, jumping out of his chair before the servants had a chance to put it down. The two men embraced while Hania and Hattusaziti looked on.

"You scoundrel," Menkhara laughed. "You've taken up the ways of the Hittite, and I see you've put on some weight."

Critias answered with a broad smile. "Spend a winter month up here, and you'll find merit in the Hittite way of life." Critias patted his stomach. "There was not much for me to do but eat, stay warm, drink and enjoy a few of the offered diversions."

Menkhara looked over Critias's shoulder. A pretty young Hittite maiden stood in the shadows of a column, long strands of her black hair flowing across her white gown. "Diversions, indeed," Menkhara answered with a laugh.

Servants took the tired party to their bedchambers. Menkhara's bed was on a raised platform fitted with heavy layers of sheep's wool and robes, and was so inviting he hardly noticed the plate of dried apples, apricots, breads, honey and the flask of wine waiting for him. Moments later he floated naked and ecstatic in a warm bath, one eye shut, the other cocked on the naked female attendants at the bath's edge, waiting to apply soothing oils to his dried and weathered skin.

Later, he climbed into bed, and for the space of many hours was lost to the world. It was only moments before he woke that he dreamt he was back in the workers' village of Deir el-Medina, dining with his parents, with Mayet at his side. He was seventeen once again, and he was happy.

⁂

Menkhara had expected to see King Suppiluliumas on the day of their arrival. The following morning there was no indication the king would give them an audience. The only people available to speak with were affable palace servants whose business it was to make their stay at Hattusas as comfortable as possible.

The diplomatic slight was offset by good food and excellent wine. Every need was attended to, including a small wardrobe of Hittite clothing more suitable to the chilly climate of the high plateau.

Finally, on the morning of their third day at the palace, the three men received word the king would grant them an audience that afternoon. After their noon meal, Menkhara, Hania and Critias were taken to the huge columned banquet hall and escorted up a long ramp to King Suppiluliumas' palace apartment.

"It's about time," Menkhara said.

Critias laughed. "Hittite customs require getting used to, Menkhara. You must not mistake the king's failure to grant an audience as a message of some kind. Most of their guests are exhausted from their journeys here, and they are offered more days to recover than a young fellow like you might need."

"A wise practice," Hania nodded. "When you're my age, you take all the days you can get."

A servant led the three men into a reception room. They waited for the king's summons. An hour passed. A servant appeared at the door to announce the appearance of the king's three sons.

They wore long, narrow garments with long sleeves and the familiar shoes with upturned toes. Two of the brothers wore their hair long, hanging over their necks, and a third had his tied in a ponytail.

One of the brothers introduced himself as Mursilis. Speaking perfect Egyptian, he pronounced his name with an air of regal pride. He was Suppiluliumas's favorite, and it was rumored he was the son most likely to succeed to the throne.

Mursilis introduced his brothers. The one called Anuwandas looked sickly, and had a drawn, pocked face with a warm kindly smile.

The youngest was Zidanza. He was playful, unpretentious, and despite his good looks and privileged life, could have been taken for a stable hand, or, at best, the son of a merchant. Menkhara wondered what prince he would pick for Ankhesenamun. It was an idle thought since he had no inkling how the king would react to the queen's letter.

"And you've met our brothers Piyassils and Telipinos?" Mursilis asked.

"Yes," Menkhara replied. "I saw King Piyassils of Carchemish less than two weeks ago. He was very gracious and treated us like honored guests. Your brother Telipinos was on route to Aleppo to receive the adulation and sovereign crown of a king."

Servants brought a silver ewer of Syrian wine and goblets on a tray. The Egyptian guests and the princes exchanged information about their respective countries. The conversation turned to religion. The princes seemed to know a lot more about the gods of Egypt than Menkhara and Critias knew of the thousand gods of the Hatti.

As the hours flew by, Menkhara had enough wine in him to inquire about a subject of interest: the gleaming sword with the light-blue blade given him by their father.

"I'll tell you this much," said Mursilis, "the blade is made of iron and another material I'm not at liberty to mention. To be frank, I can say no more, for any man or nation may one day greet us on the field of battle armed with the weapons we helped them fashion. The last thing we need is a proliferation of these swords. You understand?"

"Yes," Menkhara conceded.

"Be happy and proud my father has given you such a gift," Mursilis continued. "It's an honor, especially in light of the low regard he has for at least one of your generals and his third-rate army."

Menkhara thought the queen's foreign minister should take the lead when they met with Suppiluliumas, but there was no telling how Hania would perform. The altitude had made him dizzy.

The chamberlain, Hattusaziti, slipped into the room, his eyes on Hania. "His lord majesty will receive you."

⁂

Suppiluliumas sat on his throne in the palace audience hall. He nodded as his guests bowed politely before him.

"Welcome, emissaries of your gracious queen," he said. "You have braved the snow and cold of the Taurus. That in itself is an accomplishment. More than one envoy from distant lands has been found frozen after the spring thaw. Would you believe I've been criticized for the mountains of Hatti? They would have me reprimand the Taurus, as I would a discourteous subject." Suppiluliumas broke into a laugh. "I trust you have enjoyed the amenities of our palace?"

"We have, my lord," Hania answered. "And we thank you for the kindness."

"You've lost no time returning to me with a reply from your queen. I would imagine by now that young Pharaoh has been safely installed in his tomb?"

"No, my lord," Hania answered promptly. "Preparation of the

god for his passage west, as well as the tomb where his ka shall dwell for eternity, takes much time."

Suppiluliumas thought for a while. Finally he grinned. "Well, with respect for your gods, it's a waste of money and effort to me. When I die I'll be cremated in the manner of my forefathers. We've no time to dwell upon death as you Egyptians are wont to do."

In the long silence that followed, the bark of a dog echoed across the rocky terrain. "Now to the matter at hand," Suppiluliumas finally said. "The letter from your queen. It's written in glyphs like the last one?"

"Akkadian, my lord," Menkhara ventured.

The king glanced at Hattusaziti. The chamberlain clapped his hands. A man simply dressed in a short kilt and wool tunic appeared inside the door.

"A Hittite scribe," Suppiluliumas said. "If the Egyptian queen's ambassador would consent to a translation."

"My lord," Hania protested, "it was written in confidence."

The king smiled. "There's no one here I wouldn't share it with."

Hania produced the oxhide tube, drew out the rolled papyrus and handed it to the scribe. Menkhara bristled. Hania had capitulated too easily. Ankhesenamun would not have wanted her letter spoken in open court.

The scribe held up the scrolled papyrus. He pointed to the queen's seal. The king nodded. The scribe broke it, and unrolled the papyrus. He began in a low steady voice:

My Lord:

> *You doubt my intentions, and have sent your emissary to my court to question me. Could you believe I would deceive you? For what purpose?*
>
> *If I had an heir, do you suppose I would have sent to a foreign country laying forth these shameful facts? Would*

I have begged for a lord to be at my side in marriage?

My husband is dead, and I have importuned you my lord for a son. I cannot and I shall not take a subject and make him my husband.

I am alone, a defenseless woman. I have not written to any other country; only to you my lord! You have five sons. Send me one, and he shall be king of Egypt, and will rule at my side. I cannot be more explicit my lord. Doubt not my intentions.

Ankhesenamun
King's wife
By this seal known[2]

The king, a hand cupped over his chin, listened carefully to every word, hoping to divine some message written between its lines. He raised his eyes, and with a flick of his hand dismissed the scribe. He gazed around the room taking measure of everyone there. His eyes came to rest on his chamberlain, Hattusaziti.

Finally, Suppiluliumas sat straight up and filled his lungs with a deep breath. Looking faintly angered, he stared at Hania. "Do you really expect me to send a son of mine, a prince royal, to Egypt? He would be slaughtered the moment he set foot on Egyptian soil."

"Not so, my lord," Hania answered assertively.

"Saying so does not guarantee his safe passage."

In the silence that followed, Menkhara knew that this was a crucial point in the negotiations. He was not a skilled diplomat, but something had to be said.

"My lord," Menkhara began slowly. "What purpose would our

[2] The Deeds of Suppiluliumas, As Told By His Son Mursilis II, Tablet 7, royal palace, Hattusas

queen gain from luring one of your sons to his death? Her court is a tempest of intrigues. She has no more regard for General Horemheb than you do, and as for her grandfather, Ay, she has rejected his proposal of marriage and—"

"Marriage?" Suppiluliumas interrupted. "To her grandfather?" The frown on the king's face changed to a caustic smile, and then he continued in a softer voice. "Ah yes, I very nearly forgot. You Egyptians do that sort of thing. Continue, if you will."

Menkhara nodded and began again in a softer voice. "Our queen has rejected Ay's proposal of marriage and support. Having done this, she finds herself beset with threats to her throne. There are still many who love her. She has the support of her household guards, and advance units from the army of the loyal Viceroy of Kush are only days from Thebes."

"Our lady of the Two Lands enjoys the affection of her people," Hania interjected. "And let me say, my lord, there are rich and powerful men, including the treasurer, Maya, and the vizier of the Lower Kingdom, Usermont, who would deal forcefully with any would-be usurper."

"You ask for my trust?" the king replied with a thoughtful smile. "Hatti and Egypt have long been friends. This has been attested to by treaty." He pointed to a table next to his throne chair. "I've ordered that same treaty brought from our archives. There it sits," he said somberly, a finger pointing to the clay tablet on the table. "I myself was friendly toward your Pharaoh; yes, even loved him as a brother. But then your troops attacked the ruler of Kadesh, the same city I won by rights from Tushratta of the Mittani."

King Suppiluliumas reached over and picked up the clay tablet, glanced down at it with a sneer of contempt and then heaved it straight up.

The tablet crashed down at Hania's feet, fragmenting into innumerable pieces.

"That's what your Horemheb did to our treaty when he sent his army against Kadesh!" Suppiluliumas roared. "Whatever might be the sincerity of your plea, Excellency, Egypt no longer enjoys my trust."

A shard of clay had cut into Hania's skin above his ankle. Its sting matched the anger in Suppiluliumas's voice. Hania, unnerved by the king's angry outburst, and the sight of blood on his calf, struggled for words.

Menkhara had to defend the actions of his queen. Quickly, he considered his response. One word misunderstood, one mistake or bad judgment in phrasing a proposal, would doom his mission and quite possibly his country and his queen. Wisely, he decided not to defend the attack on Kadesh. It was a sore point with the king, and Menkhara wanted him off the subject. Better to get to the matter at hand.

Menkhara began: "Consider this, my lord. Your fear that your son will be killed or taken hostage is, with due respect, ill-founded. Our queen's plea for one of your sons to share her throne, while embarrassing to our lady, also required courage. She has no heir. Let me assure you, my lord, we went to no other country to secure a husband for our queen. We're not making our rounds, so to speak. This request pays homage to your great house. We beg of you, my lord; give us one of your fine sons and we shall make him our sovereign lord. You can only benefit from his sitting upon the throne of Egypt."

More silence. The king once again cupped his chin, his eyes cast down at the shattered remains of the tablet. "I'll give you my answer in due course."

The king got up, his eyes riveted on Menkhara and an unreadable smile on his face. Everyone in attendance bowed their heads respectfully and waited. When they looked up, the king was gone.

25

Suppiluliumas did not immediately respond to the queen's letter. The king's chamberlain let it be known that it could be some time before they got their answer. Hania showed his displeasure by retiring to his room and eating alone. Menkhara and Critias spent the following two days wandering around Hattusas.

When Menkhara and Critias returned to their palace room the evening of the second day, Hania was waiting for them. "The king has invited us to a banquet tonight. I'm told by Hattusaziti he will then announce his decision."

Critias breathed a sigh of relief. "The gods be praised. Hattusas is clean, and her people hardworking, proud and friendly, and yet I've never been so bored. I long for the black lands of Egypt."

Hania heaved a long sigh. "It'll be a long trek back if he turns the queen down."

Menkhara flashed him a cynical smile. "Back to what? There has to be a price on our heads."

⁂

"Our Hittite friends know how to enjoy the good things in life," Critias remarked as he, Menkhara and Hania entered the huge banquet hall that evening. Menkhara could not help sharing the same opinion.

There was much to like in the hall. The banquet table, so different from the low ebony serving tables of Malkata, was made of fine woods, and instead of cushions, chairs brought the guests waist-high to the table's edge. Flames spiraled up from the evenly spaced wall sconces, coloring the walls with a fluid orange-tinged glow.

On the table were wine vessels identified by Critias as

Mycenaean in origin. Roasts venting steam rested on large platters, and there were vegetable stews, bowls of dried fruit and an abundance of beans and breads.

The invited guests included a few of the city elders, palace ministers and chamberlains, the king's sons, and priests from the temple complex of Hattusas. The king's empty seat was at the center of the table, flanked by his three sons. Menkhara, Critias, Hania and the king's chamberlain, Hattusaziti, were seated across from the royal party.

Hania turned to Hattusaziti. "I assume from what you have told me, the king has consulted with his advisors and has arrived at a decision."

Hattusaziti answered with a patient smile. "That's not the way it works in Hatti, my friend. His majesty spent the day shut up in the cult room of the temple. It was from his libations and animal sacrifice to the honor of the storm-god and the sun-goddess of Arinna, that he and the priests were able to divine the right answer."

Menkhara began to feel apprehensive. He had hoped the king would base his decision on what was obviously in the best interests of both countries. But now it had come down to pure chance, poking around the entrails of some miserable animal, or being influenced by the flight of birds, or worse yet, the divination of some crazy priest.

Hania said, "Can we assume from this lovely meal that the response from the gods favors our queen's request?"

The chamberlain laughed. "No such luck. Diplomats who go home empty-handed are also treated to a banquet. Failed diplomacy has nothing to do with good manners. The amenities of our court are available to the most persistent enemies of the Hatti."

The king and his sons, attended by household servants, entered the banquet hall. The entire assemblage immediately rose to their feet and clapped their hands until the royal party was seated. The king raised his hand. The applause ended as quickly as it began. It was also a signal to begin eating.

There was much chatter across the table, with the king and his sons engaging the Egyptian delegation on a range of subjects including trade, military tactics, wine making, religion and, ultimately, women.

Late in the evening some of the merrymakers wandered around the room, engaging in private conversations. The youngest prince, Zidanza, came to where Menkhara sat. Hattusaziti had in the meantime left his chair to whisper something in the ear of the king. Zidanza sat down in the empty chair and said softly to Menkhara, "Tell me about Queen Ankhesenamun."

Menkhara smiled. He liked the prince's unassuming manner. "She's a woman of extraordinary character, and a good ruler who loves her people."

Zidanza moved his chair closer. "Yes, go on."

"She's fun-loving and loves a good joke. She's very generous and loyal to her friends."

Zidanza flashed Menkhara a sheepish smile. "Yes, these are wonderful attributes for a queen. But—"

"There's something else you wish to know?"

"Well …"

"You've only to ask."

Zidanza blushed. "Is she pretty?"

"Our country's brightest ornament. She's beautiful."

Zidanza's smile ran from ear to ear. "I'm glad to hear it. Very glad indeed. Thank you!"

Zidanza returned to his table and Menkhara turned at once to Hania. The queen's foreign minister had taken in so much wine Menkhara feared the old man would fall asleep in his chair.

"Hania, my lord minister," Menkhara whispered close to Hania's ear. "I have something to tell you."

Hania looked drunkenly at Menkhara. His head bobbed up and down. "Speak away, you great winged messenger of the gods." Hania's slurred words and voice, an octave higher than normal, and several decibels louder, began to attract attention.

"Never mind," Menkhara answered. "I think we ought to get you to bed." Menkhara looked around for help. The king was staring straight at him. His majesty winked.

One motion of the king's hand and servants were at Hania's side. The chatter of conversations fell to a soft hum as his excellency, the foreign minister of Egypt, was helped out of his chair by stalwart servants and guided from the hall.

The chattering conversations and laughter resumed. Menkhara turned back to the king. "Thank you, my lord king," Menkhara said.

The king laughed. "It is the altitude. It does not mix with good wine. Your minister is not the first emissary to collapse at our table." There was a ripple of laughter.

The king left the banquet hall, and almost immediately the guests began to leave. Menkhara and Critias headed back for their chambers.

"We're no more informed now of the king's decision than when we arrived," Critias said.

Menkhara smiled. "I am very much informed. The king will send his youngest son Zidanza into the arms of our beloved queen."

"Wishful thinking," said Critias. "You would have no way of knowing."

"Zidanza told me."

"Before his father announced the arrangement?"

Menkhara laughed. "Not directly. The prince inquired of our

queen's looks, and was grateful for my answer. You don't need the brain of an Imhotep to figure that one out."

⁂

Menkhara was right. Hattusaziti informed Hania of the king's decision the following morning. Suppiluliumas would send his youngest son, Prince Zidanza, to the court of Queen Ankhesenamun to marry her and become her husband and king of Egypt. No one was sure how much of his decision was based on divinations or good judgment, and no one really cared, least of all Hania. The good news acted like a magic tonic on his hangover. The king wanted the betrothal kept a secret until after the union, and for that reason no official notice of the marriage was given to the people of Hattusas.

The morning following the king's approval, Menkhara and Hania met with the king, his sons and Hattusaziti to toast the betrothal and reaffirm a treaty of friendship between the two countries. This was followed by several more toasts of wine and a long private conversation between the king and his parting son.

That night Critias and Hania met in Menkhara's chamber. Menkhara, seated at a table, carefully unrolled Kenofer's papyrus map of their route back to Thebes. Critias and Hania stood behind him watching the candlelight flicker across the map.

Menkhara knew the route home was a long and arduous gamble that would take them over the Taurus Mountains, eastward to the plain of Aleppo, across the Orontes river and a brief rest at Kadesh. Beyond the headwaters of the river, north of Byblos, they would cross the border into Egyptian territory and outside the protection of the Hittite king.

At Gaza they would pick up the old military road, the Way of Horus, and follow it all the way to Silé, cross the desert for five hours of march until they reached the Gulf of Suez, where they would hire a boat and head south upon the Red Sea to the port of Quseir.

The last leg of their journey was over the Red Sea hills and across the Eastern Desert. The plan was to swing south as they approached the Nile and sneak into the ancient town of Madu, where they would spend the night at a villa owned by a friend of Kenofer. The following night they would travel overland to Thebes and the relative safety of the palace at Malkata.

In the late morning hours of a misty spring day, Prince Zidanza, the Egyptians and a Hittite military escort formed up in the palace courtyard by the lion's gate. There were eight battle chariots, each with a crew of three; three Hurrian chariots, one manned by Menkhara and Critias, and the others by Hittite warriors. Four bullock carts were hitched to donkeys and filled with leather water-skins, large water pots, food, clothing and gifts for the queen.

The eight Hittite battle chariots would turn back to Hattusas once they crossed the headwaters of the Orontes. This would leave three Hurrian chariots occupied by four charioteers. The carts would be manned by the remaining charioteers. Near the Egyptian border, the Hittites continuing on to Egypt would shed their distinctive helmets, sleeveless leather battle jackets, cloaks and curled shoes in favor of the simple attire of Egyptian soldiers. Prince Zidanza would start the ride in one of the Hittite battle-chariots.

The king wanted to send more chariots across the Egyptian border, but Menkhara convinced him that a sizeable number of chariots would only draw attention to their party, and provoke the enemies of the queen.

At the long plaintive wail of a horn the lion's gate opened. Slowly the train of chariots and high-spirited horses and donkey-drawn carts lumbered down the long ramp toward the outer walls of Hattusas.

King Suppiluliumas and his two remaining sons stood in the courtyard, their eyes fixed on the chariots and carts. Menkhara gave one last look back at the diminished figures of the king and his sons. The foggy mist swept across the plateau, and in an instant his hosts, the great citadel and the lion's gate disappeared from sight.

26

The weather had improved when the caravan of chariots and carts began to ascend the Taurus Mountains. The days were clear and cold, and shafts of pale sun raked across the narrow passes and glittered on the drifted snow. There had been a melting between the hard freezes that came with the setting sun. Tufted shrubs poked through the crusted snow, and the sharp smell of resin and pine carried well on the thin icy wind.

Suppiluliumas had seen that the party was well-equipped for the mountains. Each man had been furnished with a sheepskin cloak, woolly gloves and fur-lined boots. Menkhara's optimism soared knowing that they had secured their prize, a Hittite prince for his queen. And with chariots full of hand-picked Hittite warriors, sleep came easily to him whenever they pitched tents and settled down for the night.

The Taurus Mountains to their backs, Zidanza wanted to spend a few days with his brothers at Carchemish and Aleppo. He was the youngest sibling, and Menkhara sensed that he probably had his way growing up at court. Not this time, Menkhara thought with an inner smile.

Hania was of the same mind as Menkhara. He told Menkhara that his bones ached from the bouncing of the bullock-cart, and that he missed the pleasures of his villa home and his gardens too much to allow a sallow Hittite boy to delay their journey home. Hania was, of course, more diplomatic in act than thought, and explained to Zidanza that any delay would lessen their chances of arriving safely.

Zidanza, too coddled to be convinced of his mortality, was at last beginning to feel a certain uneasiness in the strange world beyond the borders of Hatti. And Menkhara was beginning to understand just how young in heart this Hittite youth really was.

They crossed the plains of Aleppo, and on the following day reached the headwaters of the Orontes. Ahead lay the border separating the contending empires. It was time for all but three of the Hittite-driven chariots to quit the party and turn back for Hatti.

Zidanza gave each Hittite warrior his hand and thanked them. The three remaining Hurrian chariots, two occupied by the remaining Hittite charioteers, formed up in front of the bullock carts, all eyes on the battle-chariots making their way north along the riverbank. They watched until the chariots rounded a bend in the Orontes and passed out of sight.

It was decided that Zidanza should make himself comfortable in a bullock cart. He objected at first, but Hania insisted, pointing out that the prince was too important a passenger to expose himself to the danger and even the possibility of assassination. Reluctantly, Prince Zidanza climbed out of the chariot and allowed himself to be unceremoniously boosted into a cart.

The lead chariot driver raised his hand. Chariots and carts lurched forward. Ahead lay the ancient Lebanese city of Byblos, the northernmost city of the Egyptian Empire. Critias and Menkhara glanced briefly at one another. For the first time in their lives they felt like strangers in their own land.

⁂

Menkhara's party reached Silé, at the foot of the Way of Horus, and then turned south toward the Gulf of Suez and the Red Sea.

The floor of the desert was fine quartz gravel, and gave off a clattering sound from the cart and chariot wheels. The cauldron-hot expanse of desert before them was one of bleak desolation, littered with the bones of men foolish enough to attempt to cross it. Before long the horses and chariots were covered in yellow dust, and the air so hot and dry it was like breathing inside an oven.

By late afternoon they reached the Bitter Lake. Menkhara decided that they should camp on the western shore beneath a stand of shady palm trees.

The soldiers rigged a tent and to everyone's delight found a shallow well with sweet cool water. Prince and charioteers alike gathered in the tent to sleep through the long hours until dusk. A guard posted outside was changed at one-hour intervals. The transient colors of sunset covered the desert in an orange hue, and then slowly darkened to crimson.

By the time darkness closed in over the camp, everyone was awake. A fire was started from the dwindling supply of wood, and the usual fare was prepared: porridge made of barley and served with strips of dried ox meat.

Two hours before dawn the party formed up and began its trek southward. The wind blew cool in the early morning hours, and the full moon gliding between thin wisps of clouds softened the stark landscape and the low distant hills.

Sunrise transitioned quickly into another hot day, and in the space of two hours each man felt himself dried and parched. They pushed on for four hours and then stopped for three hours of rest behind the protective linen sheets of their tent.

The following day, within the space of two hours, they heard the waves drone softly over the rocky shingle of a beach.

Klysma was one of the most worrisome places in the long trek back to Thebes, the place where the party hoped to find or purchase a vessel large enough to take on the chariots and carts.

The village was a small, ramshackle place with two ancient sagging docks made from the planks of beached ships. It was inhabited by Bedouin, whose only industry was money extorted from smugglers, escaped criminals, runaway slaves and those willing to enter and leave Egypt without paying duty on trade goods.

In the hour of sunset, a delegation of Bedouin met the caravan at dockside. Three vessels were moored, but only one large enough to be of value, a freight barge that looked as old as the pyramids. Its long, slender hull had considerable overhang and space for fourteen oarsmen on each side, but only four remaining oars. The decking was full of splintered holes. The steering oars were in place, but the narrow sail hung like withered skin from the yard. The boat had no cabin and therefore no retreat from the sun. On the plus side, it was a good ninety meters long, with adequate deck space for the carts, chariots and horses.

"We wish to rent your ship," said Menkhara. He had taken off his sandals and allowed the seawater to lap at his parched feet.

One of the Bedouin stepped forward. He looked as old as the ship, and his lips were nearly hidden behind a frothy white beard. "You mean you wish to buy it, for we've no hope it will ever be returned."

Menkhara laughed. "There's some question it will survive the sea beyond sight of this beach."

The Bedouin shrugged his shoulders. "Unfortunately, it's all that's available." The other Bedouin laughed, their eyes dancing in their sockets. Entertainment was hard to come by in this desolate place, and they were enjoying themselves.

"What do you want for it?" said Menkhara.

"Two hundred kite of silver, or its equivalent in shekels."

Menkhara, realizing that they were in the company of thieves, replied tartly: "Not possible. We don't have that kind of money, either in rings, shekels or their equivalent in jewels."

Menkhara had his eye on Zidanza. The prince had been listening to the conversation. He had brought with him jewelry, gold and silver in the supply cart. Menkhara, sensing Zidanza was about to step forward to make an offer, whispered in his ear. "Offer nothing. And keep your mouth shut, if you please, your highness."

The Bedouin answered after a long pause. "I cannot offer you the boat."

"Here. Take my jeweled collar," Hania answered, raising the collar from his shoulders. "It was given to me by Pharaoh himself."

"Don't bother taking it off, my friend," said the Bedouin. "The ship stays here. I bid you goodnight."

"Wait, Bedouin," Menkhara shot back angrily. "You do not deal from a position of strength. Take what is offered, or you shall have nothing, and lose your ship as well."

The Bedouin smiled, showing his worn mottled teeth. "You have it wrong, Egyptian. We'll take whatever you have including your lives."

The Bedouin raised his arm. Shadows lanced across the

shingle of the beach. At least thirty Bedouin jogged toward them, the blades of their swords gleaming in the moonlight.

Menkhara fell back on his officer's training in the divisions of Ptah. He reacted instantly.

"Warriors of Hatti, at the ready!" Menkhara ordered. Critias and the Hittites drew their scimitars. Menkhara motioned the startled prince and Hania back into the water. "This is not your fight," he shouted to them. Then he turned to face the charging Bedouin. "We're outnumbered three to one my friends. It ought to be a fair fight." The ripple of laughter from the Hittites died with the sound of clashing swords.

The Hittites and the Egyptians spread out, their backs to the sea. They were ten strong.

The Bedouin charged across the sand, shouting their terrible war cries.

The Hittite warriors took a full step back, parrying with their swords at the same time. The Bedouin, ill-trained, either stopped short or misjudged and stepped past the defenders. It was a costly mistake.

What followed was a slaughter. The mismatched Bedouin, smiling disdainfully at their foe, were cut down like shafts of wheat at harvest time. When the remaining Bedouin lost their numerical advantage, and their numbers reduced to a dozen or so, they fled back to their camp, their spokesman, the elder Bedouin, among them. The Hittite losses amounted to one slightly wounded charioteer.

The Hittite charioteers were disdainful of the poor showing put up by the Bedouin and wanted to sack the town to show their contempt. Menkhara quieted the men with a promise to break out some of the fine Syrian wine the prince had brought with him in large earthenware jars.

"Isn't that right, my lord?" said Menkhara, looking back at

Zidanza.

The prince, dumbfounded, had not fully recovered from watching the fight. Standing at the water's edge, wavelets gliding across his bare feet, he nervously nodded his approval. "Yes, by all means," he said hurriedly. "It's a fine idea, and I most earnestly approve of it."

Critias and Menkhara inspected the ship. Fortunately the hull was in good shape, but with so few oars available and a tattered sail, they could not expect to make good time unless favored by a strong north wind.

Every man, except the prince and Hania, helped rig the ship for sea. There was not a mariner among them, though Critias seemed to have an understanding of sailing ships. He knew what had to be done.

The mast, stepped roughly amidships, had standing rigging with fore and back stays, but no shrouds. With little effort, it was unfurled and raised on the curved yard.

The chariots and carts were brought aboard, and in the gray mist of dawn, the party cast off. With little wind, the vessel was entirely dependant on the strong arms of the Hittite crew.

They had been at sea for several hours. It was calm, with not so much as a hint of a breeze. Menkhara and Critias took turns walking the deck and making sure that each man at the oars was relieved every hour.

Critias had rigged up an overhead canopy to shade a portion of the deck where the off-duty men could go to rest and drink their ration of water. The prince sat beneath the canopy looking tired, his drawn face red from the paralyzing heat. Menkhara urged Hania to avoid the sun and keep the prince company, but he would have none of it, preferring to make himself useful with the steering oar.

The sun set behind the rim of the horizon, painting the sky and distant landscape of sand and limestone hills a beautiful mix of red, pink and orange hues. A light breeze came out of the north, filling the sail. The Hittites, half dead at their oars, let out a wild cheer. To celebrate, the prince's promised wine was broken out, and each man given a good measure of it along with a meal of dried meat and figs. Even the horses and donkeys were not forgotten. Generous baskets of grain were set on the deck below their bobbing heads.

The north breeze continued into the following day. The ship made good time. Menkhara guessed that if the wind held, they would make the old port town of Quseir in six days.

The following day they left the Gulf and entered the open waters of the Red Sea, keeping their ship close to land. As they moved farther south, the sand and limestone hills grew rugged, and the humidity rose with every passing mile. The night brought with it a stillness broken only by the lonely sound of the creaking ship and the occasional whinny of a horse. Toward morning, with starlight dancing on the water, the vessel began to rock, and Critias had blocks placed under the chariot and cart wheels.

27

Simut's affair with the handmaiden Tarina proved to be more profitable than he could have dreamed. Tarina had heard whispered rumors that the queen had solicited the Hittite King Suppiluliumas to provide her with one of his sons to take in marriage.

Ay would have to do something. The queen had rejected Ay's offer of marriage and was determined to hold onto the throne.

Given her behavior, the rumors, no matter how bizarre, had to be taken seriously.

Simut was invited to a meeting at General Horemheb's villa. Three commanders from the divisions of Amun stood around a folding field table that Horemheb had set up in his villa study. Minnakht, the nominal commander of the armies, managed to arise from his sickbed to attend.

Simut was pleased. He felt himself at the center of things. The threat from the queen, and her rumored unsavory contacts with the king of Hatti-land, had united many interests, and Simut profited from the crisis. Mutnedjmet and Ay were present. Ay was seated across from Horemheb. Mutnedjmet sat by herself, away from the table, her chair against the wall.

Horemheb, as the most reliable military man, was given the task of stopping Menkhara's party from returning to Egypt. The general sat at the head of the table flanked by hand-picked commanders from the divisions of Ptah and Amun. Simut, two seats down, craned his neck as Horemheb unrolled a large papyrus map and secured the ends with granite weights.

"I will not beat about the bush, my friends," Horemheb began. "This Hittite prince and the treacherous Egyptians bringing him to our sacred black soil, must be struck down, their bodies left for carrion meat wherever they fall."

Horemheb, using a short sword as a pointer, aimed it at the Phoenician coast. "This would be the easiest route back to Egypt from Hatti. They would sail from Ugarit to Tanis, and then down the Nile to Thebes. The route is too obvious; they know they would be easily spotted by the time they reached Byblos. On the other hand, there is too much at stake to assume anything." Horemheb paused and looked each one of his commanders in the eyes. "Alert the harbor masters in every port between here and Tanis. Have them keep a sharp lookout for the Hittite prince and his party."

Horemheb stared in silence at the map. "In the event they try an overland route and follow the Way of Horus, paralleling the coast, I want the entire route patrolled from Palestine to Silé." The general looked up at the men, his eyes fixed and bright. "Any questions?"

"Yes, sir. There is, if I may say, another possibility." The officer was a commander of chariotry with arms as big around as a ship's mast. "What if they should sail down the Red Sea and take the old gold mine route east across the desert?"

Horemheb shook his head. "The route is too arduous. By the time they reached the Gulf of Suez they would be roasted alive, their water supply exhausted."

"Still, sir, we must admit to the possibility," the chariot commander insisted.

Horemheb shrugged his shoulders. "Very well then. You may draw off enough men from the militia at Thebes to ring the city, and inquire of everyone entering from off the Eastern Desert. Divide up your responsibilities, gentlemen, and make your own dispositions."

Simut was pleased with the plans laid out by Horemheb. But he felt nervous. Something wasn't quite right.

Mutnedjmet smiled broadly at the general, and would not even glance in his direction.

Horemheb stood up and cleared his throat, and then broke into a broad smile. "If I may put to words what must be obvious to all of you, Egypt without a Horus god to lead us is like a rudderless ship sailing in the night." The general paused and then turned to Ay. "My lord vizier and regent, divine father and former commander of chariotry, your succession will be just and lawful."

Horemheb clapped and was soon joined by everyone present. Simut clapped enthusiastically. If everything went according to plan, Ay would one day be his father-in-law, and he would succeed as the Horus god on Earth.

No sooner had Horemheb finished when Ay rose and asked the servants, standing at a distance, to bring goblets and ewers of wine.

"Good soldiers of Egypt," Ay began, "I am pleased to take this occasion to announce the betrothal of my beloved daughter, Mutnedjmet, to General Horemheb."

The thundering applause beat into Simut's soul. His mouth went dry, and he felt weak. Had he misunderstood what Ay had announced, or was he locked in a bad dream? A cold sweat formed on his brow. Confused, he looked across the room at Mutnedjmet. She was now standing, her face creased with a smile that seemed to stretch from ear to ear. They were toasting her.

Simut force the goblet to his lips. The wine tasted bitter. The smile on Mutnedjmet's face kindled flames of anguish. How could she smile and be so indifferent to his feelings? He bellowed silent insults: Slut! Bitch! How could you do this? Oh, godless bitch!

He waited for his first opportunity to leave the villa, mindless of the surrounding laughter. Outside the villa gates, he declined a sedan chair and decided to walk home, all the while mumbling over and over again to himself, "And for this I have killed a king."

28

Menkhara and his party reached the Port of Quseir in the late afternoon. Within minutes after securing the mooring lines, the party abandoned their ship without looking back. The horses and donkeys, sensing they would soon be back upon land, shuddered, whinnied and brayed as they were led down the gangplank.

They made immediately for the town's only inn. Menkhara,

Hania and Critias agreed that a good night's sleep in a real bed would pay off the following day.

After the horses and donkeys were attended to in the adjacent stable, the Egyptians and Hittites dined together in the inn's common room. There was no distinction of rank. Zidanza ate and drank alongside the charioteers.

The sun fell behind the hills, and by the time the stars began to shine above them, every man of the party made for his assigned bed.

With the coming of dawn, the hills softened behind a pinkish mist. Menkhara and Critias purchased provisions and water for the long journey to the Nile Valley.

While the caravan was forming up, Menkhara walked over to Zidanza's cart to inquire of the prince's health. He smiled up at the prince, who sat with his legs stretched out on top of a wooden chest, the top padded with folds of linen for comfort. He glanced at the cart behind the prince. Hania was still asleep beneath a light linen spread.

Menkhara felt guilty that he had not given much thought to the prince during the long journey. The young man in his charge was to become the queen's husband, and quite possibly Pharaoh. But despite the high-sounding titles, his only thought was to bring the journey to a successful conclusion and get everyone safely through it.

"How goes it, my lord?" said Menkhara.

Zidanza returned the smile. "Well enough. How much longer do you suppose before we reach the palace?"

Menkhara stared out across the bleak hills. "Eight days, I'd say. That is, if our maps our good."

"I've heard Egypt is best reached by sailing down the Phoenician coast to Tanis. Why sail down this sea and across such wretched country?"

Menkhara smiled to himself. He had not discussed their route home with Zidanza's father. The king would have immediately sensed danger to his son if he knew the planned route back to Thebes.

"As your highness knows," Menkhara began, "whenever a sovereign ascends the throne of any land, danger is always close at hand. This route was purely precautionary."

Zidanza seemed satisfied with the answer. "Very good," he said, staring mindlessly at the distant hills. "Let's be off then."

Leaving the limestone plateau, they threaded their way through passages of primary rock that rose up on both sides to heights of two thousand meters. Occasionally they came upon green places with concealed springs, and rested long enough to fill their water pots.

Everyone suffered from the unaccustomed high humidity. Sweat rained from their brows and chests, and the dampening effect slowed their pace to a crawl. But more importantly, they were drinking water at an alarming rate, with no assurance they would find another spring.

The descent out of the heights was gradual, but soon they were on a pebble-strewn wadi. The air was drier now, but the heat was as stifling as ever. The water supply grew dangerously low, and Critias put himself in charge of rationing.

Less than four hours of march from Gebtu, Menkhara halted the caravan and ordered a more southwesterly route which took them out of the Wadi Hammamat and onto the desert. To bolster morale, he announced that they were only a day from their destination, a town on the Nile called Madu, a bare hour of march from Thebes.

For the first time, Menkhara laid out Kenofer's plan to the Hittites. Critias translated as he spoke. "Tonight we shall spend the night at a villa at Madu, where they will receive us as honored guests. Our bodies will be cooled in baths and soothed in oils and unguents. We will rest one night and a day before leaving for Thebes."

At this news a loud cheer went up from the men, and Zidanza waved his frail arms in the air. Menkhara pointed southwest. The Hittites snapped their reins and the caravan lurched forward.

*

Bodies parched and wasted from days on the Eastern Desert, the prince's party reached the lush valley of the Nile near Madu, the city of the falcon-headed god. Kenofer had arranged for them to stay at the villa of an old friend who was not in residence when the chariots and carts arrived at the villa's front gates. Servants, anticipating their arrival, were waiting.

Following their arrival at the villa, each man was pampered with the luxury of a bath, clean clothes and as much cool sweet beer as he could drink. Their bruised, desert-scorched bodies, soothed and massaged with expensive unguents, craved the greatest of all pleasures, a deep unmolested sleep.

The villa fell silent as each man was led off to bed. It was not until late afternoon of the following day that they began to awake, all of them ravenously hungry.

29

The following evening the banquet hall was ablaze with wall sconces. The prince and his guardian charioteers felt triumphant. In four weeks they had braved the Taurus Mountains, driven across the plains of Aleppo and the long arduous Way of Horus to Silé, endured the hot, foul weather of the Red Sea and its coastal range, and finished with a long drive across the Eastern Desert.

This was a special triumph for the charioteers, for among them was the young Zidanza, his presence sure to guarantee a recording of the epic journey in the archives of his Anatolian kingdom.

The prince's color had returned. He allowed his men to honor him with toasts. When they finished, they called upon their prince to speak to them.

The banquet hall fell silent as the frail young prince who would be Pharaoh rose to his feet and made eye contact with each man, his goblet thrust forward from an outstretched hand.

It wasn't the wine. Menkhara had very little to drink. He put down his goblet and cocked his ear. Something sounded like the muffled rhythmic scraping of sandals.

He waited, his eyes on the smiling face of the Hittite prince, leaning forward with his goblet.

At the sound of a faint cry, several charioteers looked around. Menkhara glanced at Critias, whose dark eyes held his. Something was definitely amiss.

The prince had not yet spoken. He looked radiant, happy in his new country.

A piercing cry, and a clatter of weapons.

Menkhara turned.

Shadows rushed ghost-like from behind the papyrus columns, metamorphosed to men, warriors, their swords and javelins tipped in the flickering orange light of the torches.

Fear struck with such stunning force that Menkhara remained in his chair, wondering if he was living through a dream.

A ripping sound tore past, close to Menkhara's ear. He looked back to the head of the table. An arrow caught the prince square in the eye of his still smiling face. He stood at the table's edge, caught in a laugh. His body fell forward across the table. A bronze arrowhead poked through his skull.

Prince Zidanza was dead before his head hit the surface of the table with a dull thud.

The assassins descended on the banquet without warning. Hardly a sword was drawn against them before they reached their bewildered victims.

Three Hittite charioteers were run through with javelins and swords even as they raised their wine goblets to their lips. Others managed a horrified glimpse only seconds before the point of a sword plunged into them.

In the space of a few heartbeats, veteran fighters not yet drunk with wine, lay entangled in food and the severed body parts of their companions. The floor of the banquet hall was slick with the slaughter.

Hania sat with his back to the Hittites. A sword had cut into his windpipe. He fell back clutching his throat with bloody hands.

Only Menkhara, Critias and two Hittite charioteers got to their feet in time to defend themselves. The four men hit back and dropped their opponents, only to face another. Nearly surrounded by a ring of swords they fought on, retreating slowly backward to the protective wall.

Not even the Hittite swords and their superior fighting skills could throw back the horde of attackers. Where one assassin fell or lost his sword, another was only too eager to take his place.

The point of a sword ripped into a charioteer's arm. Critias bled from his shoulder. Menkhara was having no better luck. The point of a sword slashed his chest.

Critias, gasping for breath, cried out: "For God's sake, Menkhara, run for it. You must get to the queen!"

Menkhara hesitated. Leaving his comrades was unthinkable.

Critias motioned to a space separating the banquet room from a hall. "You know where your duty lies, Menkhara. Go, man! Go!"

Critias was right. Menkhara's survival was critical to Ankhesenamun. Reluctantly, heart racing with anguish, he turned and ran down the hall, the scraping of sandaled feet behind him. The hall led out into a forecourt. He ran across it, down a series of steps to an alabaster railing separating the court from a plunging terraced lawn.

Menkhara did not have time to think. He jumped over the rail, falling into the darkness, falling, he thought, to his death. He rolled partway down the terrace. He lay still for a moment, picked himself up, and, lurching crazily forward, darted into a garden.

A stand of date palms marked the end of the lush villa grounds and the beginning of the desert. Behind him came the cries of his pursuers.

A commander barked an order, and then an eerie pause in the shouting. Menkhara's wound began to sting.

Beneath the pale starlight and what light there was from the interior of the villa, he made out a familiar voice. He crept closer in. Horemheb's deputy commander spoke rapidly to some of his officers. "We've accomplished our mission. The Hittite prince is dead. What's the point of tracking down one soldier more or less. Let's get out of here."

The remaining soldiers came out of the banquet hall. It was obvious why they were late in joining the ranks. Some carried ewers of wine taken from the banquet table, and others carried trophies stripped from the Hittites.

The last man out held something in his clenched hand.

The head of Prince Zidanza.

He held it by the hair, allowing the pale grizzly thing to swing at his side.

The soldiers slowly drew up in double file. A sharp command, and they tramped away.

Menkhara was alone in the stillness, breathing heavily. He waited a bit longer, and then walked back to the courtyard.

The villa was deserted. His heart beating triple time, he entered the dining hall. The carnage at the banquet made him nauseous. The prince's beheaded torso lay sprawled across the table top in a pool of blood. He paused to turn away and rest against a wall. Death was everywhere, but most of all he felt it in the utter silence. Nothing stirred.

He walked the length of the room, gazing at his fallen comrades. In death, their eyes were wide open, caught in what was to be a deserved celebration, reposing almost child-like in their own blood.

Poor brave men, Menkhara cried to himself. This was no way for a soldier to die, butchered, without a weapon in hand, far from their Anatolian plateau, their families and their storm-god.

He turned to walk back up the other side of the table, the sandstone floor under his feet slick with blood.

"Critias!" Menkhara cried out. The scribe lay on his side, his right hand still grasping the hilt of his sword. His lips were drawn tight in a resolute act of defiance. He was alive.

At that moment three servants who had hidden themselves during the onslaught, timidly poked their heads into the banquet hall. One of them called to Menkhara.

Menkhara motioned them to Critias's side. Breathing heavily, he said, "It's not a mortal wound. Carry him to his chamber and tend to it.

A moan from somewhere in the room. The servants found two charioteers still alive. One of the Hittites was well enough to stand. An attendant guided him out of the banquet hall.

Menkhara returned to his chamber and was soon joined by a servant. He was helped out of his blood-soaked Hittite gown. The slashing wound across his chest was not deep. The servant cleaned, covered and bound it with strips of linen. Helped into a fresh tunic, he spotted a mirror on a cosmetic table and picked it up.

He scarcely recognized himself in his black beard. The beard made him feel unclean and foreign. He didn't like the feeling, and a disguise was no longer necessary. He wanted it off. He picked up a razor from the cosmetic table.

Later, Menkhara went to the chamber where Critias had been taken and found his friend conscious. "When you left the banquet hall, most of them broke off the attack and chased you," Critias said with a weak smile.

"You're in good hands," Menkhara answered. "You're going to be all right."

"The others?"

Prince Zidanza, Hania, and most of the charioteers are dead. Two are alive, and they will make it."

"You've got to get back to Malkata," Critias insisted.

Menkhara placed a purse of gold rings in Critias's hand. "The prince won't be needing this. It will get you and our Hittite friends down river to Amarna, and to wherever you want to go, with money to spare. Here is the queen's signet ring, in case there is any doubt about your loyalty to her. The priests of Amarna revere our queen, and they will give you and the charioteers shelter.

"Thanks," Critias whispered. "There's no place for me in Egypt, at least for now. I won't remain long in Amarna."

"Where will you go?"

"Greece."

Menkhara clasped his friend's hand. "I pray to God we meet again, Critias."

Menkhara found the chamber where the servants had brought the Hittites. Satisfied that they were being cared for, he left the villa.

He walked past the open gates, pausing momentarily to take in a deep breath of the night air, thinking how good it was to be alive.

It was less than one hour of march to Thebes, and he would walk all the way. He desperately needed time to think. Prince Zidanza was dead, and the mission a failure. All this he would have to tell the queen.

He ambled slowly down a dirt path beneath a canopy of brilliant stars, thinking all the while that the worst was yet to come.

30

The seventy-day ritual preparing the mummy of Tutankhamun had come and gone. Pharaoh's body was finally brought back to the palace, where it lay on a great gilt animal-shaped bed in the forecourt, watched over by the household guard.

In the early morning hours of the day of the funeral, Menkhara entered Thebes.

He walked down a dirt path at the city's outskirts. The sun was warm on his back, and from behind the tall amber reeds of the lagoon came the insistent quacking of ducks.

In the first bare hint of an unusual day, women outside their huts made bouquets for the funeral. A cart piled high with them was ready for transport to the quay for shipment over to the west bank.

The babble of humankind increased as he approached the city's quay. The Nile was crowded with ferries and lighters, and Menkhara had to wait an hour before paying an inflated fare to a private ferry owner for the privilege of being transported to the West Bank. Across the river, the ship traffic in the canals was so heavy that Menkhara left the ferry and walked across the flood plain to the palace at Malkata.

Leta helped Ankhesenamun into a simple mourning tunic of bluish-white linen. The queen tied the sash and sat down in front of her cosmetic box staring into her bronze mirror. She looked older than her twenty-four years. She applied bright red ochre to her lips. Mourning women were not supposed to wear makeup, especially the widow of a dead Pharaoh, but she put it on in generous layers, more in defiance of custom than as any sign of disrespect.

She had been in official mourning for more than two months, waiting for the priests of Anubis to prepare her husband for life everlasting. Now that it was nearly over, she felt a sense of guilty relief.

If only Menkhara would come with news from Hatti. Did King Suppiluliumas give his consent and send a son for her to wed? Was her prince with Menkhara? She hated the prospect of sharing the throne as Grandfather's wife and queen. The thought of it filled her with dread and added to her anticipation of news.

"My lady," said Leta.

Ankhesenamun looked up at her handmaiden as though she were staring through a dream. "Yes."

"He's come, my lady! He has come!"

"My grandfather?"

"Menkhara! He is waiting in the oblation room."

Ankhesenamun's heart beat with excitement. "I will greet him in the throne room."

Her dear Menkhara would be surprised by the formality of the setting. She rarely used the throne. She could scarcely understand her own motives. It had something to do with the royal personage she stood for, the symbol of the long line of kings out of which she descended, the seat of power she would not easily surrender. Whatever news Menkhara brought, she would receive it as a queen upon her golden throne.

Menkhara entered the throne room unescorted. The handsome Lieutenant of Infantry, whom she had put so much faith in, looked frail, almost haggard, his cheeks hollowed.

He bowed. "My lady."

Ankhesenamun sensed bad news. "The king of the Hittites has refused me?" she said, expecting him to nod in agreement.

"No, my lady. He acceded to your request and sent his youngest son, Prince Zidanza"

"But where—?"

"Forgive me. The prince is dead. Assassinated. We came out of the Eastern Desert last night. We stopped at a villa in Madu. A party of Horemheb's soldiers ambushed us. All were killed except Critias, myself and two Hittite charioteers."

The queen steadied herself against an offering table. "Oh, dear God of my father," she cried. "Here in Egypt he was slain? His father will surely avenge his death." She paused, placed a hand to the side of her lowered face, and then continued, barely above a whisper. "Suppiluliumas, dread king, he will send his divisions, his battle chariots against us. Those who did the vile deed must answer for this."

Menkhara's voice was ragged with sorrow and exhaustion. "I wish to all the gods that I had good news for you. It would have been an act of mercy had I been felled by the assassins." His face grew hard, his voice stronger. "I can tell you that all this was the work of Horemheb. I saw his men after my comrades were slain."

Ankhesenamun turned pale. She fell against the sloping back of the throne with its inlaid scene of the queen anointing young Tutankhamun. Menkhara rushed to her. She allowed herself to be carried to the lion couch near an oblation altar. Then he knelt beside her.

"Shall I call for your handmaiden?" said Menkhara.

Ankhesenamun shook her head negatively. She sat up. "When will I ever stop underestimating the ambition of men in search of a throne, Menkhara?"

He took her hand and rubbed it. "When you stop being good."

"Grandfather already wears Pharaoh's blue khepresh, the war crown. His image as Pharaoh is drawn upon the walls of my husband's tomb, though I, his queen, am nowhere to be seen. He is but one step away from becoming one with the Horus god. He's saving that for our marriage which is to take place tomorrow."

She paused and looked directly at Menkhara, her voice more resolute. "The viceroy of Kush, Huy, was Tutare's dearest friend. He is here in Thebes for the funeral. I'll speak to him today."

"My lady. There is something else. Forgive me for mentioning it. You have cares enough."

Ankhesenamun gave him a wan smile. "I know what is on your mind. You should have asked me straight out. Mayet has fully recovered from her wound. I've sent her to the valley to look after my baldachin at the tomb ceremonial site."

"Thank the gods."

Ankhesenamun took Menkhara's hand. "I have something for you," she said. She slipped out of the room and returned moments later holding a golden collar in her hand. She reached up and put it around Menkhara's neck. "I give you this shebu collar of honor. It signifies to the world that you are a lord of the court. It will gain you admittance anywhere."

Her hands were around Menkhara's neck. She drew his face down to hers and kissed him on the lips. Then she let go. "If all else fails me," she continued, "I will return to Memphis to assemble the disaffected divisions of Ptah and troops loyal to the memory of my father. In the meantime, you must have the means of finding a new life with Mayet if things go awry."

Gathering her strength, she waved aside Menkhara's helping

hand and went over to a low table, picked up a cotton purse tied with a white cord and handed it to him. "It contains several hundred seniu of gold. You must have it."

"My lady!"

"Do not argue with me, Menkhara. It will do you absolutely no good."

He took hold of the purse. "Thank you," he said softly.

"Stay close at hand. It comforts me knowing you're near."

"Trust that I will."

"Now I must get myself ready."

31

Menkhara sat in the shade of a weeping willow on the palace grounds and waited for the official party to leave with Tutankhamun's mummy. Many people gathered in the palace forecourts, ready to follow the funeral bier to the Valley of the Kings.

Finally, the mummy was lifted onto a boat-shaped bier and set upon a sled harnessed to red oxen, the symbolic color of Lower Egypt. Behind the sled, a procession formed, consisting, as was the custom, of nine friends of the king, followed by officials and solemn priests with their pommelled canes.

Menkhara watched from the shade of a tree as the women in their mourning dresses and headbands formed behind the priests. Then the queen was led to the front of the procession. Menkhara watched as Ankhesenamun took her place. She seemed unsteady, her face expressionless and pale.

The procession swayed forward. Palanquins, plaustrums and carriages for the rich bobbed like vessels in the sea of humanity, moving no faster than the ordinary citizen on foot.

Menkhara watched until his view was blocked by the frenetic

antics of ritual dancers in their short loincloths and tall reed headdresses. The procession passed through the palace gates, heading north to the valley. Menkhara trailed along behind. Toward dusk, Tutankhamun's mummy was removed from its bier and set standing at the tomb entrance on white strewn sand. Ay came forward, wearing the blue khepresh crown. He poured libation water over the mummy's death mask, and crowned the shrouded head with a garland of olive-leaves, blue petals and cornflowers.

Finally, the most important act of all. Ay touched the mummy's mouth with an adze. Menkhara could not hear the words spoken by Ay, but he had ritually opened Tutankhamun's mouth and eyes with the instrument of Anubis, just as Horus opened the mouth of Osiris. Then Ay cried out in a quavering voice: "You shall remain in your sweet youth, always young. You live forever."

Tutankhamun, ready for immortality, was at last one with Osiris. His body was lifted up and carried down the thirteen steps to the waiting tomb.

Menkhara had watched Ay perform the ritual restoring life to the heart and limbs of the dead Pharaoh, thinking of Ankhesenamun's veiled accusation that but for Ay, the young Pharaoh would be alive.

He searched for Mayet, working his way through the crowd until he reached the rope barrier separating ordinary people from the special guests. When the guards saw the shebu collar of honor lying across his chest, he was immediately admitted to the gathering of the select few.

Night had fallen and torches lit a huge tent erected for the funeral banquet. The cries of the mourners were finally silenced as the guests adorned themselves with floral collars of willow leaves, cornflowers, blue lotus and slices of mandrake.

With the smell of roast oxen, lamb, and wild duck in the air, Menkhara continued looking for Mayet. He wondered if she had gone back to the palace.

Something touched his arm.

"Mayet!" he cried out.

He stretched his arm around her waist and raised her off the ground with a cry of delight, then set her gently down, still holding her close. By the light of the flickering torches, he studied her sparkling eyes and her pretty, innocent face; and then, remembering all that was dear to the memory of their youth, he kissed her, and his head was so filled with a new promise that he wanted to cry out to her, a promise that he would vow never to break.

The sudden reunion was too much for Mayet and she wept. Menkhara drew her close, her sobbing muffled against his chest. He waited for her to calm down, and then he thought of Ankhesenamun. On her husband's day of entombment, the unfortunate woman had to worry about an unwanted marriage.

Menkhara took Mayet by the hand and guided her out of the banquet tent. "We must find the queen," he said.

"She's not here."

"Of course she is. I saw her in the procession."

"Then she has since left. I've looked everywhere."

"She could be anywhere. Perhaps she is in the tomb tending to things."

"I inquired. She's not there. I only know that before leaving the palace she met with the viceroy of Kush. The meeting could not have gone well. According to a handmaiden, when the viceroy left she was crying."

Menkhara shook his head. "The viceroy was Tutankhamun's friend. She was counting on military support from him. Apparently he didn't give her any encouragement."

"And tomorrow she must wed Ay, though she swore on her life never to enter into such a union."

Menkhara gave Mayet a tender smile. "You've become friends."

"I owe her my life, and now I fear for hers. Oh, Menkhara, we must find her."

Menkhara's eyed narrowed. "Yes, even as we talk!" He clasped Mayet's hand. "Back to Malkata."

They hurried down a winding dirt path, dodging people as they went, turned off the trail and took a shortcut, picking their way over the treacherous, rock-strewn floor of the valley, grateful for the soft moonlight flooding down on them.

⁂

Queen Ankhesenamun had complained of illness after the funeral procession. She told the high priest Inmutef that she wanted to rest in a cool bath for a while before returning for the funeral banquet. But it wasn't a physical illness that had caused her to return to Malkata. She sat at her cosmetic table and stared mournfully at a polished bronze mirror, staring as though she were a stranger to herself.

"You have failed," she said to her reflection. "You cannot fight them." She set down the mirror and thought: Now is the time to die and hope for the promised life in the sweet fields of Yaru. I am a queen. When they find my body, surely they will have to prepare it for the afterlife.

She had an urge to write to Menkhara. He would understand. She walked to her writing table. Her ink palette and reed brushes sat on top, but there were no spare strips of papyrus. Impatient, she stood up and turned over a chest, hoping to find a sheaf of papyri. The chest contained clothing and jewelry, and nothing else.

"I am the queen of everything except a scrap of papyrus," she cried out.

She went to her bed and lay down. "I will never see Menkhara again," she said aloud. "Oh please, dear God of my father, let me see my Menkhara again." But then another voice whispered in her ear. *He is no longer yours, my lady. You gave him to Mayet.* The queen nodded. "Perhaps she was always his. The gods must believe this, most certainly."

She called for her handmaidens, Auti and Leta.

"I will be going to the Gempaaten," she told them. "Have a sedan chair ready and waiting."

"East Karnak, lady?"

"Yes."

"Are you all right, lady?" Leta asked.

"Yes." Ankhesenamun wanted to cry. She had so often confided in Leta and Auti. They had shared so much over the years. She was hoping that they would stay and talk, without being commanded to do so.

I have failed, but at what? she thought. She was stuck in Thebes because of her husband's funeral, and every day the priests at Karnak and their insufferable pantheon of gods assumed their old role as the center of Egyptian religion. One day the Aten would be all but forgotten, and her father's holy city of the Aten in Amarna would be sacked and burned to the ground.

Thoughts of escape came to her unbidden. She could fly to some far-off land such as Punt, or some place across the Green Sea, and there live out her days married to a peasant farmer, growing wheat and being happy for it. She thought of these places while at the same time she smoothed out her simple funeral gown. They expect me at my husband's funeral, she thought with a sad smile. Instead, I go to my own.

She was warmed by the thought of the old temple of the Aten built by her father in his youth, when Amarna was no more than a dream. The old temple of the Aten, overrun with camel-thorn, its interior ransacked for precious stone, deserted, wind whistling through its open court and humming in the roofed colonnade of square piers.

"Yes," she thought, "there I must go."

32

Simut felt like a fool. He had presided over the funeral of the king he had murdered, and his payment for regicide was humiliation. He had expected the hand of Mutnedjmet, and believed he himself would one day ascend the Horus throne. That was not to be. Mutnedjmet had betrayed him. No doubt she had had no intention of marrying him, but merely led him on. If he could have gotten out of joining the funeral entourage, he would have done so.

The procession made him sick with guilt. He did not want to face the royal mourners, especially Mutnedjmet. She would undoubtedly find some sort of ironic humor in the whole thing, and he would have to take it in silence.

To make matters worse, Queen Ankhesenamun had left the valley after the funeral rituals, complaining of exhaustion. She had told the high priest Inmutef that she would return in time for the banquet. It was already sunset, and she was nowhere to be seen. Ay blamed him.

"I've sent a squad of soldiers to the palace," Simut had volunteered, nervously gauging Ay's reaction to each word. "If she's there, she'll be brought back."

"You damned fool," Ay had answered with a scowl. "No one lays hands on a solar queen! She is to remain under guard, untouched, until I pass through the last phase of enthronement and receive my five titles and the aura of Amun. Then we shall be at once united in marriage."

"Yes, of course, my lord," Simut had replied.

He remembered Ay's warning finger pointed at him. "Find the queen!"

Simut's heart was in his mouth when he looked at Ay's craggy face and those glaring dark eyes of his. It was the face of the man who would soon be transformed into the new Horus god on Earth, Pharaoh. If he hoped for a better life at court, he would have to put his own misfortune behind him and find Ankhesenamun.

Nauseous with fear, Simut summoned his sedan chair. He had no sooner climbed in than someone called out, "Holiness!"

It was Tarina, and she had that familiar look on her face.

"You have something to tell me?" Simut said with an air of impatience.

"You asked me to keep an eye on our queen, and report everything to you."

"Yes."

"Well, I can tell you that she has no intention of returning to the banquet."

Simut's mouth fell open. "What's this?"

"She left the palace and went straight for that old temple east of Karnak."

"The Gempaaten?"

"If that's what they call it."

"She's still there?" Simut asked in a demanding voice.

"She said goodbye to her favorite handmaidens, Leta and Auti, and asked them not to follow her. She said she was going to a better place. Auti told me this, and then she began to cry."

"Thank you, precious Tarina," Simut said, sitting erect in the sedan chair.

Simut's mind raced as the carriers trotted over the rocky narrow trail slicing through the barren hot terrain of the valley. First he would stop off at Karnak long enough to assemble a company of temple guards, and then off to the temple of the Aten.

This was a chance to redeem his honor. His personal safety no longer mattered to him. He was tired of being played for a fool. His father had been murdered in the oblation room of his own temple, on orders of Queen Ankhesenamun's father. Perhaps Ay was in on the murder too. And where was the queen on this solemn day of her husband's funeral? Praying to her damned Aten!

He thought again of Mutnedjmet and her betrayal.

An imperfect idea began to form in Simut's mind. He had wanted Ankhesenamun dead from the very beginning. He had no use for the daughter of his father's assassin. Now he had the opportunity to avenge not only his father, but also himself for the belittling humiliation he had endured. He would strike a blow for Amun-Ra and all the gods of Egypt. He would kill the daughter of Akhenaten.

33

Menkhara and Mayet raced across the palace forecourt and through the spacious corridor to the main ramp that led up to the royal apartment. The audience room was deserted. They checked the oblation room. No Ankhesenamun! Reluctant to enter the queen's chamber uninvited, they called her name.

Menkhara and Mayet raced to the queen's apartments and found them empty.

Mayet's brow furrowed with an idea. "The Temple of the Aten."

"Why?"

"I was told that when she was depressed she found solitude in her father's temple, the Gempaaten. It's across the river, east of Karnak."

They left the royal residence and ran down the long ramp to the large entrance hall. A detachment of household guards, twenty-five men in all, passed through the papyrus columns of the front portal. They were led by an easily recognizable figure, the household guard commander, Siptah.

"The queen is nowhere to be found," Menkhara cried out. "We think she's at the temple of the Aten."

Siptah, followed by his men, joined Menkhara and Mayet as they hurried to the ferry bobbing on its mooring lines at the Lake Tiye docks.

The ferry captain sat at the stern, drinking beer from a pewter jar.

"Do you know the whereabouts of the queen?" Menkhara asked the captain. "She's not at the funeral and doesn't appear to be in residence."

The captain was half drunk and slurred his words. "Yes I do. But I dare not say since the queen herself put me under a cloak of secrecy."

"Did you take her to the East Bank?"

"Well, lad, you mustn't put my loyalty to the test."

"I'll put this sword to the test, you old bastard," Siptah shouted, drawing his weapon. "Where's the queen?"

The captain's hand shook so much, he lost nearly half of his beer. "The Gempaaten!" he cried out. "They didn't ask me to stay. The queen said I would be fed to the desert jackal if I breathed a word."

"What do you mean by they? Someone was with her?"

"A priest."

"Take us there at once," said Siptah. He ordered his men onto the ferry. They jogged two abreast up the gangplank.

The captain rubbed his neck. "I've sent my crew to the funeral. I'll need a hand."

"My men are at your disposal," Siptah shot back.

Moments later they were underway. Siptah operated the tiller. The captain stood at the prow barking orders. The canal workers, always ready to give preference to a royal barge or ferry, seized hold of the boat's lines. The ferry glided down the ship's canal toward the river.

Akhenaten's temple of the Aten, an abandoned complex of buildings known as the Gempaaten, dominated the eastern edge of the precinct of Karnak.

The ferry docked on the East Bank and Menkhara, Mayet, Siptah and his guards raced down the quay to the temple. They jogged down colonnades, across chambers, through small chapels and receiving rooms, their sandals slapping rhythmically against the sandstone floors.

They reached the inner temple, stopped short outside, and peered in. The huge room's open ceiling allowed sunlight to pour down upon the hundreds of offering tables and the long ramp and balustrade that led to the canopied altar. Behind the altar was a slab of granite with the disc of the sun and the arm-like rays chiseled in bas-relief upon it. The rays of the sun were capped with tiny hands. A colossal statue of Akhenaten dominated the temple.

Ankhesenamun stood at the altar, her arms raised in supplication to the Aten. The flickering torchlight liquefied her translucent gown, causing it to shimmer.

Menkhara stood watching. She looked fully recovered and as strong as ever, her face bright with life. He had never seen her looking so beautiful, her features finely chiseled, everything about her so mature, wise and divine.

And then he saw the fine scarlet stream flowing from her wrists.

"Ankhesenamun!" he cried out.

⁂

Ankhesenamun smiled at her friends and at the young men near the pylon entrance to the temple. They were clad in their white kilts, red sashes of the household guard across their chests. She was at peace with herself and wanted them to know it. She slowly lowered her arms.

She opened her mouth to speak just as a glaze of cloud drifted into the temple, filling it with its soft whiteness. She tried to see through it, but there were only shadows, except for momentary breaks, revealing familiar grieving faces.

Queen Ankhesenamun wanted to tell them that everything was going to be all right, but she could not speak. With one last effort, she forced words to her lips. "I am leaving you, dear friends. Remember me as you knew me once; by my true name, my father's child, Ankhesenpaaten."

She heard a plaintive cry muffled in the gloom. She moved in the direction of her father's colossus, arms outstretched, down a ramp that would guide her to him. She wanted to be with her father, the child of the Aten and the source of her light. She knew where it was, if only she could …

The clouds, white as the purest cotton, enveloped her now, and from somewhere grains of sand driven on a whistling wind bit into her skin. The wind sang in her ears. She imagined other people assaulted by the desert wind and wanted to stay their fears, but could not summon up the energy to speak. She felt her body floating down through the mist, heard the soft cry of many voices, and then the gentle feel of arms taking her by the waist. The wind had stopped and she felt a joyous languor. Her breathing seemed to end in the middle of a long sigh. Above her, waxing and waning in the white mist, the calcite stone majesty of her father, Akhenaten.

And a long golden shaft of dazzling light before the dark.

⁂

Menkhara had sensed early on that the queen was not herself, that something had seized upon her heart and soul. His worst fears had been confirmed when he saw the thin stripe of blood coiled around her forearms and flowing away from her feet.

Menkhara raced forward, jumped from the floor to the midpoint of the ramp, encircling Ankhesenamun before she fell. He scooped her up in his arms, as light as a feather, carried her down the ramp and gently laid her at the feet of Akhenaten's statue.

Menkhara stared down at the queen. Her face was aglow with a youthful exuberance. She looked asleep. For Menkhara it was as though the queen drifted out of life and into a different state not even death could claim. He felt an awful hatred for Ay, for Horemheb, and ashamed for his own sex; all of this as the soul of his queen oscillated between light and darkness.

Mayet ran to Menkhara's side. She reached down and took Ankhesenamun's hand, and then filled the temple with her melancholy crying.

Siptah knelt next to the body. He examined her slashed wrists, listened for a pulse, and, shaking his head, placed his hand over her brow drawing the palm gently down over her eyes, leaving her face in a sweet repose.

The household guard formed a protective ring around the silent scene.

A priest in a clean white gown shuffled over to where the queen lay. "I could do nothing to dissuade her. From whom shall I beg forgiveness? Our faithful daughter of the Aten is dead. I could not stop her."

"Who are you, old man?" Menkhara said, rising to his feet.

"I'm Anias, son of Pawah, high priest from the temple of the Aten at Amarna. The queen invited me to Thebes, and on this day asked me to accompany her here. I had no idea she—"

"And there was no one else?"

"No one."

Menkhara stared down at Ankhesenamun. Mayet crouched by the body, holding the queen's head protectively in her arms.

Menkhara looked over at Siptah. "The queen's handmaidens will tell everyone. By now Ay and Horemheb know. Suicide did not figure in their plans, Siptah. They are dangerous, ambitious men. Who's to say what they'll do now."

"I don't imagine they will come here."

"Indeed!" A familiar voice cried out.

Menkhara turned. Simut stood at the entrance, behind him a knot of Theban temple guards, swords drawn.

Simut swaggered over to where the queen lay. He lifted her hands, stared at the ragged wrist wounds, and then dropped them cruelly to the floor. To this he added the insulting gesture of stepping over her body, his sandaled foot brushing hard against Mayet's cheek. Menkhara heard him whisper, "Whore."

"We've come to claim the body of the queen," Simut announced with an arrogant smirk. "And as for you, Menkhara, son of Pawero, you're going to answer to your commanding officer, General Horemheb, as well as our new Horus god on Earth, Ay. I have a verbal warrant from the vizier to take you into custody."

"Which vizier?"

"Why, the vizier of the Upper Kingdom, the queen's own grandfather, our most beloved heir to the Horus throne."

"In which case, you can't take me into custody."

"How so?"

"Your authority derives from one who has usurped the Horus throne. A felon cannot do the work of the law."

"Old friend, you've just added another count of treason to a list long enough to take your head from your shoulders ten times over."

Menkhara flashed Simut a caustic smile and drew his sword. “Not by your hand, priest. Your fate was sealed when you insulted the body and person of our queen, and destroyed the lives of my parents.”

Suddenly the sound of sandals clapping in unison on the temple's tiled floor. Temple guards poured into the chamber.

Taking up the challenge, Siptah wheeled around, sword drawn. “Household guards!” he shouted. “Teach these men a lesson, lads. Up swords for our queen!”

Menkhara took his measure of Simut, the cruel triangular face, the beady black eyes. He guessed that Simut realized that death was at hand. The second high prophet of Amun-Ra hobbled backward on his clubfoot, his pale chubby face filled with panic and fear. It was too late.

Menkhara's Hittite sword hummed in a glittering arc that ended with a sickening thud.

Simut's head sailed through the air, a puffed-up orb that bounced off the opposite wall in a splash of scarlet. His headless body, hissing blood, teetered drunkenly in a dance of death before collapsing to the floor.

The household guards, outnumbered four to one, were chafing for a fight. They at once took advantage of the narrow entrance to the chamber. As Simut's men passed through the entrance, many were cut down before having had the chance to form up. By the time all of them entered the chamber they had lost twenty-five men. So great was the carnage, the soldiers, backing up, slipped on the blood-slick floor.

Siptah held his household guards back, allowing what was left of the temple guard to escape. He counted his dead. They had lost sixteen men, the other side five times that many.

Menkhara walked over to where Ankhesenamun lay, Mayet still at her side. Two guardsmen stood protectively over her.

Siptah came out of the shadows, his tunic stained with blood. "They will come back," he said, his eyes fixed on Menkhara. "They'll send a whole damned battalion this time."

Menkhara gazed down at Ankhesenamun's crumpled body. "We can't leave her here."

"We'll bury her in the desert. It's the best we can do."

"To be denied an afterlife, buried like a common thief, only to be dug up and eaten by the desert jackal? No, Siptah. She is our queen."

Siptah raised his hands in a gesture of frustration. "I've got to think of the living." He pointed to the remaining household guards at the opposite wall, some sitting from exhaustion, others barely able to stand at all. Their limbs, some bandaged, were covered in grime, sweat and congealed blood. "How much more can they give?" Siptah asked in a quivering voice.

"There is another way." The voice belonged to Anias, the high priest of the Aten. Mayet had pulled him down to her side during the fighting. The old man watched it all in a daze.

"Speak, priest, for God's sake! We are running out of time," said Siptah.

"It has always been the queen's wish that her body be returned to her beloved city of the Aten, there to be entombed with her father, mother and her four sisters."

Menkhara said, "All well and good, but it's several days down the Nile to Amarna. Her body would be corrupted before the funerary priests could do their work."

"There's a way," Anias answered assertively. "This temple has its seldom-used House of Vigor. Admittedly it has fallen into a state of disrepair. But I have seen it. The tools of the priests of Anubis are still in their cases. In a matter of hours, all things corruptible could be removed from the queen's body, and then it could be quickly cleaned with water, natron and palm oil. There would be no rituals or spells cast. All of that can wait. Her body could be hastily wrapped in temporary cloth and covered in dry natron. I've seen wooden coffins stacked in the chamber of the controller of mysteries."

Menkhara's face softened with relief. "You can do this?"

"In an hour's time, with help. Two hours at most."

"One hour," Menkhara insisted.

Anias answered with a reluctant sigh. "So be it."

Menkhara called for the nine remaining guardsmen to gather around him. "There's no place for any one of us here in Thebes. We're as good as condemned by Ay, Horemheb and their henchmen. Still we have the honorable task of delivering the body of our queen to the city of her father, Amarna. There, you'll find friends who love our queen. They'll show their gratitude and help you, and hide you from the long reach of those who want us dead. If any one of you desires to remain in Thebes, speak now." After a long silence, Menkhara smiled. "I thought not. Let's get on with the business at hand."

Four guardsmen eagerly came forward to bear the body of the queen to the temple's House of Vigor. Menkhara and Siptah left the temple, and in the Theban darkness headed toward the docks in search of a boat that would take their party downriver to Amarna.

34

Nothing comes easy, Menkhara thought as he peered out from behind a sailmaker's shop. He and Siptah had found a suitable vessel, and now it was only a question of boarding her undetected.

Up until now everything had gone well. Ankhesenamun lay nearby in her natron-filled coffin, with Menkhara's party nestled close by, eager to slip out of Thebes. It might have been a perfect night to steal a boat, but for one problem. Given the number of visitors to Tutankhamun's state funeral, there were more armed harbor guards to watch the ships than usual. Also, so many vessels were stacked together that navigating the narrow channel, a difficult task by day, would be nearly impossible at night.

"This will not be easy," Siptah said, staring out at the quay and the line of blazing torches placed every two hundred cubits. "The place is lit up like a banquet hall."

A smile spread across Menkhara's face. "Why not make the entire dockside as bright as day?"

Siptah's brow furrowed. "You mean wait until daylight?"

"Create a distraction, my friend. And what better distraction than a ship set ablaze at the other end of the quay. It would draw every guard in the dockyard." Menkhara pointed at the docks. "The ship we've decided upon could be boarded and rigged in no time at all."

Siptah thought for a while, looked back at the tattered remnants of his guards, at the old priest and Mayet, and then set his eyes on the vessel. "What have we to lose? I'll go."

"No! Leave this to me," Menkhara insisted. "Wait until there's a good blaze and the guards leave their stations. Then get everyone aboard. I'll race back." Menkhara paused, then added: "Wait for a count of one hundred after you're aboard. If I don't return, leave without me."

"But I—"

"Your word, Siptah!"

"I give it."

Menkhara crept back to Mayet. He whispered in her ear, "I love you." He took her face in his hands, kissed her, and then stole away before she could answer.

He returned to the back end of the sailmaker's shop. "The gods go with you," Siptah said, taking Menkhara's hand.

Menkhara ran a kilometer down a path before turning out towards the docks. Nile ships, lighters, barges, ferries and transports were pressed close together causing the hulls to grind against one another with the screeching sound of tortured animals.

The vessel Menkhara decided to set afire was a large sailing ship loaded with provisions and cargo. A torch blazed from its quay socket-stand at the stern of the vessel. A perfect choice. He looked both ways. A harbor guard one meter down the quay walked in the opposite direction. Menkhara made his move.

He seized the torch, pulled himself over the side of the prow and dropped onto the deck. Two sailors left to guard the vessel slept at their posts on deck, smelling of stale wine. Holding the torch low, Menkhara slipped past the sleeping men and made for the deck cabin at the stern. Outside the cabin were wooden chests containing food, linens and clothes. Much to his surprise, he found an amphora of sesame oil. He set down the torch inside the cabin and poured the oil across the deck and over every piece of cargo that seemed flammable.

He went back for the torch and touched it to the oil-slick deck. A line of fire raced toward the bow, widening as it went until flames covered the entire surface.

The guards woke up and struggled groggily to their feet. Menkhara drew his sword. Their kilts on fire, they screamed, and leapt into the water.

Menkhara used his sword to cut through the single mooring line. Helped by a good breeze, the ship drifted down the quay, its deck and mast a flaming inferno.

He jumped to the dock from the prow and sprinted back down the dirt path. Looking back, he saw that two other vessels lying alongside the burning ship had caught fire. The harbor guards shouted, their sandals slapping hard on the sandstone quay as they ran toward the doomed ship.

Menkhara breathed a sigh of relief. Siptah had gotten everyone of his party aboard the commandeered ship. He bounded up the gangplank just as the guardsmen were placing the coffin inside the cabin.

Despite the light variable breeze caused by the fire, he kept the sail furled out of fear that it would be set ablaze by the glowing embers floating through the air.

Without being told, the guards took their places on the eight rowers' seats while a guardsman untied the mooring line and jumped aboard. Siptah handled the rudder, and Menkhara stationed himself in the pilot's box at the prow.

Slowly, the vessel moved away from the docks. Menkhara called out instructions to Siptah to insure a safe navigation of the ship-gorged river. Many of the vessels were lashed to one another, and in turn tied to a vessel lucky enough to secure a dockside mooring line.

Ahead, they could not distinguish the ship originally set afire from the others now ablaze. The fire, aided by the breeze, spread down the docks and fanned out to ships, barges and lighters farther from the docks. The crackling sound of burning dried pine and Lebanese meruwood mingled with the cries of the aroused sentries and guards.

At one place along the docks, the fire had leaped across the quay and set a warehouse on fire. In the eerie glow, streams of curious Thebans poured down side streets toward the docks.

As the ship headed downstream, the acrid smell of smoke filled the air, causing everyone's eyes to tear up. The rapid spread of the fire amazed Menkhara and his party. It was as though an Anatolian forest were set afire and the flames, variously yellow, orange, and crimson, leaped up to the sky, sending squadrons of firebrands floating effortlessly in the dark.

Some of the blazing vessels now floated free, presenting a danger to Menkhara's pirated vessel.

"Steady! Steady!" Menkhara cried out to Siptah and the guardsmen at the oars. He picked out two vessels on fire, the flames muted behind a screen of dense smoke. One was dead ahead and the other to their port side. Navigating toward the docks was impossible. Somehow they would have to snake their way between the two vessels. Menkhara breathed in the smoke-filled air, searing his lungs. He gestured and cried out to Siptah, who in turn barked orders to the rowers. There was only a slim chance they could avoid a collision. Menkhara staked out an opening and called to the men at the oars. "Lay on hard, guardsmen." The vessel lurched forward.

The ship they had come upon was now slightly off their starboard side, blazing like a cauldron of fire. The oven-heat of it burned their skin.

The ship began to slip by on their starboard bow, its tall mast ablaze. The mast cracked at its base and fell in an awful blinding flash, swishing down violently near Menkhara's pilot box.

Finally they broke free, the burning ship behind them.

Menkhara turned to his crew and pointed northward. "Give it everything you've got, my friends," he cried out. "We've the open river ahead, and that way is the City of the Aten and freedom!"

As the ship glided forward, the air began to clear. Siptah waved his hand in a sweeping arc of triumph.

Menkhara looked back at Thebes. The entire dockside was on fire, and in several places it had skipped over the quay, the flames scouring the empty stalls of vendors, warehouses, ship repair shops and the harbormaster's quarters. Burning Thebes was the city of his birth. He felt guilty, but only a little. He turned away. Ahead lay the quiet of the countryside, the distant restful cry of oxen, the occasional cawing of a kingfisher and the sculpted beauty of a gray heron soaring beneath a canopy of bright stars.

35

They were six days out from Thebes. The commandeered ship bearing the body of Egypt's Queen Ankhesenamun, made good time running downriver with the current. North of the town of Zawty, the limestone cliffs plunged down close to the river and then receded to a semicircle, forming a bay.

The High Priest Anias joined Menkhara at the prow. "Here you and your crew will find a place to live if that is your choice. Each man will be given a new identity and a place of honor."

"Very kind of you, Anias," said Menkhara, staring respectfully at the aging priest from the pilot box. "I can't speak for the others, but no place in Egypt will be a safe haven for me. Anyone willing to shelter me would do so at his peril. I could not do that to you or the people of this lovely city."

"Where will you go?"

"I can't tell you that, for your own good. Torture has a way of loosening even a good man's tongue. It is best you don't know."

"And Mayet?"

"It's a decision she will have to make. But there's one favor I would ask of you."

"Name it," Anias answered with a smile.

"A fresh crew to take me north to Tanis."

"You'll have them, and I'll see to it this ship is furnished with fresh provisions." Anias fell silent and then said: "You'll stay for the queen's funeral?"

Menkhara shook his head. "Nothing would please me more, but I cannot. It'll take many days to prepare our queen for her tomb, and Amarna, being the city of her father's design and burial place, will be the first place they will look."

Anias nodded. "Ankhesenamun will not share her father's tomb here at Amarna. There's no telling what Horemheb and Ay might do to her tomb if it were discovered. They'll never find her, Menkhara."

❧

There were no officials waiting at the Amarna wharves when the ship bearing Ankhesenamun's body arrived. Dock hands treated the vessel like any other as they reached for the cast ropes and secured them to the berth.

Anias asked everyone to remain aboard ship while he informed the temple of their arrival. The old priest, waving away assistance, walked unsteadily down the gangplank, summoned a dockside sedan chair and was carried down the Royal Way, past the palace of Akhenaten which ran 1500 meters along the length of the quay.

In a short time Anias returned at the head of a column of priests of the Aten. They were followed by a crowd of townspeople, their numbers swelling as they approached the quay.

Menkhara stared at the priests and townspeople. Anias must have told them their dead queen was aboard. A plaintive wailing seemed to flow out of every corner of the town.

Anias organized a boarding party of handpicked priests. The guardsmen, some still sitting on their trestle seats, others standing, watched in awe as the white-robed priests, their shaved heads shining in the sunlight, lifted their queen's coffin with reverence and carried it down onto the quay.

Menkhara, Siptah and Mayet followed behind the priests. The last to disembark were the guardsmen.

The procession moved slowly down the Royal Way toward the temple of the Aten. The guardsmen, never having been to Amarna, looked in awe at the palace with its topless columned temples and bright white limestone walls.

They entered the temple of the Aten and crossed its spacious forecourt, continued down a walkway open to the sky and finally into a massive room with a high altar reached by an alabaster ramp. On both sides of the ramp were hundreds of offering tables. The priests alone climbed the ramp to the altar, where they gently set their precious charge on a bier. Then they formed up behind the coffin, their heads lowered.

The coffin lay in the bright sunlight like a golden bar. Menkhara, moved by the affection shown the queen, the dignity of the procession and the sheer beauty of the temple, could not stop the tears that filled his eyes.

Later, Anias offered the ship's party a well-deserved bath, soothing oil massages for their tired bruised bodies, fresh garments, and later, a dinner in the palace. Mayet, her gown still stained with the queen's blood, was gently led away by two women.

Toward sunset Menkhara asked Mayet to walk with him through the Maru-Aten, a region of Amarna near the southern cliffs. The place had a reputation for its lovely lake, colorful gardens and sunken water-courts.

They walked hand in hand, following a path around the lake. The sun, falling below the horizon, plated the mountains crimson. The lengthening shadows cast by the sycamores fell unevenly across the rippling lake. They sat on the stone quay, calmed by the gentle slapping of the water.

Menkhara's eyes were on Mayet. It was the first time he had had a chance to be alone with her, free of the distractions that threatened their lives. She wore a fresh new gown, and her face was less careworn. She looked at him with that shy, perky smile he knew so well. And then he remembered all of the very good reasons why he had fallen in love with her when they were so very young. He put his arm around her shoulder, leaned over and kissed her on the cheek.

"You must know, Mayet," he began somberly, "I can't remain in Egypt. Sooner or later they will come looking for me, and indeed they may have already organized a party to find and bring me back to Thebes and the House of Maat."

Mayet shook her head. "But they may not connect you with the fire."

"It doesn't matter. They know me as the queen's good friend, her emissary and a representative in the court of Suppiluliumas. I'm by that fact alone a co-conspirator who tried to bond in marriage an Egyptian queen with a foreign prince. They'll come for me."

Mayet clasped Menkhara's hand and brought it to her breast. "I'll go with you, Menkhara. No matter where you dwell, I shall dwell. If you will have me, I'll be at your side all the days of my life."

Menkhara wondered for the first time if the life he planned for himself looked that good for Mayet. It was selfish of him to think so. Now he wanted her to understand what lay ahead in that new world both of them knew so very little about.

"You need to understand, Mayet. I intend to leave the country of my birth. I'm an Egyptian, and I know that all Egyptians despise the thought of living in foreign lands. It must be the same for you. You would find yourself in a strange place. Your words will not be understood. You will come to hate me. I've decided to go first to Crete. They are a good breed of men, and one in particular offered me the comforts of his home. I don't know where I shall go from there, except that I'll certainly sail the Great Green Sea and trust to the gods for guidance."

Mayet's eyes filled with tears. She took Menkhara's hand. "I have loved you all my life. Not a day has passed when I did not think of you, wanted you, pleaded with the gods for you. Your life shall be my life."

Menkhara gave her a tender smile. They were the words he had hoped to hear. His heart sang with joy. He pulled her close and kissed her on the lips.

Anias had planned a banquet in honor of his guests. Menkhara declined, fearing that agents of Ay were in hot pursuit.

Anias said, "Sailing these parts of the Nile at night is difficult enough for the most experienced pilots. To make matters worse, this is the season of low water. It is dangerous, Menkhara."

"Forgive my bad manners," Menkhara answered. "You deserve better of me. But we must leave."

Anias's smile conveyed his understanding. "It's this old man who is selfish. I will not detain you. But come then, both you and Mayet must eat your fill now, and in the meantime your ship will be provisioned and the new crew made ready. Also, the temple will furnish you with rings of gold. You're deserving of so much more."

"I thank you and your temple, Anias, but the queen, before her death, awarded me this shebu collar of gold. It will see me past the frontier. Tied to my waist is a purse filled with gold; another gift from our late queen. You have amply repaid me with your kindness; that is what matters most."

An hour later, toward dusk, Menkhara and Mayet stood next to the short gangplank of their ship. The new crew was already aboard. Strong experienced mariners sat at their oars. There were two officers, one at the rudder and another in the pilot's box. A small party was on the docks to say their farewell.

Menkhara took Anias's proffered hand and thanked him. Then he embraced Siptah. The young commander of the household guards had made possible their escape from Thebes. Menkhara took each guardsman's hand and thanked him for his courage and loyalty.

Menkhara took Mayet by her hand, and together they climbed up the wooden gangplank and stepped onto the deck. The mooring lines were cast off, and the rowers worked their oars. The ship slid away from the dock. Standing at the prow, they waved to those on the quay a last farewell.

36

The Nile ran swift on its course to the sea. Helped along by the sturdy rowers, Menkhara and Mayet reached the familiar busy docks of Tanis without incident. They thanked their crew and watched from the quay as the vessel drew apart from its wharf and turned south, back toward Amarna, pushed along by a north breeze. The couple stood watching, their eyes fixed on the diminishing stern decorated with a lotus blossom. It rounded a bend in the river and was lost from sight.

Mayet's hand tightened around Menkhara's. He knew what she was thinking. The ship was their last link to the world they knew, the world of their native Egypt. Even in the wilds of Anatolia, Menkhara had not felt so completely alone.

His first thought was to confer with the harbormaster on sailing ships bound for Crete. He would have a list of all vessels assigned a berth, and would know which one took on passengers. But there was a problem. The harbormaster or one of his deputies might remember him, and recall that he inquired about a Cretan-bound vessel. At this point the agents of Ay and Horemheb had no idea where he was. For all they knew, he could be in Libya, Kush or Babylon. But they would be relentless in their search. He would not make it easy for them. No clues would be left to find.

Menkhara took Mayet's hand, and together they walked down the quay. Mayet stopped at a vendor's stall to admire a purple linen scarf. Menkhara haggled with the Assyrian trader then bought it for her. He drew it around her neck, pulled her close and kissed her. They continued down the quay, stopping at a beer vendor's stall. They sat at a battered acacia wood table drinking their jars of sweet beer and watched kingfishers and seagulls above the calm water.

Afterwards, Menkhara inquired of ships' crews about their destination. Most often the ship's captain was in town and the seamen unable to converse in Egyptian. Occasionally he was able to make himself understood, only to learn that the vessel was bound for a city on the Phoenician coast. Two hours searching the docks had yielded nothing.

Menkhara began to despair at the thought of spending a night with Mayet in Tanis without a ship, one day nearer to being caught.

He spotted a familiar vessel near the end of the quay. It was slender, with a spoon-shaped hull. The stern was bluff, and it had a large deckhouse. He recognized the deep maroon cloth covering the entrance. His heart began to race. He took hold of Mayet's hand, and together they quickened their pace.

The ship's name was carved into the stern: *Mallia.*

Menkhara recognized a familiar face. "Theas!" he shouted. The Cretan mariner set down a crate, ran to the prow of the vessel and returned with the captain.

The broad smile on Menkhara's face was infectious. "A friend?" Mayet asked excitedly.

Menkhara squeezed her hand. "The captain, Pasias! I've sailed on his ship!"

Pasias motioned Menkhara and Mayet on deck. Hands were taken all around.

After a moment of busy conversation, Pasias grew somber. "Listen, Egypt, if you're looking for passage up the Phoenician coast, I am afraid this time I am unable to accommodate you. I've a full load of papyrus and jars of ink. We are sailing back to our home port—to Crete."

Menkhara laughed. "And that's our destination, dear friend. May I talk with you alone, Pasias?" The two men strolled aft.

Moments later, they returned. Pasias turned to Theas. "Find Lasos. He's somewhere on the quay. Drinking beer, I'll wager. We'll cast off before the hour is out."

Theas started down the gangplank. "Oh, and one more thing," Pasias called after him: "We've taken on passengers. One is a woman of quality. You tell the men, especially those damned Mycenaeans, I'll have no foul language aboard my ship. Now get on with you."

Theas scampered joyfully down the gangplank.

⁂

Within the hour the ship was ready to get underway.

"It would be nice if you told me where we're going," Mayet said, curling her arm around Menkhara's waist.

Menkhara did not immediately answer. He was watching the dock workers cast off the mooring lines.

"Pasias is from Khania," he said at last. "It's a seaport on the northern coast of Crete. He's the same sea captain who took Critias and me up the Phoenician coast. We became friends, and he offered me the amenities of his home should I ever desire them. I told him everything that happened. He asked me if I was in trouble. I held nothing back. He knows about Ankhesenamun. He treated me like a brother and reaffirmed his offer. He's truly the best of men, Mayet. We shall go with him to his home in Crete. Perhaps we shall find a reason to stay. I can only tell you that it's a world very much different from our own."

Mayet turned to face south and stared back at the busy port of Tanis. "Egypt grieves the death of its Pharaoh, Tutankhamun, even as it grieves the death of our queen. What will Ay say to the people?"

Menkhara squinted at the busy seaport. "I don't know. By now Ay has been proclaimed Horus god, and he'll say whatever pleases him. But in the quiet hours he will think how he came by the sekhem of power, by murder and by fraud."

"Murder?"

"It was no accident that killed our young Pharaoh, Mayet. There was no proof either way, but I now know in my heart of hearts it was by Simut's hand, the same man who led to the ruin and death of my parents. I'm ashamed to say that Simut and I were friends once."

"You must leave that behind you now."

"Simut is dead," Menkhara continued. "In a way he's lucky. Ay will live with his criminal ambition, and he'll remember Queen Ankhesenamun—or should I say Ankhesenpaaten? The deaths of the royal couple will burn out his heart, and his reign will be short."

They stood together in silence, and then Menkhara's face softened. He turned Mayet around so that they faced north. They stood in silence, watching the watery delta lands slip by, and soon there was nothing but the brackish water of Lake Menzalah. A sailor brought them jars of pomegranate wine.

They walked over to the deck cabin. Mayet looked tired from

standing. Menkhara took her by the waist and hoisted her up onto the roof. She sat holding her wine jar, staring out toward the wide expanse of sea that lay ahead. Menkhara stood below her. She ran her fingers through his dark glossy hair and then draped an arm over his shoulder.

After a while Mayet said, “Given the life I was forced to lead in Egypt, and your own misfortunes, our new life will not be so bad. But, Menkhara, tell me about these Cretans and the Greeks.”

Menkhara looked up at her and winked. “Well, I can tell you they are large-hearted children of the mind, and they love to play.”

Lake Menzalah, its shores a bare sliver of mud, slipped behind them. The pewter-colored water transitioned dramatically to turquoise. The ship rolled upon the crest of the waves, their lives joyfully and inexorably drawn toward the dwelling place of other gods.

And down from a bright blue sky, soft shafts of sunlight sparkled bright upon the Great Green Sea.

Postscript

Shortly after Tutankhamun's death and burial, Ay became Pharaoh, moved the court back to Thebes and ruled Egypt for five years.

When Suppiluliumas learned that his son Zidanza had been murdered on Egyptian soil, he directed his forces to attack the Egyptian frontier in the ante-Lebanons and lay waste the cities of the Amki. The two armies engaged, but in time both sides lost heart and broke off the engagement, leaving the results inconclusive.

Ay was succeeded by General Horemheb. Shortly after his ascension to the throne, Horemheb married Ay's daughter, Mutnedjmet. In the fifteenth year of his reign, Mutnedjmet died. Horemheb, the last Pharaoh of the Eighteenth Dynasty, proved to be an able and just ruler. Seventeen years into his long reign, he razed Amarna to the ground, and destroyed all traces of the Aten religion. The tomb of Queen Ankhesenpaaten (Ankhesenamun) has never been found.

Menkhara and Mayet lived with Pasias in Crete for two years, and then established their own household and had four children, three sons and one daughter. With the help of Pasias, Menkhara became a mariner, and then a successful merchant. He never returned to Egypt.

Critias recovered from his wounds, and was helped out of Egypt by the priests of Amarna. He made his way back to Greece, where he settled down as a teacher in a sleepy little fishing village called Athens.

Author's Note

Little is known of Tutankhamun's widowed queen, Ankhesenamun, but there is agreement on most of the bare essentials of her too brief life. I have spent a good many years researching and writing this novel, and have kept, as much as possible, to the historical record. But as a novelist, I have reserved the right to choose a sequence of events that seems to render more plausible and more interesting the life and times of Ankhesenamun.

Curiously though, some of the historical characters of this novel seem too bizarre to be real. By way of example, the lascivious dwarfs Pera and Rehenen were, in fact, pet-servants of Princess Mutnedjmet. My protagonist, Menkhara, was pure invention, as all heroes of historical fiction must be when put to the task of managing a drama so far removed from our own time.

Ankhesenamun's remarkable letters to the king of the Hittites are faithfully rendered and supported by reference to their source. Identifying the historical record is a practice best left to scholars. In this instance, however, I wanted to remove all doubt of literary license, and establish the historical truth of a frightened widowed queen driven to beg the protection of a foreign prince.